PRAISE FOR THE NOVEL OF
TIM McGUIRE

"*Danger Ridge* belongs on any list of frontier classics."
—Loren D. Estleman

"For those who like action in their Westerns, Tim McGuire's first novel has plenty of it, from start to finish."
—Elmer Kelton

"*Danger Ridge* is one of the best Westerns I've read in years."
—Jack Ballas

"*Nobility* is fast-paced and action-packed. Read it—the Rainmaker will latch right onto you."
—Robert J. Conley

TEXAS WEST

TIM MCGUIRE

BERKLEY BOOKS, NEW YORK

THE BERKLEY PUBLISHING GROUP
Published by the Penguin Group
Penguin Group (USA) Inc.
375 Hudson Street, New York, New York 10014, USA

Penguin Group (Canada), 90 Eglinton Avenue East, Suite 700, Toronto, Ontario M4P 2Y3, Canada
(a division of Pearson Penguin Canada Inc.)
Penguin Books Ltd., 80 Strand, London WC2R 0RL, England
Penguin Group Ireland, 25 St. Stephen's Green, Dublin 2, Ireland (a division of Penguin Books Ltd.)
Penguin Group (Australia), 250 Camberwell Road, Camberwell, Victoria 3124, Australia
(a division of Pearson Australia Group Pty. Ltd.)
Penguin Books India Pvt. Ltd., 11 Community Centre, Panchsheel Park, New Delhi—110 017, India
Penguin Group (NZ), 67 Apollo Drive, Mairangi Bay, Auckland 1311, New Zealand
(a division of Pearson New Zealand Ltd.)
Penguin Books (South Africa) (Pty.) Ltd., 24 Sturdee Avenue, Rosebank, Johannesburg 2196, South Africa

Penguin Books Ltd., Registered Offices: 80 Strand, London WC2R 0RL, England

This is a work of fiction. Names, characters, places, and incidents either are the product of the author's imagination or are used fictitiously, and any resemblance to actual persons, living or dead, business establishments, events, or locales is entirely coincidental. The publisher does not have any control over and does not assume any responsibility for author or third-party websites or their content.

TEXAS WEST

A Berkley Book / published by arrangement with the author

PRINTING HISTORY
Berkley edition / May 2007

Copyright © 2007 by Tim McGuire.
Cover illustration by Bill Angresano.
Cover design by Steven Ferlauto.

ISBN: 978-0-425-21571-5

BERKLEY®
Berkley Books are published by The Berkley Publishing Group,
a division of Penguin Group (USA) Inc.,
375 Hudson Street, New York, New York 10014.
BERKLEY is a registered trademark of Penguin Group (USA) Inc.
The "B" design is a trademark belonging to Penguin Group (USA) Inc.

PRINTED IN THE UNITED STATES OF AMERICA

10 9 8 7 6 5 4 3 2 1

Mike O'Daniel

1944–2006

fan of Westerns; man of music; son of Waxahachie, Texas;
friend of mine and all he met.
Love ya, man.

ACKNOWLEDGMENTS

My agent Cherry Weiner for getting me this project. *Frank Flores, Janie Arreguin y Jose Lara gracias por la ayuda con el español*. Always thanks to the DFW Writers' Workshop for their eternal support and encouragement. And a special notice gratefully given to Megan Doren, the blue-eyed angel on loan from heaven who pushed me to finally finish this project and get on with the rest of life.

1

ONE MORE STEP. One more mile. Just over the next hill. Maybe another dune or two. Squinting squeezed the sweat from his eyes and allowed him time to think. Even before he found himself on hands and knees among the scrub and sand of the Texas west without a drop of water left, he knew this was a bad idea. Chasing after money brought the fool out in him.

Despite the prideful notion that the ten thousand dollars was rightfully his property, won on a wager of who owned the fastest horse in Texas, it may have been a bit too hasty to leave San Antonio in the dark of night with only his saddled dun and a single canteen, dressed in fine clothes, which now resembled rags. The matching derby was long since lost and would come in handy now, since the sun was determined to stew his brain. He was so sure he would catch that stagecoach.

Even if he didn't know its precise destination.

Despite not knowing the lay of land.

Or the distance to the nearest town or settlement.

Having never traveled farther than twenty miles on horseback by himself.

He shook his head. Droplets spilled from his brow, impacting the dust to leave tiny craters, only to dry into crusty residue in an instant. A one-eyed peek to the front showed blue skies. Not a hint of clouds to reprieve his mistake. He closed his eyes in hopes for a better result. When he opened them, the view was the same.

Blinding reflection from the parched ground stung his

vision. Only a few spots of cracked sage, void of any green, dotted the sparse landscape to the horizon. The sole tempting illusion of water wavering in the wind just above the ground never seemed to get any closer. Maybe it was for the best.

He had a good life, of what he could remember of the last twenty-four years. If this should be the end, what better fit than to pass on to the great beyond in this miserable, dusty desolation. If the numerous heraldings of his fate by those of the God-fearing flock about his practices with women, whiskey, and wagering were to be true, then this must be the doorway to the infernal depths. Hell couldn't be any hotter than this.

As he recalled such memories, a smirk grew over his cracked lips. His journey to this spot was anything but predictable. Clever determination coupled with youthful arrogance gave him the gumption to pursue the life of a sportsman. Certain to make his living by leeching off those with less guile, he left New Orleans with the same education normally earned at great expense to those seeking knowledge in the pages of textbooks.

The war made the Crescent City a haven for all seeking greater fortune. As the gaming parlors became too crowded, he set his sights on the games conducted on the riverboats, hoping to spear a few fortune seekers on their way to work for a living. It was then when his plan took a turn.

A tip of the fortune reaped from Texas cowboys at the Kansas railheads sent him west. Along the way, a finicky redhead caught his eye and sought his intimate affection. Those few minutes in Miriam Schaefer's private car set him seeking escape from Hiram Schaefer's railroad thugs for nearly three months. On the prairie of Indian Territory he met Leslie Turnbow.

A cloud blocked the sun's barrage upon the ground. It was enough to give him a minor allowance of air and sanity. Again, he peered to the front. The distance to some shade couldn't be very far. He could make it. He scrambled to rise onto his knees. If an hour's time could be spent in determination, he might survive. After all, wasn't this late winter?

The cloud passed. Like a bullet, the rays shot at his back, sapping what strength he just convinced himself he possessed. Rest is what he needed. Perhaps just if he lay in the sand to allow tired muscles a chance to recuperate. It wouldn't be for very long. Just a short afternoon nap.

Jody Barnes rode up to the rotting carcass. At first sight, he shook his head at such a disgusting vision. After a deep intake of fresh air, he dismounted to take a closer look. The hide appeared partially eaten by vermin, but some resemblance of what once lived and breathed could be recognized.

What a waste. He peeked at the sun with one eye. If the drought continued, there would be more like this. Despite more to be learned by turning it over, he didn't want his hands fouled by the process of decay. Knowing what scavengers it would attract, there was little he could do to make a difference.

With his lungs urging additional air, he stepped away from the body and went back to his horse. All that he could do now was return to the house and report the news. He stepped into the stirrup and turned the reins back to the north.

During the trip, he ran words through his mind on how to describe what he'd just discovered. Certain his ma would take the news hard, he sampled some phrases that might lighten the impact. Whichever order he put them in, there was no way to make it sound pretty.

When at the rail fence, he slowed the horse to a walk, still unsure how to explain. However, with the aroma of midday dinner cooking, he knew he'd be spotted when he was late at the table. It was best to get it over with as quick as possible.

Off the saddle, he tethered the reins to the pillar. Once up the stairs, he took another deep breath, grabbed the latch, and entered the house.

"Better hurry, son," warned Jessie Barnes. "Food will be on the plate soon enough. Go fetch your pa and that girl and see they ain't late." A glance at his mother was all he needed to be reminded that she took it personal if her meal was to let cool and spoil the taste. The three half-Mex kids set the plates as dutifully instructed. He saw Little Mary as he passed. That girl said more with her eyes with one glance than most women could gab in a day.

Jody removed his hat and went to the rear of the house. The door to his sister's room was closed. Despite the familiarity, it wasn't proper to bust it open and chide the girl for being late once again. Rather, he rapped his knuckles on the door. "You in there?"

Moments passed before there was a sleepy reply. "What do you want?"

"Day is nearly half-gone, and it's time for dinner. You better be at the table right quick, or you're going to have to fight the hogs for the slop." Standing at the door for more than a few seconds didn't get even a nasty retort. Normally, he would put up more of a fight at the lack of respect for missing a meal. However, he didn't have it in him to tangle with her. Since he'd known her, there was always spite to her manner, and she usually took more spit than an ornery bull to turn in the proper direction.

He abandoned her to the fate she would suffer and went about to find his father. Through the hall and den, he went out the back door and saw his pa splitting logs. The old man swinging an ax still had the strength of a colt. Sweat dripped from his brow, but not a beat was missed in the rhythm. Jody took another breath, still not sure what to say. He didn't have to.

Jack Barnes paused his swing and faced about to his son. A warm grin crept from beneath his wide, thick mustache. It soon faded when Jody didn't return it. Jack let the ax slip to the end of the handle. "Another one?"

Jody simply nodded. It was all the answer needed and all he could muster. Jack exhaled in a snort. With a single hand, he raised the ax and plunged the edge into the stump. No other disappointment need be shown. He took the hand cloth from the pocket of his overalls and wiped down the back of his neck. Jody stood in the doorway, knowing what it meant to his pa and to his family. Jack came to the door and stepped past his son. "Better get to dinner. No sense making this day worse."

They both entered the house and found their respective places around the table. The kids sat with napkins tucked inside their collars. As Jessie doled out a heaping serving of potatoes and carrots in brown broth, the empty chair across the table was hard to ignore. Jody peeked at his ma, who took the seat at the end of the table. He fought the urge to rise and march again to that closed door but knew any more attention brought would only spark more fuss.

He stabbed his fork into the plump boiled potato chunks. As he put the tasty bit on his tongue, the concern of the day didn't wait for the sovereignty of the midday meal.

"So, how many you reckon are left, son?"

Jack's question spoiled the taste of the mouthful. Once he swallowed, he hesitated to spear another chunk. "Under four hundred."

The answer stopped Jack's fork, too, but only for a moment before it appeared the concern was over the meal. "Damn," he muttered.

"What's ya'll talking about?" asked Jessie.

Father and son shot glances at each other in silent agreement to not explain the truth. "Oh, nothing much at all, Mother," replied her husband.

After chewing her food, Jessie took her napkin with a polite manner and dabbed the side of her mouth. "Son, I bore you twenty years ago, and I have lived with your pa for going on twenty-seven. In that time, I have learned when I'm being lied to. Now, if you menfolk believe that it is not a woman's place to be treated the same, then I'll go on and pretend that I haven't a brain that the good Lord gave me, and sit here and smile and be only concerned with feeding you two and making sure this house doesn't fill with dirt, and seeing to washing your clothes no matter how filthy you are able to get them, and I'll go about finding out what it is I need to know likely faster than if you were to tell me." She ended with her sweet smile still in place and took another bite. The kids kept eating their meal undeterred by the conversation.

Jack's and Jody's heads both turned in unison from looking at her to looking at each other. It wasn't a chore Jody felt like taking on, and with a cock of his head, he showed Jack the burden was off his shoulders. "Like she said, you've known her longer."

"Yeah, but you're more of her than I am." Jack took another bite and cleared his throat. "It isn't that we were trying to hide nothing from you, Mother. Just that there," he paused with a slight wag of his head, "might be some things you'd rather not know."

Jessie dropped her fork. "Jack Barnes, when have I ever been in such a state of delirium that I didn't want to know what concerned my own household?"

The answer was quick to Jody's mind. He spoke before thinking. "There was that time that you couldn't go out to the corncrib for three weeks after I told you I seen a copperhead out there."

Jessie grimaced. "Snakes ain't the same. They're an unholy scourge put upon the land to remind us that we are constantly surrounded by evil and temptation." She paused a moment and picked up the fork. About to stab another chunk, she looked to the both of them. "I have a weakness against evil. That's why I sent your father to kill it." She stabbed the potato and put it in her mouth, taking the napkin and wiping her mouth. "That doesn't change the subject. What's got you two with your noses pointed down like I was holding a spoon of ipecac syrup?"

Jody peeked at his father. Jack nodded, acknowledging it was his duty. "Jody and me have been watching the herd for some time now." He grunted his throat clear. Jody knew there was a fuse about to be lit under his ma. "We've lost a few head. Some were to be expected. Coyotes, bobcats taking the new calves, some get snakebit, the older ones take sick and die."

Almost like walking across a rickety roof, Jack appeared to be walking softly, but as he made progress without cracking a board, he commenced to getting on with the story with some confidence.

"But lately we've been seeing a few that we don't like." He eyed Jody, and they both looked to Jessie, who appeared content to continue eating. Jack kept walking on that roof. "There have been a few that have all gone down from something we ain't certain. Almost like they took sick from something that ain't real easy to see. And not just the old ones, but some of the young ones, too. Whatever it is, it took enough of them to notice."

"Anthrax!"

The voice brought all eyes to the hall. Standing with the look of shock stood that girl.

2

JODY'S CHEST SQUEEZED from the mention. He stared at that girl standing in her shirt, britches, and suspenders, trying to get the words out of his mouth to stop what he knew was coming. The instant he uttered a sound, his ears rang from his ma's shriek.

"Anthrax!"

The kids stopped their chewing and all looked to each other at the clamor. Jody felt sorry for the orphans. They had no choice in the matter of living in a house with this bunch. He, on the other hand had more say. "It ain't anthrax," he said in an attempt to dismiss the danger.

Still, that troublemaking girl stood in a trance, eyes wide, mouth ajar. She spoke with a haunted tone. "Drought. Grass as dry as matchsticks. Cows dropping like locusts. I heard the talk in Abilene from the drovers through town."

One glance at his ma's horrified face was enough to get Jody to his feet. Anger stirred his voice. "Les, stop your fool mouth and come to the table to eat the meal was ready for you ten minutes ago." Quiet claimed the room. Only after a few minutes did she gradually make it to the table to take her place across from Jody. When she finally sat, her face still etched with panic, Jody took his seat. A quick glance to his parents saw his ma with her mouth slowly coming to a close, and his pa in stoic silence.

"It ain't no anthrax. We just got a few dead steers, is all." Despite his own brave front, the notion started creeping into the back of his head.

He picked up his fork and jabbed a chunk, but another glance showed him to be the only one tending to his meal. Even Mary, Theresa, and Little Hank couldn't eat. Their eyes weighed the fork down so much he had to drop it back on the plate. Again, he looked into the eyes of his pa. Jody leaned back in the chair and observed the silent ponderance on that face he'd witnessed for all of his twenty years. "Well, since I see nobody is going to eat dinner, I'd soon go outside and get some air." Jody rose from his chair and tapped his father on the shoulder. His try for a discreet meeting was rewarded when Jack put the napkin on the table and followed him outside.

At a slow gait, they walked to the corral down the slope from the house. As was his habit when he needed to think, Jody reached into his shirt pocket for the wad of tobacco chew. He bit off a piece, then offered the wad to his pa as he approached. Jack shook his head. Jody moved the chaw from side to side with his tongue as he slipped the remainder into his pocket and propped his elbows on the top rail while placing his right boot on the bottom one.

"I didn't want to say anything in front of ma," he said, peeking at Jack, who assumed the identical pose. "But that fool girl's notion may not be wrong."

"I was thinking the very same." Jack's answer was a surprise.

"You was? How come you hadn't said nothing until now?"

Jack kept staring at Brewster, the longhorn bull, the corral's sole animal. "Not something a rancher wants to give too much mind to. Les is right. I heard the same talk as she must have run into. Steers snapping the heads about with their tongues hanging, cows and calves bawling for hours. Within a day, they settle on the ground, barely able to keep their heads up until they can't no more. Some just fall dead straight out. I heard it can wipe out a thousand head in a week. Them that survive can't never be used as beef, so the hands have to slaughter them just to keep the disease from spreading. It'll take ten years to get a herd back. By that time, a man's debt will take all he's worked for his whole life."

The strong words spoken in such a soft tone ran chills through Jody's spine. It was a seldom sight to see his pa admit to any fear. He spat to the left to allow time for the haunting speech to pass, then faced his pa on the right. "Well, what do you think we ought do about it?"

Jack shrugged. "I don't know if there's anything we can do. Ain't no cure for it. Can't round them all up in a bunch just to watch them. No telling if that will help or infect them all quicker."

Jody stood astonished. He shook his head at the passive attitude. "We can't just lose the herd. We can't lose all you and ma worked for." His own strong stance melted when his mind scrambled for an answer. Just as his pa, he had no easy plan waiting to be announced. The only one that seemed a possible option was so rash, he didn't want to admit to hatching it. However, the more thought he gave it, the less foolish it became. "What if we drove them?"

Jack cracked a grin. "Where? How?" He shook his head. "Wrong time of year. It will be March in a few weeks. Heifers will be carrying their first calf soon. Can't be driving them with swelled bellies."

Jody wasn't going to allow the idea to be dismissed so easily. "We still got time before that. We can take them now before whatever it is spreads. Get the jump on the rest."

Jack still shook his head. "What if only our stock has it? Ain't nobody else going to want to mix their herd with ours if they turn sick."

"Well," Jody started, trying to think of a suitable answer. When none came to mind, his stubborn streak blurted a bold reply. "We'll take them ourselves. Have our own drive."

"Jody." Jack sighed in a fatherly manner to a child's foolish idea. "You can't take just a few hundred head of longhorns north. You wouldn't pay for the hands needed. The supplies alone would cut your profit down to the bone. Besides, all the hands you'd need would join up with Frank Pearl's drive. He's the one that's going to pay the best and can get them through the Indian Territory. You know yourself that he's trusted by all them tribes."

That stubborn streak kept talking. "Then we'll go around it."

Jack faced him upon that notion.

"We'll go around Indian Territory."

Jack raised his brow but didn't open his mouth to shoot down the idea.

It was enough encouragement to keep Jody's mouth moving. "We'll take them west. Take the herd up to Denver. I heard from more than one set of folks about a new trail. Give the name of the men who first used it. The Goodnight-Loving trail."

Jack's eyes darted from Jody's for only a moment. A small nod became a bigger one followed by a few more. "I have heard of it." The nod twisted into a shake. "But that goes west of Fort Concho, and there ain't nothing much else out there. That's western Texas, son."

Jody's enthusiasm bubbled his blood. He wasn't going to let a few unsolved problems put down the idea. "Plenty of grass that ain't been trampled by other herds. We'll follow the Pecos all the way up into New Mexico."

Jack pointed his nose to the ground while staring up at Jody. "What spring grass there is out there is still yellow. It's mostly sand and cactus, and the Pecos River is over two hundred miles from here."

"The Nueces ain't. There's plenty of streams and creeks between here and there and yonder."

"Yup, and injuns, too. Apaches raiding the west. Quanah Parker and his Comanches roaming the high plains."

"We'll take plenty of rifles. Besides, all they want is a few beeves and they'll let you pass."

"You hope that's all. They may just decide to kill you and take the whole herd."

Jody grew more frustrated. Again, he turned his head to the left, spat, then faced his pa. "May? Might be? Can't say for sure? Hell, you sound like ma." When Jack bobbed his brow, Jody knew he'd struck a chord. "To just stay here and let them steers die off ain't what I thought you'd be saying."

Very few times had Jody ever given his father an argument. It wasn't a feeling he took mildly. However, it was a matter of urgent need. Day after day he'd ridden the boundaries of the ranch and seen what was coming in the next few weeks. If there was something in the air or the sparse water, they had to act or lose everything.

He kept his eyes paired at Jack's. Seconds passed by with the speed of hours, but with determination, it was Jack who first looked back at Brewster. "Tell you what. You ride about and get a gauge on what other folks think of what you're fixing to do. You'll still need at least a thousand head to make the trip worth the trouble. You get enough folks to follow," he faced his son. "And we'll go."

Rocking from side to side stirred his brain. Moisture on his lips brought his tongue out of his mouth to lap up the precious water. In a short time, he noticed the sun no longer beat on his skin. Was he dead?

The suggestion opened his eyes. He stared at the green roof. In seconds, his face felt the stifling heat. He rose up onto his elbows. His eyes focused on a snake coiled to strike.

He let out a panicked scream, twisted about onto his knees, and escaped to the nearest sunlight. As his vision improved, he saw the back end of a team of mules. Through the collection of wildly colored articles, he saw a driver of considerable years holding the reins. He patted his waist and felt the familiar shape of the .44 and the pepperbox against his ribs. If he was meant to be robbed, the weapons would have been taken. Unless this one had no fear of earthly defenses.

"Excuse me," he said as polite as he could under the circumstances. "Please don't take offense. Are you the Grim Reaper?"

The reply was preceded by a brief chuckle. "Now there's a name I've yet to be called. Have had a few aspersions heaped upon my character, but I've yet to be accused of carting the dead. No, young fellow. My name is Booker. Professor Orville Booker, to be precise. And just who might you be?"

The answer required a bob of the head. "My name's Cash. Rance Cash." He looked about the wagon full of painted crates and metal rods. Again, he focused on the snake but was able to recognize it as an accurate depiction on the side of a box. Memories slowly leaked into his mind. "I suppose I owe you a debt of thanks."

"That you do." The driver's back was all that could be seen. However, the voice was loud as a bugle. "What were you doing out in the middle of the desert dressed like you are? You running from the law?"

It was a fair inquiry. Especially since he was found in a ridiculous predicament, and the complete answer might include some legal entanglements. "Not exactly. I was in pursuit of a man who stole quite a sum of money from me. He was heading west, and I hoped to catch up with him and recover my money." As soon as he answered, he regretted the disclosure.

"How much money did you lose?"

The question was obviously from curiosity. To distort the amount by lying, it would have to remain enough to require such a desperate action. Five hundred dollars as a minimum, but still too much to admit. "Please take no offense, but I'd rather not say."

The driver nodded. "I can understand. If I was you, I would never have said nothing about losing money. I suggest you don't mention that fact in the future." Despite the same admonishment he'd just given himself, Rance was encouraged by the similarity of the response. Perhaps this fellow was a bird of the same feather.

"So what did this man who took your money look like?"

There was more than one version of the description. "Actually, I'm not too sure."

"He knock you on the head from behind, huh?"

"No," Rance replied shaking his head. "No. This man is a master of disguise. I first met him as an old-timer playing checkers with a rooster. I thought him senile. But I soon discovered he was of very sound mind. Later, I met him as an agent for the sale of a horse." Rance thought about what he just said. "Of course, I didn't know it was him. It was only when I saw him with my bag, did I realize that the two were the same."

"Checkers with a rooster. Haven't heard of that one. What was his name?"

Again, the answer wasn't simple. "He first introduced himself as a man named Dudley. That was when he was an old-timer. As the agent, he told me his name was Rodney Sartain. Rodney Ambrose Sartain. He acted every bit the annoyance.

That's why he was so convincing as an agent." Once more, Rance ran the events in San Antonio through his head. His last day there was spent earning the fortune, and the last night there spent with the most exotic beauty in all of Texas. There was never a bigger regret, but he couldn't live in peace if he were to dismiss the loss and stay with her. Still, he would always wonder what life would have held with her.

The daydream was shaken from his head by a jolt of the wagon. When several more followed, the natural question came to mind. "Excuse me, Professor Booker. Might I inquire exactly where you are going, since it seems I may be joining you?"

A giddy laugh erupted. "Yes, you may, my good man, Rance Cash. We should soon find ourselves in the oasis of the Texas desolation: El Paso."

3

THE BRISK MORNING air stopped Jody at the door. He took his coat from the peg on the wall and slipped it on as he went down the steps. Headed to the barn, again he was stopped, this time by the voice of his father.

"Ain't you going to eat breakfast?"

Jody faced about while still backpedaling toward the barn. "Got plenty of ground to cover today. I'll be home for supper."

When Jack shook his head, Jody faced about again in an attempt to get to the barn before he knew what was coming. He didn't make it.

"Now, just wait a damn minute."

Jody stood firm but did not turn. Soon, he heard the clop of boots on the dirt. His enthusiasm for the notion had pushed him beyond good sense. If the idea had a chance, his pa would have to agree. He faced about once more.

Jack came toward him with his hat and coat. "I ain't going to listen to your ma whine about how her boy snubbed her morning meal." He stood just inches from Jody. "So I'm going with you." Jody's eyes widened with the news. "If you're so headstrong that you feel you have get along with this foolish notion, then you'll need somebody to lead it."

"That mean you're going too?" asked Jody with gleeful surprise. As he'd only known for a few times in his life, his pa's bushy gray mustache crept up on one side.

"Do you think I can stand to listen to that woman if I was to let you go by yourself?"

The two Barnes men together turned for the barn. In a matter of a few moments they emerged with their horses saddled. Their giddy mood shrank upon sight of Les and Jessie standing on the porch, both with hands on their hips.

"What are you two doing?" asked Jessie.

Jody looked to Jack, who looked back at Jody. "Nothing much," they answered in unison.

"Jack Barnes," said Jessie with authority in her voice meant for a child. "Don't let on that you're a-fooling me. Does this have to do with your mumbling about some crazed cattle drive to Colorado in your sleep last night?"

Just as if he were a child, Jack only peeked to the side at Jody, cleared his throat, and then spoke in a husbandly manner to his wife. "The boy thinks there might be something to the cattle gone sick. I given it mind that we might ought to find out if others have the same trouble. Might be they think the idea a good one and share the load." He grunted again. "I just . . ." he paused, looking at his son. "We just thought it worth the ride to find out."

Jessie's face soured. Her hands left her hips in a wave of relenting. Jody knew it wasn't all about missing breakfast. Whatever fight might come later, it would be between man and wife and not mother and son. As Jessie went inside the house, Les darted for the barn.

"Where you going?" Jody asked as she passed.

"I ain't staying here with her like that."

"You ain't going with us," he called inside the barn. "We got ground to cover and can't be waiting on you." He curled his lip at Jack. His father turned his head. Jody knew this fight was his as Jack's was with Jessie. "Come on," he said to his pa. They nudged their mounts. About the time they passed the house, the pounding of hooves made them look back. Les rode the paint from the barn and reined in as they gawked at her.

"What did I say?" Jody sniped.

"I don't know," she answered. "I wasn't listening."

Jack laughed. "Sounds familiar." Jody looked at his pa with disgust at his nonsupport. Jack continued to huff a chuckle, then shrugged. "You brought her here. Besides, anyone, gal or not, that can saddle a horse so quick deserves a break from chores."

"You ain't helping," said Jody to Jack.

"I can ride a horse, Jody Barnes. Maybe not as good as you. But you weren't worried about me when we was coming back from Kansas. When you thought I was a boy."

"When you was a boy," he answered with just a peek at Jack, "I was more worried on how a young fellow could be so green. Only after did I know you was a girl did my mind have peace knowing that all the menfolk in Kansas weren't as inept as I thought."

Les raised a brow. "It was no man that rode Lone Star. Remember?"

Jody shook his head. "That ain't real riding. That's race riding. All you did was hang on."

As Les heaved a breath for another volley in the fight that had gone on near nine months, Jack raised his hand. "I thought we was trying to get a jump on the day. If Les wants to go, I see no reason for her to not come along."

With his father's decision, Jody whipped his horse's head about. "Fine," he chided. He took the lead as the three made their way down the path.

Hours ate into the distance traveled over the mix of yellow and sprouting green hills. Jody looked ahead, but his pa's call to stop had him pull back on the reins.

"If we're going to make any use of the day, we're going to have to split up."

"Sounds like a good idea," Les replied. Jody looked away from her.

Jack continued. "What say you go by the Adair spread. I'll make my way over east and stop in on the Pleasants." He peeked up. "By the looks of how much time we got, seems like all we going to get around to today."

Jody took a peek at the sun, too. He didn't like to admit it, but the plan seemed the right course. "Sounds good." He looked to Les and pointed at Jack. "You go with him."

"Oh, no," Jack replied. "I'll be needing to make some tracks, and I'm sorry to say, little lady, you'll just slow me down."

Les opened her mouth, as it was her nature to complain. So Jody spoke first. "She ain't coming with me. She's the reason we've only got this far."

"Well," Jack responded. "She's your guest. Has been all along. It's your responsibility."

Jody shook his head. "I ain't—"

"To hell with both of you," Les shouted. "I know when I ain't wanted, and I'll not be bargained against like some pig squalor." She kicked the paint and sent it off into the east.

Jody watched as the paint's hooves kicked up dirt in its wake. He looked to his pa and shook his head. "I wonder where she learned to talk like that."

Jack shook his head and shrugged.

Normally, Jody would have trouble with the girl riding alone. However, he had a heap of miles to cross and not a long time to do it. He settled his mind on the notion that the girl was like a cat with at least half its lives left. She'd been through worse than a day on her own. He'd have to depend on that confidence and get along with his business. He gave Jack a nod and turned his horse. "See you at the house for supper."

Jody rode through the gateless fence to the ranch of Marvin and Mary Ann Adair. As he slowed the horse to a walk to approach the house, he saw Enos Adair wearing only his pants and suspenders and standing a little less than six feet tall chopping wood at the side of the house.

"Hello, Enos," Jody greeted with a wide smile as he reined in the horse and dismounted.

Enos stopped the ax as if hit by lightning. "Jody Barnes," he called, drawing his parents from the house. Both Enos and Marvin shook Jody's hand, and Mary Ann gave him a motherly hug. They invited him inside, but Jody declined, describing the sight of the dead calf and the reason for his visit.

"A cattle drive!" shouted an excited Enos. "You betcha I'm going."

"Sounds like a pretty risky thing to do to me," Marvin replied. "We barely have five hundred head. I was thinking of joining Pearl's drive in the spring. Half of them I was thinking of keeping for ourselves."

"Ah, pa," Enos replied with some angst. "We have plenty for just you and Mother. Besides, it was you telling me you didn't know where we would get the money for the lumber and supplies to fix up the house and fences."

Jody saw the questioning eye of Marvin to his son. It was clear there was disapproval for the idea, and they needed to talk about it just as he and his father had. "I'll need an answer by the end of the week." He went back to his horse and stepped up into the saddle.

"That don't leave much time," said Mary Ann.

"No, ma'am. It don't. Our plan is to leave before summer hits the western plains. By the time it does, we'll be in a mite cooler weather." He looked to Marvin. "We'll have our cattle in the pens in Denver enjoying the cool air by the time Pearl and his bunch are sweating on the way to Waco." He tipped his cap to the woman. "With all due respect, pardon my leaving so soon. I have to get to the other ranches to spread the word." He steered his horse about and rode past the gateless fence.

Long into the afternoon, Jody passed the creek that bordered the Cochran property. He guided the horse through the grove of trees, passing by a barking dog warning of his arrival. The house had weeds as high as the porch. As he looked around, numerous rails were missing or rotted at the end and had slipped to the ground. The disrepair of the place gave Jody an ill feeling.

Daniel Cochran came out of the house. He wore no shirt over his long johns top with small holes in the sleeves and dirty gray pants held up by suspenders. Three years younger than Jody, Danny had only grown an inch or two since the last time Jody had seen him at Sunday sermon years before, to only stand maybe five and a half feet tall.

He walked onto the porch followed by another man of similar age, height, and build wearing a tattered hat and rust-colored shirt and brown trousers, sporting a holstered pistol and a full face of stubbled whiskers.

"Well, if it ain't Jody Barnes as I live and breathe."

Jody nodded to the both of them, and he stopped the horse. "How do, Danny."

"It's Dan now. Danny ain't a name I answer to no more. It ain't a man's name." He glanced behind him. "This is my cousin from down south near the border, Tucker Winston.

Jody nodded again. "Good to meet you, Tucker."

The stubbled face didn't flinch to return the gesture.

"What's your business here?" asked Dan.

"My pa and me are planning a cattle drive to Colorado." He looked closer into the contemptuous glare of the cousin. "We lost a few head to sickness. We feel it best to drive them now rather than wait. We're going to take the Goodnight Trail west and take them up into Denver. I'm spreading the word to get as many as we can to join in."

"And you're going to lead them there?" The cousin chuckled.

Jody sensed the dare. "That's right," he said with a bob of his head. "My pa, Jack Barnes, will boss the drive. I'm going to ramrod it."

"Colorado is a long way." Tucker paused as he eyed Jody on the horse. "You ever rid that far?"

Jody took a deep breath. It wasn't the first time his skill as a young trail hand had been questioned. However, usually it was from someone he held more respect for at first meeting. "Don't let it fool you. I rode with Pearl's drive just last year and have been working our range since I was ten. I'll be riding long after the sun goes down and long after someone like yourself is whimpering from saddle sores."

"Well, I don't know about that," said Dan. "Tucker here is a few days past eighteen. I think he knows a few things about riding horses. He come from near the Rio Grande," he paused to glance at his cousin. "And most times at night." Tucker gave Dan an odd stare as if his riding at night weren't to be known.

Jody nodded at the seeming truth of the remark of a man noted to ride the border at night. "No matter. I come to see if you want to throw in with us. I've heard tell the army is looking for beef. We think we can get fifty dollars a head."

"I ain't going," Dan said shaking his head, but he was quickly interrupted by his cousin.

"Fifty dollars!? Hell, we'll throw in with you."

Dan turned to Tucker. "I only got about forty head of cattle. I ain't seen most of them since last fall."

"Fifty dollars a head is a heap of money," Tucker argued. "For that, we'll find your cattle."

"Good," said Jody taking another look around the place. "Be at our ranch by the end of the week. We need as many head as we can drive to make it worth everyone's time."

"We can scrape up forty or more by that time," said Tucker. "I mean round up that many."

"Fine," answered Jody, still uncertain of Tucker's past. As he steered the mount around, he pulled back on the reins. "Hey. Where's your folks?"

Dan's head sagged. "They put my pa in jail about a year ago. My ma died shortly after from heartbreak of seeing him behind bars. I'm by myself now. Besides Tucker who come to live with me."

Jody gulped. "Sorry to hear of the sad news," he said with respect. "I remember them as good people. I won't burden you recalling bad times. I'll see you at my ranch at the end of the week."

4

BY THE HUFFING of the paint, Les knew she had tired out the horse, not to mention her backside from pounding against the saddle. However, the steam between her ears hadn't yet cooled below a boil. The men's quarrel over who had to drag her about still ate at her gut. She never liked being considered a burden and didn't feel it warranted. Ever since she'd been revealed as a female, Jody's treatment of her was like that of a skunk. When she pretended to be a boy, she had been accepted as a green cowhand who needed the help of the seasoned cowboy. He showed that glowing smile and obliged. Almost six months had passed since then. Now, all Jody wanted to do was rid himself and his family of her.

She pulled up on the reins.

When she crossed the creek that marked the boundary of the Baines place, her mind switched to the memories stamped out just a few weeks before. Before he died, Hank and his mix-breed kids had to live on this hardscrabble place without much hope there would be a next day. If it weren't for the gamble of a racehorse called Lone Star, those kids might never have had the cooked meals given now by Jessie Barnes since his death. It was strange how luck could change fortunes from bad to good and the other way around.

Les let the paint nibble on the grass near the bank. The sun began its dip toward the west. While sipping from the canteen, a distant hum crept into her ear. Just as she once heard Miss Maggie back in Abilene, she recognized the sound as a woman's voice. Curious, she steered the paint toward the sound. Through the high yellow grass and into a grove of trees, she approached the hill that rimmed the spread. Once on top, she gazed down to spot a single horse and buggy near the corral and a lone blonde woman sitting on the rail.

The sight intrigued her enough to nudge the horse down the slope and toward the house. The clop of hooves turned the blond woman's attention. As Les came near, she saw the face. "Miss Greta? What are you doing out here?"

A simple embarrassed smile was the first reply. "Oh, my, what are you doing here?"

Les pulled up on the reins when she got to the edge of the weed-infested corral. "Oh," she paused, thinking of a better reason than was the truth, "I was just out enjoying the good weather. Seemed like a good day for riding. What about you? This is a long way from the kitchen of the Menger Hotel."

Again, there was the blushing but brief smile. "Same for me."

Les recognized the simple answer as the same she'd just given. Her eyes drifted to the tattered wood of the house. It wasn't much to admire. The dilapidation didn't hold her imagination. Only a couple of months had passed since she herself had scampered away from the place in fear for her life when Don Pedro Cuellar's men had come to claim Lone Star. It was then when a piece of the puzzle fit neatly into Les's mind. She looked to Greta. At first, she didn't want to say it, but the melancholy expression appeared to confirm the suspicion. "You miss him, don't you?"

Surprise raised the German woman's brow. "What do you mean?" she asked with a slight giggle as if to dismiss the accuracy of the question. Les knew a lie when she heard it.

"Ah, you don't have to fool me. I know he left you. He left everybody. He owed me enough money to get back to Abilene. And Jody he owed a thousand dollars. No sir, don't mention Rance Cash around Jody Barnes." Since the admission didn't change the blond's mood, Les again peeked at the house. "You know, you can come by the Barnes's place anytime you want. To see Mary, Theresa, and Little Hank. They're doing fine. I'm sure they would jump up and down like toads just to see you again."

Greta nodded her head. "Someday I will."

"You don't have to be shy, you know. It ain't like you done nothing wrong." Although it was easy to say, Les knew it was another matter to act it. "That no-account gambler Rance Cash. He's the one that should be hanging his head. And he ain't got a brain in it neither to leave you in the way he did."

"Stop it," said Greta, lifting her head to face Les. "I know you are trying to make me feel better, yes. But I had no claim to him. He was not my husband. I did not have the right to believe him when . . ." she paused, trying to think of a word. "When . . . we . . ."

Les had heard about the gossip in town. For an unmarried woman to speak about sharing a bed with a man with or without loving intentions wasn't a matter to be spoken. Reputations sank below worms' bellies if it was thought a woman had been intimate with a man not her husband. This fine lady had all the manners of those sitting in the front pews on Sunday. There stood no reason to think her different in any way.

Since Les didn't want to irritate, she thought of another way to distract the blonde lady from thinking about Rance Cash, one that came easy to mind. In fact, the more she thought about it, the less she could keep her own mind from swinging in the same direction.

"All men are no-accounts." When she realized the words were in the air, she peeked at Greta. A raised brow from her only spurred Les to take no shame in the announcement. "Well, they are. Each time just when you think you know what they're thinking, they whip around like a rattlesnake and show you their fangs."

Greta giggled. "I thought it was women who are to blame for changing their minds and moods so quickly."

"Well, I guess men aren't any better." More giggles turned infectious. As Les tried to restrain hers, she found more to free from her chest. "Sometimes when they look at you, and you think," she paused and shrugged, "they be paying attention. Just when you think that, they're off talking about raising cattle, or how to ride a bronco, or some such nonsense. And they make sure for you to know that they are the only ones on

God's green earth that know exactly how it is to be done."
When she finished, Les let out a giggle, in part to keep from
bawling.

Greta arched a brow, then faced the ground as she spoke. "It
sounds like you have noticed quite much." She peeked at Les.
"Maybe a little too much. Or maybe too little."

The odd remark sparked Les's ire and curiosity equally.
"What is that supposed to mean?"

Greta's eyes darted back and forth between Les and the
ground. "Well. This man you speak about, who I am sure has
no name, might be thinking the same of you. No?"

Les cocked her head to the side like a puppy.

Greta nodded, realizing her message needed to be said differently. "If I remember, you are to be seventeen soon, yes?"
When Les nodded, Greta grunted her throat clear. "Well, then,
you are a young lady."

Les peeked down at herself. The man's shirt and suspenders
along with dungarees didn't have much lady in them.

By the time she could face Greta again, the words came at
her like a gale. "You should act like one if you want to have
men notice you as one."

Although the German woman's English chopped a bit at
the ends of words, Les would have understood in any lan-
guage by just the snap of her speech. The pit of her stomach
felt like a hole had been burrowed clean through to her socks.
It was one thing for a man to say those things, but for another
female to mention it hurt the worst. About to turn the paint for
home, Greta's voice stopped her.

"I could help, maybe."

Les held the reins firm. She never liked talking about herself. However, if she were to ever change her frustration with
Jody, she needed to do things she didn't like. "How?"

Greta stepped down from the rail, brushed off her backside
and her hands, and motioned for Les to dismount. At first a little fearful, Les reminded herself of the silent resolve she'd just
made and slipped off the saddle. When she stood next to the tall
blonde, she remembered being in the presence of an older,
wiser woman, the Shenandoah Lady on the far side of the Abi-

lene train tracks who would lecture about how men were just a
patch of ripe strawberries just waiting to be picked if you knew
just where to put your fingers.

Greta loosed the chin cord and pulled the hat from Les's
head like a lid off a coffeepot. "You are letting your hair grow,
yes?"

Upon leaving Abilene, Shenandoah had cut Les's hair to
give her the look of a cowpoke. The lady was no barber by her
own admission. It had taken almost nine months for Les's hair
to get beyond the bottom of her ears. "When I ain't having to
be a man."

Greta stroked the strands to a part. "Hair is one of the
things men notice. It must always be groomed in a way that
shows the woman takes care of things." She straightened the
collar of the shirt, pinching at the shoulders to pull out the
wrinkles, then buttoned the top button. "A woman never
shows a man what he must not see." Her own remark made
her pause, but for only a moment.

With a mild push to Les's shoulders, Greta forced her to
stand straight. "Do not slouch. Men slouch. They do not like
women who slouch." She took a step back and modeled the
pose. "Be proud you are a woman." Whether it was meant or
not, the straighter the tall German stood, the more her bust
stuck out. Les couldn't help but peek at her own modest pair
of protrusions from her shirt. The difference depressed her so,
her stance eroded, causing her to slouch, and her small bust-
line was lost in the wrinkles.

Greta stepped forward and forced Les's shoulders back
once more. "Do not worry." She positioned her hands parallel
to Les's front. "These are not what make a lady."

"No," Les lamented, "but I've seen men look at them just
the same. They are what makes a woman. You ever seen Liz-
beth Carter?"

"No," Greta answered shaking her head, still straightening
Les's shoulders.

"Well, she has the dandiest pair a girl could want. Birds
could use them as a perch."

"Do not think of such things." Greta stepped back and motioned to the side. "Now. You walk." Les turned and went a few

steps. *"Nein,"* said the blonde German. "Do not walk like you are some cowboy. You should walk on the front of your feet. You want to show the man how light you are."

"But I don't weigh much."

"Not like heavy." Greta shook her head. "Men stride. Women should prance. Especially when they are being noticed."

Les took the advice and walked in a manner she hadn't thought she could. In fact, just to walk in this manner, she had to think about it.

Greta nodded. "Better."

The blonde woman went to Les and took her hands, stepping back as Les walked forward. Feeling a fool, Les kept reminding herself of the pledge she'd taken. As she stepped, she felt the less she was walking and the more she was dancing. In order to continue, she had to keep herself from noticing.

"So how do you talk to them?"

"Talk to who?"

Les bobbed her head left and right. "Talk to men."

The dancing stopped. She looked up into the blonde woman's blue eyes. During their entire conversation, it was the first time she felt a bond.

"You must first consider them your friend."

Les dipped her eyes for a single moment. While doing so, she asked herself whether she felt that way. She looked up again at Greta and nodded. "I'm all right with that."

Greta inhaled, then released a sigh. "I have always found it difficult to talk to them from the start. You know, to begin. But you must. A man is very proud. Besides his attention to a woman, he also feels attention toward his work. It is the other half of his life. The first is his family. The next is his work. It is something that if it is done good, it is not for him to tell you about it." She patted Les's shoulders. "It is for you to notice."

Les wasn't quite sure what Greta meant.

"You must say something good about it."

"Say something good about Jody Barnes!?" She quickly shook her head. "I mean the man that don't exist?"

Greta rolled her eyes up then bobbed her head slightly. "Yes, yes. Even that man that does not exist." While Les inhaled, cursing herself for letting the name slip from her mouth, the sting from the mistake eased away when she thought about how she herself just got done trying to pretend not to know about Greta's time with Rance. It was time to admit she had a shine on Jody. "All right. Go on ahead."

"Well," Greta started in a mild tone. "It might not hurt so bad if you were to say nice things about what he does."

"Oh," Les began looking to the side. "It ain't like he ain't got everybody with a mouth saying how good he is. Me saying anything ain't going to mean nothing."

Greta put her finger to Les's lips. "Stop talking like that. You must not believe that. You must believe that what you will say will matter a great deal. That is when you will know."

They stood in the dimming light holding hands. Les knew she must appear foolish, but at that moment she didn't care. She peered into the tall blonde's eyes and soaked up each word.

"A compliment is the most precious gift given, and it costs nothing. But if it is not given with the heart, then it means nothing. If you say what you mean, then don't be afraid at how it is accepted. That is when you will know."

Les stood bewildered at the last part. "Know what?"

Greta smiled and squeezed Les's hand a mite tighter. Her eyes beamed from the angled sunlight. The soft reply sounded clearer than a blare. "That is when you will know whether it mattered." She paused and nodded only once. "Trust me. You will know in your heart."

5

SUNDOWN CAME TO the front door of the Raven Saloon. Expecting an evening crowd eager to shed their sobriety as well as their good sense after a day's work, Avis McFadden bided her time shuffling cards for a game of solitaire. Despite its small size, the Raven stood as one of the premier gambling halls in all of El Paso. And it was all due to her.

She glanced into the mirror behind the bar. The auburn hair maintained its curl at the ends. She adjusted the pendant necklace to center above her cleavage peeking above her red neckline. She needed every advantage while playing poker. She counted on the distraction when a man decided which raise was more important. In fact, most of them didn't mind when they lost, as long as they enjoyed the play and the view.

She dealt a single column when loud voices approaching drew her attention. The first figure through the door was known by all. Clyde Farnsworth filled the threshold with his size and reputation. The straw Panama hat's brim nearly creased the edges of the doorframe. His red-blond beard hid most of his face.

Behind, like a barking dog, walked in Horace Willoughby. Usually one of the town's keepers of local conscience, the thin-framed lawyer chattered at the burly Farnsworth.

"I want you to know, Mr. Farnsworth, that I intend to file a complaint with Sheriff Tadbury on behalf of my clients. You cannot ignore the laws of this county and state. Rustling other people's cattle isn't a matter to be treated lightly."

Farnsworth walked to the bar and peered into the mirror.

Avis met his eyes in the reflection, but for only a glance. She averted her eyes to the cards, but there wasn't any ignoring the scene as Willoughby continued.

"Do you intend to stop your thieving?"

Sam the bartender brought a bottle of rye and a single glass. Farnsworth took it from him with a decided grasp, ripped the cork from the spout, and filled the glass. When full, he put the bottle back on the bar. "Your clients, huh," he said without facing about.

"Yes, my clients," Willoughby responded. "Law-abiding citizens who deserve protection under the law. And I intend to give it to them. Now, do I have your word that these raids will stop?"

Farnsworth kept drinking and pouring.

"I see," said Willoughby. "Well, then. I'll just stay here until I get my answer." The lawyer took a seat at the nearest table to the bar.

Avis didn't care for the fuss. Squabbles were best settled outside. The more they were to continue, the less money would walk through the door. She thought about offering a free hand of poker, just to let tempers cool. However, the longer the silence, the less inclined she felt to be in the middle.

Farnsworth threw down another shot. "Your clients are Mexican greasers."

Willoughby leaned forward on the table. "That may be. But they are due the legal process of the law, none the same. And what about the white man's cattle you steal to sell in Mexico?" His tone and dress of flat-brimmed hat with a round crown, white shirt buttoned at the collar, and simple black cloth vest made for an impression more as a pious preacher. "Don't let it be overlooked how broad your reach is into other men's pockets."

With a huff, Farnsworth poured another shot.

Just when it appeared over, Avis's worst fears were realized. Two regulars approached through the door, took one look at the burly figure at the bar, and reversed course to the next nearest establishment. The deck spilt from her shuffle in a flutter.

"Don't be so easily fooled, Farnsworth," Willoughby said. "Without your personal guarantee, I am prepared to seek the help of Texas Rangers to stop your rustling business. And if Rangers aren't enough, then I will call for the governor to seek the help of the army at Fort Bliss. Whatever measure is needed, I will not hesitate to use it to stop you and your minions." With a smug grin, the lawyer wagged his head from side to side. "What do you think of that?"

Without so much as a terse word to reply to the dare, Farnsworth poured himself another drink with a firm hand to fill the glass to the very rim. He carefully put the bottle down, picked up the glass, and threw the liquor down his throat. With a wheeze from the whiskey's bite, he swiped his sleeve across his lips to sop away the dribble. He slapped the glass back onto the bar and turned about. With fluid motion, he drew one of the pair of .44 pistols tucked beside his soft leather vest, aimed the weapon at arm's length, cocked the hammer, and squeezed the trigger.

The shot boomed through the air. Smoke streamed from the muzzle. Willoughby's forehead suddenly showed a red, round hole, and the back of his head exploded with blood like a cannon with fire. The lawyer fell back, chair and all, to collapse on the ground in a dead heap.

Avis's heart pounded. Her chin quivered. Gradually, her eyes turned back to see Farnsworth standing there holding the pistol. His piercing stare shot through her eyes to the back of her brain. Calmly, he holstered the pistol, glancing only once at Sam behind the bar.

"You all saw it. It was self-defense, pure and simple." He picked up the bottle again and poured another drink. As he turned to Sam, who nodded like a frightened child, Farnsworth turned his leer at Avis. His reddened cheeks squared his face like the devil himself. He picked up the full glass without breaking his stare, throwing down the liquor without once blinking away from her. Once he swallowed, he exhaled in a snort, drops trickling from his chin and into his thick beard. "Ain't that right, woman?"

Jody reined in at the front of the house as night fell. He knew he was late, but the success of the day's travels made for a good excuse to be late. Once tethering the reins to the pillar, he stepped onto the porch and opened the door. His parents sat in their usual places. The three kids had already dug in to the pot roast. His place had a plate in front of it. And so did Les's.

"Well, what'd you find out?" asked Jack.

The voice brought him from his notice of the empty chair. "Oh," he said removing his hat, "I have some news." He hung the hat on the peg and went to his chair. "I seen Danny Cochran," he said putting the cloth napkin in his lap. The instant silence drew his attention to Jack, who looked at Jessie. "Did you know about his ma and pa?"

Jack nodded, about to comment, but it was Jessie who spoke first. "I don't want no talk about that. Not here."

Jody saw the look was meant not mention such a subject as jail and death in front of the young kids, so he picked up his fork. "So, I saw him. He's there. With some saddle tramp of a cousin from down south. Not sure about that one. Seems a mite shady. Just the same, Danny, er," he paused, then bobbed his head. "Dan, as he goes by now, says he has forty head." He took a bite, chewed, and kept talking. "Don't appear he had much to keep him there. So I think we can count them in."

He took another bite and let his eyes drift. They centered on the empty seat across from him. His curiosity formed a question, but before he could ask, Jack spoke about his day.

"Good to hear. I stopped by the Pleasants'. Seems they have over a hundred steers they say they know of. Might be more that crossed over their spread without a brand. Charles said he would talk it over with his wife and child and let me know in the morning."

The mention stirred Jody's mind in another direction. "Penelope Pleasant?" He grinned. "That girl still with her folks?"

Jack nodded with his mouth full.

"I heard she's turned into a right pretty-looking girl," added Jessie, while wiping the face of Little Hank. Jody turned back to his pa.

"That right?"

Jack shrugged, and he swallowed. "Well," he started, "I only got a glimpse of her. She has grown out of the little blue spotted dress. Has the blond hair of her mother and took her father's slim frame."

"How old is she now?" Jessie asked like dangling a worm. Jody knew his ma's tactic, hoping he would bite. Despite the trick, he couldn't help wanting to know. They all looked to Jack. He shrugged again.

"Don't know. I don't ask men how old their girls are."

"Well," Jessie said, "she's got to be every bit of nineteen. Don't you remember so? You two went to Sunday school together. Might be a mistake to leave a cute little lady behind while you're off driving cattle off the end of the world."

Jody glanced at Jack. "Now, Ma. I know you're not of the same mind as Pa and me. But it ain't like we got much choice. If we don't drive the cattle now, then we might lose the whole herd."

Jessie put her finger to her lips to shush the talk in front of the kids. After she changed her face and her mood, she put another biscuit on Little Hank's plate. "I was just thinking, you might pay her a visit before you gallop off."

Jody stopped his fork. He knew how she ended every word and how it was meant. He first looked to his ma, then his pa, then back at her. "You ain't going?"

She shook her head. "I can't leave the kids, and they can't go off into the wilderness." She peeked up only briefly. "Your father seems bent on leading this drive of yours. Me and the kids will be fine. It will be just like when you and your sister were little."

The idea of his mother alone with three little children while the menfolk were gone for three to four months didn't comfort Jody's gut. Suddenly the gravy wasn't as tasty. He looked to Jack. "You know about this?"

His father nodded in his normal reassuring manner. "We talked about it. She's right. The young 'uns can't make that trip, and there's no one around here she'll trust them to. I talked to Charles Pleasant. He said he'd make it a habit to stop by."

"Charles Pleasant?" Jody asked in confusion. "Ain't he going?"

Jack stuffed his mouth full and shook his head. When he cleared his throat, he answered. "Nope. Got a bad case of fever last winter. Can't be out in rain and wind no more, or he'll shake like a rattler's tail. Don't have no trouble when he's indoors after a day's work. But he told me he would send a hand along to tote the load of his beeves."

"Might have a chance to see Penelope after all," Jessie said with a lilt in her voice.

"Oh," Jack grunted, "I think he may get that chance."

Confused why there was that mention, Jody opened his mouth to ask, but the door flew open.

Les walked in, hat in her hand and hair smooth of any tangles. "Good evening, everybody," she greeted in an unusual tone for her. "I apologize for being late to your supper, Mrs. Barnes." Her polite voice startled Jody. He quickly glanced at Jack and Jessie to see them with puzzled faces, too.

"Where you been?" Jody inquired with some irritation.

"I was riding," she replied, taking her place and doling out a helping onto her plate. "Since you two wanted to be off on your own, I thought I would take a nice little ride by myself, smell some air that ain't been smelled."

"They run off and leave you?" Jessie inquired with the same voice Jody just used. He looked to his pa, who quickly stuffed his mouth. Jody looked to Jessie.

"Well," he said. "It ain't like we run off from her."

"No," Les said picking up her fork. "Actually, I did. Just after they argued who was going to be stuck with me riding with them," she ended with a smile.

Jody frowned at her.

"Jack and Jody Barnes," admonished Jessie. "Shame on you both. Shunning her off in the middle of no place."

While Jack kept chewing without any change in expression, a habit from a lifetime of living with the woman, Jody felt a nip of guilt. He looked to Les, who appeared not the same girl that ate breakfast that morning.

6

THERE WAS NO rest to be gained while the rickety wagon bounced over every stone on the road west. Rance peeked out into the brilliant, unceasing sunlight. Earlier, when he attempted a nap and failed, he'd last seen some shades of green growing up from the desert floor. But now, some three hours later, the green turned to dust and sand.

Surrounding the valley in every direction were distant mountains resembling mounds of dredged dirt. Those that they passed closely by revealed cracks and gaps between the boulders chiseled by centuries of wind, rain, and of course unflinching heat.

Between the rocks sprang the only visible signs of foliage managing to survive here. Thorny scrub and yucca plants inhabited the hills like defiant natives that didn't know of the better climate only a few hundred miles away or certainly they'd pull up roots and move there. Every view showed desolation filled with hard edges and sharp points. Who would want to live here?

"Should see the town around this next bend coming up."

Professor Booker's announcement came none too soon. The meager water keg showed only a dark ripple at the bottom as any sign of moisture. "There's a river there, right?"

Booker kept his eyes on the team. "Oh, the Rio Grande's still there. Don't carry much of a flow, though."

"You've been there before? Am I understanding you correctly?" Rance had to yell to be heard over the rattles of the numerous wooden crates clinking of glass.

"Oh, I make it every couple of years as I make my rounds."

As the professor steered the team around a boulder as large as any building, Rance took hold of the few sturdy beams on the interior. As he felt gravity pull him to the other side, he braced his boot against one of the crates. Like a spoiled pet, it screamed in protest.

"Careful back there. You got to buy what you break."

With the distinct lack of any means to pay for a stick of licorice, he eased his boot off the crate and grasped the beams tighter. Just when he was certain he was to crash headfirst on the opposite side of the wagon, gravity yanked him back level on his rear with the force of a mule kick. "Damn!"

The professor's cackle at his discomfort sparked Rance's temper. However, since he couldn't risk being left in the sand, he turned his anger at the professor's source of pride. "What's in there?"

The cackle grew into a hoot. "You're about to find out."

The pronouncement drew his attention out to the front. Objects disturbed the plain, so Rance cautiously maneuvered to gain a better view. Down in a valley were profiles of wooden structures. Compared to the treeless terrain, they appeared as tall as any cathedral.

As the wagon descended, the steep angles pushed him from his perch. With only a few miles to the end of this jarring journey, he settled himself in the most secure position.

The sun would be overhead soon. The loss of time disturbed Jody. He knew that most drives needed to make tracks in the dawn hours before the heat slowed man and animal. As he sat in the saddle, he shook his head at the bad omen.

Jack Barnes rode near. "They're a-coming. Be over the hill in less than an hour."

"We should have left without them," Jody said in disgust. "Let them catch up. We're going to lose the whole day."

Jack shrugged. "Just one day, son."

"One day creeps into two. Two makes a week before you know. At this rate, we'll be in Denver with a foot of snow on the ground."

"Ah," Jack said with a raised brow. "Now you sound like Frank Pearl."

Jody was ready to bark back but held his tongue. He recognized the tone in his own voice, yet the resemblance wasn't of the trail boss Frank Pearl, but was of the man who he came to know only as Smith over the return trail from Abilene.

At first, all he thought of Smith was that of a crusty old-timer set in his ways. As the days melded together to make weeks, which clumped into a month, it was the constant nagging to get things done right that now governed his own thoughts this day. He wouldn't admit it, but it was those lessons that gave him the confidence to make this cattle drive.

"I guess we can't change nothing." The lament filled his head for only a few seconds, when rising dust caught his attention. By the appearance, it was a single wagon coming toward the house. He looked to Jack. "Is that the chuck wagon?"

Jack squinted in the direction, then shrugged. "Let's go find out." They steered their horses and rode toward the wagon. As they approached, Jody confirmed his suspicion. The short, high-wheeled wagon with the bowed canvas cover could only be a chuck wagon. Now as they reined in, he knew what the wagon was, but he didn't recognize the man in buckskins driving it.

"Hello," was the greeting in a booming voice. The full beard matched the curly hair poking out from beneath the round-brimmed, short-crowned hat. A wide, friendly smile was a good sign, but the unfamiliar face didn't ease Jody's gut.

Jack nudged his horse to come along next to the driver's seat. The driver extended his hand. "I am Jon Sanderson. Trail cook, part sawbones, and passable fiddle player to keep the cows calm."

They shook hands. "Jack Barnes, pleased to meet you." He bobbed his head. "That's my son Jody. He's ramroding the outfit." Jack peered at the wagon. "Who have you worked with before?"

Sanderson inhaled as sign the question took some thought to answer. "Well, sir. I worked for none other than Jesse Chisholm back in '66. Cooked for his outfit all they way up to Wichita."

"That was four years ago," Jody said. "Where you been since?"

Sanderson looked to him with a bit of surprise to his grin. "Oh, here and there. Lately been cooking for a rancher in east Texas for the men riding the line." When it appeared the answer didn't suffice, the bearded man again grinned. "But I have been on some drives since. I was hoping to be on Chisholm's drive this year when I heard from the army post that you were looking."

The reply didn't seem to alarm Jack, but Jody's gut turned over. "Jesse Chisholm died two years ago. Every cow man in every direction knows that."

The grin turned to an open mouth of awe. "Rest his soul. No. I had not heard that. Must have been cooped up in that line shack too long."

Jody peeked at Jack. His pa once more curved his brow at the question, then grunted his throat clear. "Well, Mr. Sanderson, we're planning on taking the Goodnight Trail to Colorado. Likely take three months. Trying to get into the high plains before the summer. We're going to need food that's hot, tasty, and quick, if we're going to make it there on schedule."

Sanderson nodded. "Yes, sir. I know exactly what you mean and what you're needing. I guarantee three meals a day. Breakfast before sunup. Dinner by noon, supper when you've got them bedded down for the night. Biscuits, bacon, beans. Eggs when I can get them. I carry salt pork and with a little molasses make a mighty tasty stew. For that, I take six cents a plate."

"Six cents, huh," replied Jack. "That's a high rate."

"Yes, sir. But I am a fine cook. You'll see. How many hands you got?"

Jack peeked to Jody. "Oh, 'bout an even dozen."

"Dozen?" questioned Sanderson. "That's all?" He cocked his head to the side. "That's hardly enough for a man to make a living."

"Well, then maybe we don't have a deal, 'cause that's all that's coming," Jody answered firmly.

The cook eyed him, and Jody returned the stare.

"But," Jack said breaking the silence. "Maybe that's a fair trade. You wanting six cents a plate and us only having twelve drovers." He steered his horse about. Jody met him not far from the wagon. Before concern could be voiced, Jack whispered his reason. "I know what you're thinking, but we can't leave without a cook. We'll watch him for a while." He finished with a wink. It wasn't the solution Jody first wanted, but his pa had been right about so much in the past, he trusted his instincts.

Rattling turned their heads back to the wagon. From beneath the canvas cover emerged a young woman. A young Indian woman. Her black hair hung braided from each side of her face. She wore buckskins as well, but her straight single-piece dress draped at sign of a female figure.

"Who is that?" complained Jody.

Now standing on the side of the wagon, Sanderson looked to the woman, then showed his grin at them. "She's my wife. Her name is Dorothy."

The name sounded peculiar for an Indian. "Dorothy?"

"Jody," Jack said in a shaming tone.

Despite the question, Sanderson's tone remained friendly. He nodded. "That's right." He again looked to the Indian woman now standing at the boot. "She kind of reminded me of a girl I knew back home in Tennessee. The name was appealing to me, so I call her that." The grin gradually shrank from his face. "Is that a matter of concern to you, Mr. Barnes?"

Jody needed a deep breath. As he looked to the woman, his first thought was of the long trail to Colorado. How this Indian would mix with the rest of the drive stood as an unknown risk. However, despite their appearance of at least fifteen years apart, the man introduced her as his wife. To voice a complaint could spark a fight and cause more of a loss than just that of a trail cook. He shook his head.

"No. I apologize if there was any offense taken. It wasn't meant. It's just that cow drives with a bunch of ornery drovers ain't a place for a woman, if you get my meaning."

The grin returned. "Don't you worry about Dorothy. She is a member of the southern Cheyenne tribe. She can walk twenty miles a day toting a fifty-pound pack if she has to." Sanderson looked to his wife. "The Cheyenne raise their women as workers, Mr. Barnes. She ain't no dainty miss that needs any tending to. She'll earn her keep." The cook finished with a nod. The praise sounded more fitting of a fine mule.

As silence took over the next few seconds, Jack broke it with his own friendly tone. "Mr. Sanderson, we'd be happy to have you along. Meet up with us about three miles over that ridge to the west in about the next hour."

The cook again nodded. "I'll meet you there. Just want to feed and water the team. I'll be moving before long."

Jody relented to the choice of his pa. They both turned their horses back to the ranch. A peek above showed the day quickly passing. It galled him to have such a bad start, but he took another deep breath, realizing the more worry he gave it, the worse the trouble grew, but only in his own mind. As they approached the corral, he reined in and was about to dismount for some much-needed water. However, a peek toward the barn only galled him more. "Where do you think you're going?"

Astride the paint, Les led the racehorse called Lone Star toward them. "He's going with us."

"He's going with us? The question was to you. You ain't going."

Les looked to the house where Jessie came with the little kids near her apron. "Dang if I'm not," she answered. "Somebody got to tend to this horse, and I'm the only one that can handle him. It was your ma's idea."

Jody looked to Jessie. She nodded.

"I don't want that horse here. Don Pedro could send his men after it. I don't want no fuss while I'm here alone."

Jody looked to Jack, who shrugged as he dismounted. "Your ma is a strong-willed person," he muttered.

Despite the decision made without his knowledge, Jody stared back at Les. "I can take that horse. We'll put him in the remuda."

"And have ten thousand dollars worth of animal just free to roam? Maybe get bit by a rattler?" She shook her head. "No. I'm the one that will watch him." Jody's grimace only fueled her tone. "I ain't staying here, Jody Barnes. I've been telling you since I got here that this ain't a place for me. Rance Cash promised to get me home. Since that rascal done ran out on all of us, I'm taking his horse as proper payment to use to get back to Abilene."

Jody shook his head. "If you bellyache one time, I'll put you on that racehorse and slap its rump in the opposite direction."

The terse words seemed to steal some of her breath. Once she got wind, she mumbled the reply. "Fine by me."

"Here they come."

7

JACK'S ANNOUNCEMENT TURNED all heads to the west. Four riders came at a lope. Jody recognized Mr. Pleasant in his wool dress coat. Another rider stayed close by, and two other riders trailed behind. Jody slid off the saddle and went to get that water for his parched throat. When he reached the pump, he cranked out a gush and stuck his head into it.

When he shook the drops from his cheeks, he squinted back into the light to see all four riders now at the corral. Jack had already greeted the bunch.

"I'm sorry I'm not able to go with you," said Mr. Pleasant. "But I brought along some trail hands to use in my stead."

As Jody approached, he blinked twice to focus his bleary vision. To the far left he saw two Mexicans wearing broad sombreros and thick leather chaps. The sight was a welcome one for the work ahead. As he stepped closer, he blinked again to get the drops off his eyelids. When he could see clearly, he noticed the rider to the left of Mr. Pleasant. The floppy hat hid the face from immediate notice, so he needed another step to identify why the white shirt appeared peculiar. When he reached that step, his eyes went wide. The reason the white shirt poked out as it did was due to an ample bosom. He went closer to the fence to see the face. The smudges on the cheeks didn't hide the smooth skin nor the strands of blonde hair straying from beneath the hat.

"Penelope!?"

"Howdy, Jody," she replied in a stoic tone.

In disbelief, he somehow held his tongue, although there were many thoughts to voice. He looked to Jack. "We need to talk." He marched back to the front porch of the house with his pa not far behind. When he faced about, he stuck his nose to a point with his father's, trying to keep his voice low between his gritted teeth. "You knew about this, didn't you? Have you gone plumb loco?"

"You were saying you were aiming to see her once more. I told you you'd get your chance."

Jody huffed out a breath. "We wasted a whole day. And come to find out you hire a cook who don't appear to know the cow business. He's bringing along an Indian wife looks more like a daughter's age. Then Les thinks she's coming to nursemaid that racehorse, which ain't going to be no good on this drive. And now you bring us little Penelope Pleasant, thinking she's some sort of trail hand?"

Jack nodded. "I don't know if you've seen good, son. But, she ain't so little no more. Especially in more places than others."

"Three women?" Jody whined. "Three females. Les ain't so bad. At least I know she can tote water and stir beans. She ain't much for roping or chasing strays, but at least I can control her." He took another breath. "That Indian girl. She don't look right. Hard to know what she's like. But Penelope? She's likely to be moaning for home after the first week."

Jack put his palm up to stop the barrage. "Now, hold on there. I think she's changed quite a bit since last you saw her. When her ma took sick, she had to take over all the chores of the place. Her pa tells me she can ride as good as any man." He paused to dip his eyes to the ground. "Matter of fact, she tends to act more man than gal. Give her a chance. With what's showed up today, we may need every butt in a saddle we can get."

"That's another matter. Have you thought about what it may be like with men and girls out there on the range? I know. Just like when mustangs come across the remuda. One night, when we ain't all looking," he stammered, "men get to dreaming. Pretty soon, their drawers get too tight. You know what I mean."

Jack nodded. "I thought of that. But we'll have to make do. Like I said, we ain't got a lot of choice. You were the one hollering about getting the cows to market as soon as possible. There are sacrifices got to be made." He patted his son's chest with his palm. "Let's just get these dogies moving. We'll see what happens. May not be as bad as you think." He finished with the wink that had convinced Jody all his years that his father knew best.

They went back to the corral. "Sorry, folks. We just needed to get the route down that we'll be taking. We're going to swing the herd due west of San Antonio and pick up the Goodnight Trail there."

"Sounds like a good plan, Jack." said Mr. Pleasant. He pointed at the two Mexicans. "I brought along Noe and Alejandro from my spread to go with you. They're seasoned vaqueros and know how to handle these longhorns. They'll be a great help to you. I've told them I'll pay them when they return."

"Mighty fine," replied Jack. He arched his thumb behind him. "My son Jody will ramrod the drive." He motioned in the direction of the barn. "Les will handle most of the remuda. That there horse she's got needs special care, so she'll need some help from time to time."

"Won't get no help from me," Penelope announced. "I'll be too busy driving our cattle."

When not staring at the sky in disbelief at the situation, Jody noticed Les and Penelope eye each other like two hens. Their reaction to each other rivaled two bar hussies fighting over the same drunken cowpoke. It was all he could do to keep his mouth shut.

"Well," Jack said once more to break an awkward silence, "let's get to driving." He turned to his wife. "Mother, you take care of these young 'uns and I'll bring something pretty back in about four months." He gave Jessie a peck on the cheek.

Jody went to his ma and pecked the other cheek. "Keep the door latched all the time. Any smell of trouble, you hightail it to Mr. Pleasant's place in the buckboard."

"Don't fret over us, son," said Jessie. "I've been taking care of myself and kids out here since you were younger than them." She pecked Jody's cheek.

He smiled at his mother. He faced about and went to his mount. When he climbed into the saddle, he peeked to his right. Penelope's stern jaw rivaled the jowl of the crusty old Smith. Without a hint of sentiment of leaving her pa, she turned her horse toward the prairie.

Jody cocked his head to the side at her unusual manner. His eyes caught Les's as she stared from under the brim of the floppy hat. Her silence was as loud as any yell. "So, what are you waiting on?" he said as he turned his horse to the corral. He opened the gate and looped his lariat. With the ease of leashing an old dog, he slipped the loop around Brewster's neck and led the old bull from the corral.

"You're taking him?" Les asked. "Ain't he more good here?"

Jody shrugged. "No sense in leaving him behind to take sick." As he passed, he ran his eyes to her, then Lone Star. "Besides, seems we're taking along a whole mess that don't make sense on this drive."

Rance peeked from side to side as they entered town. Mud adobe huts with logs sticking from the sides sat next to more civilized structures resembling some American culture. However, if this was El Paso, it was no San Antonio, and San Antonio was certainly no New Orleans.

As the wagon mercifully came to a stop, Professor Booker hopped from the seat, arched his back in a painful motion, then walked out of view. Rance anxiously waited as the rear doors opened, casting brilliant light inside. The immediate illumination almost blinded him. With considerable effort, he struggled to move his aching legs to climb out of the back of the wagon. Once outside, his knees buckled, sending him to the ground.

"It is like a religious experience," said Booker. "Glad to see you are a God-fearing man, Mr. Cash."

Although his posture wasn't what he intended, he didn't argue for fear of spoiling any benefit he may have gained. Slowly, he claimed a wobbly stance as Professor Booker began unpacking the crates from the wagon.

"I thought I might venture about to see if I could get us some food."

Booker shook his head, dismissing the notion. "Can't spare a minute. They'll be here soon."

Rance scanned about the empty street. "Who might that be?"

"The locals." Booker pulled out the wooden box with the snake painted on the side. "One thing about coming into town. It don't take long before human curiosity takes over and brings them about like pilgrims to a church on the Sabbath."

Rance still stood confused. "Brings them to what?"

Booker snapped two buckles free from leather bindings and unfolded a large plank hinged to the rear doors, all painted in the same distinctly annoying color green. Reaching inside, he drew out two more sturdy planks, which fit neatly into slots cut into the underside of the first plank. In moments, he stood atop what appeared to be a stage. Booker now walked into the wagon and began stacking the crates. On the side of the crates, stenciled letters painted the words, Booker's Life-Altering Potion No. 16. A premonition pushed Rance to the side of the wagon. Framed in the same color green, a rendering of a coiled snake with dripping fangs portrayed in a submissive position to a portrait of the one and only piously posed Professor Booker holding a bottle amid the bright promise of the painted sun shining over a fertile valley.

"Oh, no," Rance muttered under his breath.

"I could use a hand here," said the professor while stacking the crates.

Rance walked back to the rear and noticed a few townsfolk heading in their direction. "I think I got the wrong impression as to your professor's degree. I'm not—"

"Not what?" said Booker. "Not eternally grateful for my kindness to save you from thirst in the middle of the desert? Not willing to help repay in some meager way your indebtedness to the man who could have let you languish until you were nothing but withered bones? Not able to call yourself a gentleman, so you'll welch on your honor to reciprocate in any means possible in order to show your gratitude?"

Despite his questionable morals, Rance never sat comfortable with the accusation of a welcher. He turned his head side to side as more of the population came near. "All right. What do I have to do?"

Booker's face went from stern to pleased satisfaction to one of concern. "We haven't got time for the spinning wheel of fireworks." He reached into the wagon and tossed Rance a set of overalls. "Strip to the skin and put only these on. And hurry."

Confused as to why, Rance complied by retreating to the front of the wagon. Quickly, he pulled the coat from his shoulders and unbuttoned his shirt. Professor Booker's loud barking was hard not to hear.

"Friends and neighbors, please gather near. It is so good to be back in your midst once more. My name is Professor Orville Booker. Physician, scientist, and inventor. Alchemist of all elements on the planet. Apothecary of exotic medicinal solutions of my own discovery to help heal the infirm. I have come to your humble hamlet located here in the wilderness of the Southwest to spread the bounty of my labors dedicated for the relief of the ailments and maladies inflicted upon you good Christian people."

As Rance pulled his trousers off and climbed into the overalls, he couldn't help admire the oratory.

"Now, friends," Booker continued. "It has been my mission, as dictated to me by the man above, to search the earth for a cure to the plethora of diseases sent here from Lucifer himself afflicting the Lord's flock. I have gone around the globe in service to the kings and magistrates of Europe and the Orient, practicing my unique skills from the Court of St. James to beyond the Great Wall of China, collecting remedies from those royal surgeons to all that plague mankind. In my noble quest, I came upon the knowledge bestowed for generations upon the maharajahs of India of their secrets of eternal health and was able to harness the healing power of the most deadly of venoms the world has ever experienced. This bottle, which I now hold in my hand, is the result of two decades of research. It contains what was once an agent of evil in the form of crippling poison from the fangs of the king cobra of India."

Rance threaded the thick buttons of the straps over his shoulders. The oversized garment sagged to expose his matted chest. Despite what modesty sacrificed, he crept closer to the wagon as twilight fell, sensing his cue in the act. He listened carefully to the Professor's dissertation.

"Fellow Christians, with the Lord's guidance, I was able to tame this most vile of nature's weapons, like Daniel in the lion's den, and transform it into the nectar of peaceful well-being. Fifteen attempts were needed before I was able to gauge the precise formula of many exotic extracts in order to invent Booker's Potion No. 16. Now, don't just take my word for it. Earlier this day I came upon a man of destitute circum-stances. I believe he is in the crowd among you. Where are you, Mr. Cash?"

8

"I SAY, MR. Cash. Are you out there?"

The cue given, Rance slowly crept into the dimming light. He rubbed his jaw, old habit when pressed into unfamiliar situations. The stubble about his chin and cheeks certainly gave him the look of destitution. Despite the proper appearance, being cast as an unsophisticate wasn't a complete comfort. He didn't enjoy being a supporting player in another's performance. It could make for difficult confidence building among these locals should he get the chance. Nonetheless, the part of the shill was an act he'd performed before.

As he stepped about the stage, Booker towered above, projecting an open palm like some divine angel. "There you are, sir. May I inquire again as to your vocation?"

Rance's eyes widened. This hadn't been rehearsed. As he peeked to the crowd, he mumbled the possibilities under his breath. Sportsman? No. Who would trust him? Maybe a farmer, a planter? What would be the first answer to any question about that life? No. Cattleman? Same problem. No. Lawman? What if asked about where he was the local law authority? Someone could be from any place he might mention. He peeked to their inquisitive faces. Another peek above showed Booker's impatience with the delay. What were the choices again? Lawman? No, not that one again. Law, law, law . . .

"Lawyer." The blurt was out in the air. It couldn't be retrieved. Might as well push it out once more to see any objections. "I was a lawyer." No shaking heads. Perhaps it was destined. But from where? When in doubt, the truth sometimes could prove useful. "From New Orleans."

"Lawyer?" Booker repeated. "Yes," the professor shook his head. "I remember you telling me now. What a noble profession." The professor's smile turned to a scowl. "And now look at you. Gone from a successful debater of the law to a poor, directionless drifter of no visible means. A pitiful example of an adult male. Is that not right, sir?"

The pride Rance felt for thinking up the perfect profession now sank with every verbal stone the professor hurled. Betrayed, Rance could only nod his head. The shame on his face was genuine.

"Earlier, as I conversed with Mr. Cash, I spoke of my magic elixir, which lifts spirits, rejuvenates the body by eliminating all the pathogens of the pathetic, which thrive in the souls of the disillusioned." He leaned closer toward Rance. "Take one sip of this salvation, sir. Imbibe the illumination of liquid sunshine."

Rance took the bottle. Apprehension had to be conquered in order to pull the cork. The deep breath was no act. However, as all eyes intently watched each move, he put the spout to his lips and raised the bottle.

At first, a hint of flavor splashed his tongue, almost like fresh-churned butter. As it quickly passed, the caustic burn of alcohol singed his taste buds, eating into the membrane of his mouth, dissolving all protective guardians of the throat, burning its way to his gullet. Air passages blocked, he coughed through the pain, eyes wide, certain this was his last moment of life.

"You see, friends," Booker announced, snatching the bottle from Rance's hand and raising it aloft. "See the cleansing taking effect on this poor man. All the evil and despair being boiled from the body."

Rance's eyes rolled in their sockets. Dizziness crept in his head, his brain starved for oxygen. He took a step back to keep his balance. If he fell, would he be buried at that spot?

"Don't be alarmed at the response to the treatment, friends. That is Potion No. 16's patented effect, scouring the soul of all which means it harm."

A desperate grasp of the wagon wheel saved Rance from spilling backward. The jolt was enough to allow him to swallow. The burning cleared his throat, allowing for a gush of air to spiral into his lungs, and he sounded a howl for all to hear.

"How do you feel, Mr. Cash?"

Tears blurred his vision. He blinked in an attempt to focus. Another gurgle spilled from his lips. His first thought spilled from his mouth as well. "Alive!"

"You see, friends!" Booker proclaimed. "An honest testimony to the miracle that is Potion No. 16. It treats if not outright cures gout, rheumatism, colic, jaundice, yellow fever, scarlet fever, and fever of all shades. It is effective against smallpox, cholera, whooping cough, and lumbago."

Rance inhaled his initial intake of fresh air. He swiped his arm against his brow to clean the sweat and tears from his eyes and cheeks.

"Look at Mr. Cash, friends. He is overcome with the rebirth of his health. Step right up and get your bottle of this miracle. Potion No. 16 is the godsend you've been waiting for. Not only is it a savior against sickness, not only does it chase away the aches from your joints and muscles, it also revitalizes the enzymes in the blood, producing vigor and a snap in your step. Ladies, it will make your mother's milk taste better to your offspring, while also warding off excessive body fluids and slimming your figure. Gentlemen, it will produce the same vitamins usually only found in the tropical fruits of the Amazon, thus awakening long-dormant nerves in the loins. I guarantee it will trim ten years off your normal age." He looked to Rance. "Don't you feel that's right, Mr. Cash?"

Barely revived, Rance could only nod and agree. "Oh, I'm sure it will take at least ten years away from you."

"You see, friends. Another honest testimonial from just one sip. Step right up and invest one dollar in the remainder of your life. Potion No. 16, when mixed in proper proportion, can also be used as a suitable fertilizer for your crops, clean your plow, and dissolve the filth jamming your farm machinery. It even tenderizes meat so it doesn't have to stay so long in the pot. Step right up, friends. Let this be the day that changes your lives. One dollar a bottle. That's all it costs you."

As Rance recovered, his part fulfilled and debt paid, he watched as the professor snatched the silver coins from the hands of the masses with the proficiency of any field hand picking cotton. In little time, one crate emptied and another was pried open. As more whisked away their share of salvation, the count doubled to fill the open spaces in the line. A frenzy ensued as more townsfolk rushed down the street.

Rance could only shake his head. Initially, he didn't care to be a player in the professor's show. The more he pondered his role, the greater the satisfaction he took in its success. If this town was so gullible as to throw their money at this charlatan, there may be a future here.

Like a furious storm, the wash of believers subsided to a slow trickle. With the final customer serviced, Professor Booker again arched his aching back.

"Seems you could use a taste of you own medicine."

Rance's remark surprised and appeared to alarm the professor. Another moment later, Booker understood the ironic intent. He shook his head. "None for me. Can't drink the profit. Besides, I know what's in it."

The mention brought the question to mind. "You know, while I was struggling for life, I did wonder as to the ingredients."

Booker shrugged with a smug grin. "Trade secret."

"My guess is a little Jamaican rum spiced with a dash or two of chili pepper?"

Booker counted the stack of coins in his hand. "Could be something like that. Don't spare the few drops of opium. Dulls the effect."

"And the mind, I'm sure," replied Rance.

Booker kept bobbing his head as to the accuracy of the accusation. Once counted, he slipped the coins in his pocket. "Sixty-three new dollars. Not a bad night."

Rance realized as the professor began stacking the empty crates back into the wagon the chance for a cut of the profit wasn't likely in the plans. With the stage emptied, the professor hopped off and went about striking the planks to pack the stage.

"Maybe we could share a meal?"

The professor once more shook his head. "No. No time for that." He folded the plank into the frame of the rear door and closed up the back of the wagon. "In this profession, it's a little dangerous to linger about. We'll make camp a few miles out of town. I do have a few scraps of enough to make a stew."

One word stood out among all the others. "We?"

The question stopped Booker in his tracks. "Well, you're coming with the show, aren't you? The whole of New Mexico beckons to be saved."

The offer surprised Rance. He hadn't given much thought of continuing his role. The time recalled spent in the back of that wagon ached his back just standing still. He shook his head. "I think I might just stay here a few days. Might be a market for those with elocutionary skills. I can spin a few words myself."

Booker smiled. "I have no doubt." He pointed at the spot where Rance previously stood. "That performance was remarkable. You even had me convinced of the power of my potion. You're a natural."

Rance smiled. "That was no act." He retrieved his clothes and gun belts from the street and shook them clear of the dust. "Appears they will need some brushing."

Booker reached into his pocket. "Here, take these," he said handing over two dollars to Rance. "Get them cleaned. Maybe a shave, too. Keep the overalls as a souvenir."

Rance forced a smile at the gesture of the puny gift. "How generous of you."

"Don't give it a second thought. Only fair." Booker walked to the front of the wagon. He climbed into the seat and wasted no time in taking the reins. It must have been a lesson learned in the past that the best chance to leave might be the only one. He shook the reins, and the team responded. He steered to the right, picking up the road out of town. With a wave, he gave a silent farewell.

Rance watched as he disappeared into the darkness. Then he looked to the shiny silver coins. Caution told him to take a bite of the edge. When the coin didn't bend, it was nice to learn that even the noted professor had some professional ethics. He looked again at the ruts in the sand left by the wagon. And so concluded his experience with Professor Orville Booker peddling his tainted tonic.

Rance faced about. Fortune had placed him once more in unknown surroundings. Torches stuck from pillars lighted the boardwalks. He strolled through the night, the brisk air cooling his exposed skin. Another peek at the coins sparked future plans to multiply them. As he neared the center of town, a pair of swinging batwing doors drew his attention.

Jody swung his leg over the horn and slid off the saddle. The pitch of night had settled, bringing a stiff north wind with it. However, it wasn't the chill putting a spite to his lips.

He marched toward the campfire. Sanderson's wagon meant he had fulfilled his promise to meet up with the drive. However, it wasn't much of an achievement. Jody came near the flames, pulling his hands from his pockets and holding out his palms to absorb the heat. He took a tin cup from the line and with the hook, tipped the pot to fill the cup.

Hooves pounded from the dark. He turned to see Les leading Lone Star near the chuck wagon. She tied the reins of the paint and the lead on the racehorse to one of the wheels. For just a moment, she stared at him but didn't come near. As she walked in a different direction, he wanted to tell her he was sorry, but he just didn't have the words formed on his tongue. Besides, she had seen him mad before. There would be other times for them to talk.

A glance to the right showed Sanderson and his Indian wife mixing their wares in different bowls. It made no sense to pry into their business. As long as there was food for the night, it was all he cared about at the moment.

Another rider emerged from the night. Jack Barnes came into the light. Jody went up to him. "We didn't make three miles today."

Jack shrugged. "We knew we wouldn't get far. Don't think of it as losing a day. Think of it as making a start."

His pa's words didn't cool his temper. Having been part of a successful trail drive run by the legendary Frank Pearl, he saw only the wrong about this one. A deep breath took away some of the edge that poked his gut. The steaming brew might do some good as well. He sipped at the edge of the tin.

The first taste was like that of flowery paint. He spat it to the ground. "What the tarnation is that?"

"What's a matter, Mr. Barnes?" asked Sanderson in an unconcerned tone. He continued chopping stems. "Ain't you had chicory before? I didn't have time to get supplies for this trip with us moving out so sudden. Tomorrow, I'll search out a general store to get some coffee."

Jody shook his head. He watched as the steam blew off the top of the cup. He wondered if the breeze could cool his temper in the same manner or if it was going to blow in more unexpected trouble.

9

THE SIGN OUTSIDE called it simply the Raven. Rance Cash peeked above the batwing doors. He had visited bigger closets in his past, normally those of wives with absent husbands and too much time and money on their hands. Still, it stood as a break from the breeze, so he entered. A simple and plain bar stood to the right with a four-foot-wide mirror hanging on the back wall. The barkeep must have heeded nature's call, because there wasn't anyone tending the bar.

He glanced about to see the room empty. Perhaps it was worth the risk just to sample the local whiskey. Some saloons watered the liquor to the point of delusion. He took one step and then another and soon found himself behind the bar and within easy reach of the bottles. He reached for one with an interesting label. He needed something to wash that awful taste of Potion No. 16 out of his mouth.

"It's four bits if you're taking a slug from the bottle." A turn to the left showed a woman in a red dress not fit for a Sunday sermon. From the distance, she stood five feet six, maybe five. What held his tongue was the blended complexion of olive and brown. The auburn hair showed she wasn't a native. "Two if you want a glass."

The pricing brought him from his daydream. "Thank you. I was just curious as to the selection." He casually moved in front of the bar. As he moved, the beauty took a chair at a table. The deck encouraged him to think he'd found a kindred soul. "You must be the local player to beat."

She took the cards, shuffling, and threaded them all the

while wearing an enticing smile. "Why? Are you looking to play, or you needing to get back to your chickens?"

He peeked at the overalls. "Oh." He took a few more steps toward the table. "Actually, this is sort of a costume." He pointed to the folded clothes hung from his arm. "In truth, I am a sportsman myself." He tossed the bundle into an empty chair and took a seat. She didn't appear impressed and kept shuffling. With a closer view, she held the remarkable features of a fine white woman in shaded skin. He couldn't be sure if she were a Southern mulatto, an exotic import from the Far East, or if she just carried a Mediterranean heritage. Either way, she was captivating to the eyes despite being surrounded by some of the harshest conditions mankind dared to inhabit. "So, how did such a pearl as yourself find her way to such a dusty pit as this?"

The question was meant as a compliment. However, the curve of her brow showed she didn't accept it as such. "Pit? You have a strange way of making yourself welcome, mister . . ."

"Cash," he finished her sentence. "Rance Cash. Not only a name but an eternal pursuit. And what may I call you?"

She kept shuffling, then dealing the cards faceup with a decided snap to her delivery. "Cash, huh? Doesn't look like you got any. Or have you?"

The delay in the introduction only served to draw him closer. He recognized the play. The longer he lingered watching her handling the cards with her delicate lace-gloved fingers, the more eager he should become to seek a game. Despite the temptation, the two dollars weren't worth risking unless he was the one dealing the cards.

"Well, let's say I am a man of varied means. Currently I am waiting on a shipment of dry goods to arrive here so I can open up my store." He pointed his nose at the cards as she chewed on the lie. "You know, you are doing that wrong."

"Dry goods?" she questioned.

He nodded with confidence. "Yes. I own a chain of stores in the East. St. Louis, Memphis," he paused to smile, "New Orleans. I have just established the latest one in San Antonio, run by my good friends Paul and Mary Collum. They suggested I come west and seek new customers." He slid his hand along the table and stealthily eased the deck from her grasp. "Any day now, you should see a caravan of wagons, all loaded with flour, linen, and sundry items." He shuffled the cards. The edges slipping through his thumbs were like therapy, renewing his spirit and giving him the confidence to continue. "However, since that may be days away, I may need an activity to bide my time." He stacked the cards and slapped the deck in front of her. "Do you care for a game?" He arched a brow at her. "Stud," he said, then paused, "has always been a favorite pastime."

The confusion faded from her eyes and mouth. Her face eased into that of an equal player. "Oh, I bet it is." She placed her hand atop the cards, then stopped. "But I never cared for it. Only suckers play into that game." About to cut the deck, she paused again. "Usually, I like to play for bigger stakes."

The dare was intriguing. While Rance thought, the barkeep returned to his post with one suspender hanging limp. The woman peeked at the bar.

"Since you obviously are a man with holdings, and willing to take a chance, especially since you are bringing your money to such a pit as El Paso, I'd like to make it interesting." She eased the deck from his hand and reshuffled. Rance watched the cards carefully, since his stack was being dismantled. "Since it seems like it's going to be a slow night, I think a man such as yourself might be willing to play for the high card. Two out of three." She paused. "For a hundred dollars? Are you game?"

Rance coughed. The staggering amount was out of place for such a small establishment. Not even in the finest gambling parlors of New Orleans was there such an opening bet. Despite the stakes, he sat and pondered. While watching her shuffle, he considered her tactics.

As evidenced by the near-vacant hallway and the size of the Raven, the lack of steady business meant that she might be trying to make her wages for the next two years all in one night, just as a swamp cottonmouth sought a single kill to sustain itself for several months. He cocked his head to the side to buy more time.

There was another possible reason for the large bet. She may be trying to see if he really had the money. His own lie must have whet her appetite to bite into an Eastern mark. He certainly would desire so. Should he have such a sum in government greenbacks, it would answer the question. Of course he did not. He curled the ends of his lips for a few more seconds.

Finally, the last angle of the possible ploy made more sense. She wanted to rid the table of him. After all, he was dressed like a sodbuster. The days spent riding in the back of Professor Booker's wagon must have taken a terrible toll on his appearance. A casual rub of his chin reminded him he hadn't shaved in weeks. On careful inspection, the texture of the stubble had softened to a curl just in the few minutes since he left the professor. It must have been quite a toil on her eyes to focus on his grotesque features. The longer he thought about it, the more convinced he was that this was the reason she would name such a high amount.

However, he was tired and needed a place to rest that didn't include his legs being bound in cramped conditions. He glanced about the room. There didn't seem to be prospects for another game walking through the batwing doors. He faced her. "My dear . . ." He stretched for her to fill in the blank with her name. She remained silent as a mute. "I'm sorry. I didn't get your name."

"No, you didn't." Her firm reply left little hope she was to answer the question. He took the hint.

He leaned to take the bundle from the adjacent chair. "Although I would love nothing more than to risk fortunes with such a lovely woman." As he lifted the coat and trousers, the .44 came into view. He peeked at her, confirming she had noticed as well. Never enjoying to worry a woman, he quickly wrapped the weapons inside the bundle. He bobbed his head to the side. "My apology. One can never be too careful while traveling to the outreaches of civilization." He put the clothes in his lap, gauging his chances of finding a convenient alley in which to spend the night. "I must seek proper lodging for a man of my station, and in this town that may take some time. I don't suppose you have any advice?"

Initially, her polite but insincere grin didn't show much promise. With his bluff called, he was about to rise when heavy boot steps on the boardwalk signaled new customers were about to arrive. He glanced over his shoulder at the front batwing doors. Two men in broad hats and bandannas about their necks stopped just short of entering. The doors blocked the view of their torsos, but it stood a fair bet they carried the appropriate firearms needed for daily life in the frontier. Below the doors it could be seen that both men wore high, unpolished leather boots. It was the customary uniform of the Westerner. However, their scruffy whiskers didn't impress Rance that these men were cowhands or bull whackers. They peered about the room, then walked from view, their pounding steps reverberating through the wooden walls.

Rance faced the woman. Her eyes were wide and her mouth slightly ajar. After a moment, she looked into Rance's eyes. "I can recommend a place for you to stay, Mr. Cash. With me."

The offer was stunning. Rance blinked twice. He again glanced at the door and realized the reason for her mood change. Those strangers must not have been friends.

"I beg your pardon?"

She looked once more at the door while she spoke. "You know how to use those irons?"

Rance peeked at the bundle in his lap. The inquiry would normally be absurd. Would a man own a horse if he didn't know how to ride? Would he wear a pair of pistols if he wasn't proficient with their use? Unfortunately, the more he thought about his decided lack of skill with either tasks ceased his self-assessment. Instead, he relied on his one instinctive talent. "A man would be a fool if he carried a gun and didn't know how to use it."

She steered her panicked face at him. "Avis McFadden." Her hand jutted out like a sword. "Pleased to meet you." Her palm opened, and Rance gently accepted it. "You know, it is getting late. Doesn't look like there's much to hang around here for." With a quick swipe of her hand, she collected the deck and slipped it into a side pocket of the red dress and stood. Rance sat dumbfounded at her harried behavior. After a moment, while her attention was mostly directed at the front door, she finally looked at him with disgust. "What are you waiting for? Think you're going to get a better offer tonight?"

Like a soldier snapped to attention, he rose to his feet. "No, ma'am," he answered swiftly.

She walked around the table, retrieved a shawl from the arm of the chair, and headed toward a back unlit hall. "Sam," she said, maintaining her pace. "I'm calling it a night. We may have better luck tomorrow."

Rance peeked at the barkeep, who continued wiping out shot glasses and didn't appear surprised at the woman's manner. Rance followed her into the darkness. The lamplight from the bar barely illuminated what appeared a storeroom full of crates of liquor. A moment later, the creak of a door preceded the sight of outside moonlight. The woman poked her head to each side to view the alley. Apparently safe, she stepped outside and waved Rance to join her.

He came alongside her. She wrapped the shawl around her shoulders. The action and his close proximity drew his eyes to the low neckline. As he focused for a better appreciation, she drew the end of the shawl over the attraction. She led him to the street and up onto the boardwalk. Unsure exactly what was in store for the evening, he walked with her at a leisurely pace while she preferred a quick step. About to increase his gait, she slowed upon view of two figures barely visible in the moonlight standing across the street.

In an instant, he felt her arm tucked around his elbow and her shoulder huddled closer to his. Ever the chivalrous gentleman, he aimed his most ominous facade at the two across the street, despite being dressed like some hayseed holding his laundry in both hands.

When they passed the stationary figures, she tugged toward another alley. The tall buildings blocked the light, and it was all he could do to just follow her lead and not stumble over the obstacles in their path.

They reached a staircase attached to the side of a building. Without hesitation, she hiked her dress so as to scamper up the steps. Uncertain if the invitation included his attendance in her home, Rance didn't wait for clarification. After a quick peek behind to see if they were followed, he went up the stairs behind her. Once at the second story landing, she drew the key from her top and inserted it into the lock. A simple turn and a slam of the shoulder popped open the door.

Rance took one last look at the street below. At the instant he saw it was empty, a hand clutched his collar and dragged him inside.

10

THIS WOMAN NAMED Avis pulled with the force of a ten-mule team, then slammed the door behind him. "What are you doing? Trying to make sure they know where I live?" She cracked open the door for a quick peek.

Rance angled his head for a peek himself, then found his attention drawn to her arched anatomy. "Let who know where you live?"

"Those two men," she answered, shutting the door. She sidestepped him while removing her gloves. In a moment, a match was struck and a lamp lit. Rance noticed the interior. The humble dwelling had a porcelain basin and pitcher atop a thin-legged table where the lamp sat. A simple square table sat at the near wall. An angled ceiling showed water stains between the planks; however, it likely wasn't important to worry about rain in the middle of the desert. In the rear of the place was a room draped by a ring-hung curtain. He concluded it to be the bedroom, whatever its size. A glimpse would've been nice to gauge his chances for a peaceful night's sleep, but the curtain filled the opening. "You didn't see them?"

He shrugged. "I saw two men. Not an unusual sight in a town. Why? Who are they to you?"

She took a deep breath. When she exhaled, she flashed that enticing smile. "Well, I'll tell you," she said, her hand brushing against the side of her dress. Her palm stroked her hip and then her thigh. "But first, I think we need to get to know each other." She pulled up the side of the dress to expose long black net stockings. Rance was frozen in place. However bad he thought his luck when he arrived in this town, he rescinded every curse previously thought. As he watched more of her leg come into the light, he felt his jaw drop. As quick as she had hiked the hem, she drew a cap and ball derringer pistol from a garter holster, cocked the hammer, and pointed the barrel at him. "Hand over your clothes."

It took a moment before he awoke from the daze and realized she had aimed a firearm at him. "What?"

"Don't play dumb with me. Hand over those clothes, and let's find out who you really are."

"But I told you, my name is Rance Cash."

She took a step closer, carefully steadying the aim at his gut. She reached for the bundle of clothes and clutched them to her chest. "That might be your name, but you ain't no store owner. By the looks of you, I'd say you're a gambler down on your luck and looking for an easy way to make some money."

With another bluff called, he thought it time to finally show his hand. In a natural motion to convey the truth, he took a step toward her as she looked about the clothes. As soon as it was taken, she saw the move, dropped the clothes to thud against the wood floor, and pointed the single-shot pistol at his nose. Rance retreated.

A peek below showed the .44 Colt lying on the floor. She bent to pick it up. The heavy weapon wobbled in her hand.

"Be careful with that. Make sure you know where you're aiming it at."

"Hush, or you'll wake the old woman downstairs." She tucked the Colt .44 under her arm and poked about his coat and trousers, knifing her hand into the pockets. "What I figured. Not a nickel."

The discovery didn't help his self-esteem. Yet he still had his wits. "As I said, I am a man of varied means."

"Does that mean you don't have very much?"

Her remark curled his lip. "Well, what about you? If you had a gun, why did you want me to come with you with mine?"

She looked at him and shook her head. "Because this only shoots once and ain't no good beyond ten feet." She resumed her search of his clothes. "If those two were about to commence shooting, I wanted another target for them to aim at."

He bit his lip and nodded. "Thank you for your generosity in thinking of me."

She rose, holding out the shoulders of his rust-colored coat. "This is yours?" she giggled.

"That's a very expensive garment. It came from a friend of mine, who I followed on the way out here. His name is Rodney Sartain, but he sometimes dresses as an old man goes by the name of Dudley."

She shook her head while bending again and picking up the pepperbox in the holster. "This yours, too?"

"Whose else would it be?"

Again she giggled and shook her head. "I remember my grandpa telling me about these. I think I recall him telling me they were the most useless gun a man could own."

Rance inhaled deeply. "All right. Are you going to continue to ridicule every possession, or can I have them back so I can leave?"

She pointed the pepperbox and the derringer at him. "You ain't leaving."

"Oh no?" Disgusted, he went to where she had dropped his coat and trousers, picked them up, and turned for the door. "You seem perfectly able to ward off any trouble." While walking to the door he heard her scurry behind him.

"Take another step, and I'll put a hole in you as big as one of those empty pockets."

Still determined, he reached for the knob. "No you won't. That will certainly wake that old woman downstairs." When he sensed she was right behind him, he whirled about, swatting the pepperbox from her hand and snatching the derringer from her fingers. The Colt dislodged from under her arm and fell onto his toe.

"Oooowwh," he grunted. She instantly covered his mouth with her right hand. The agony of his throbbing toe angered him so, he grabbed her wrist and pulled it away from his mouth. When she put up her left palm to stop his groaning, he wrapped his elbow around her arm, seizing it and bringing her closer to him. With both her hands disabled by his grasp, she leaned closer to him and covered his mouth with her own to muffle his moan.

Her warmth distracted him from the pain. After an instant, her harsh slam against his lips turned tender. It took only moments for him to forget about his toe, perhaps due to blood rushing to another appendage. When he stopped even the lightest of noise, she still kept her moist lips upon his. It wasn't until both needed to breathe that they parted.

He sensed her heavy breath wafting into his face. "Why, Miss McFadden, not that I'm complaining, but why did you do that?"

"That woman downstairs is the landlady. She told me if I wake her once more, she'd make me move. Why? Don't you feel better?"

He tasted her lips again. "As a matter of fact, I feel a renewed sense of strength." He swept his right arm beneath her legs, lifting her into his arms. She clasped her hands around his neck as a sign of agreement to his silent suggestion. With an internal clock ticking in his head set to the pulse pounding through his veins, he carried her, first to the table to quietly deposit the derringer on the table near the basin, then went to the curtain.

He angled his shoulders to wedge his elbow at the end of the curtain and straightened to send them to the side. The small room was no more than three walls and a bed little bigger than a cot. He placed her on the mattress and lay on his side next to her. Quickly they joined lips once more. He rubbed her side. She ran her palms along his arms and shoulders.

He sensed a slight shiver to her nerves when he probed about the frame of her body, but she didn't protest. As he discovered each inch of her flesh, he reminded himself of his obligation as a Southern gentleman.

During his exploration with his mouth and fingertips, it became apparent she trembled while wrapped in his arms. It was not an unknown reaction. On the occasions when he shared bedsheets with women for the first time, he found they were in need of more than just carnal satisfaction. Those women sought the closeness of a man, the security of a masculine embrace, the need to succumb to a dominant force. Yet, also there remained their unspoken demand to be treated not just as a weaker gender, but as a trophy, to be relished, earned, and respected.

As he lay next to her, he peered deeply into her eyes. The faint light from the faraway table didn't allow for him to see, but the texture of her skin and the contours of her feminine form guided him better than any map.

Where there was cloth and metal clasps, they were soon removed either by his clumsy effort or her graceful motion to escape their bounds. He felt her fingers run through his matted chest and a forceful yank to slide the straps of the overalls from his shoulders. She quickly saw to its continued path to the floor.

Once he was completely freed from the overalls, she aggressively scanned his body with her palms and with no time lost found what she sought. He didn't protest. She made it clear to him with her pace that she wanted the same treatment. He did his best to comply.

With the neckline stretched to its limit, he squeezed the dress past the thin shoulders and once her arms slid from the sleeves, he peeled it all the way to her waist. Only a few wiggles were needed to be get it beyond her hips and off the bed.

While Sanderson stoked the fire under the kettle, Jody went to the wagon for his bowl of stew. With his hands around the rim, he stood at the back of the wagon where the Indian woman stood with the ladle.

She dipped the crooked spoon into the mix and drew out the ration to fill the bowl. Jody averted his eyes from her stare. He reached for a hardtack roll, but she did as well. Their hands brushed, and for an instant, she ran her fingers across the back of his hand. Surprised at the accident, he looked to her. She averted her eyes from his.

Confused as to what might have been meant and still perturbed over the events of the day, Jody cleared his mind of the incident, taking a peek at her husband, who returned to the wagon.

"Get all you want?" asked Sanderson.

Jody hesitated at the question. He glanced at the woman, then back at the cook. "Yeah," he answered with a nod. "All that I was needing."

Sanderson greeted the remark with a grin and a chuckle.

"Well, this ain't the best that I can cook. Due to the late start, I had to whip up something quick. Tomorrow, it'll have a few spices that I've been saving up. If we make enough time tomorrow after dinner, I can have us a praline pie waiting."

The reminder of the late start poking his gut, Jody turned for a seat by the fire while he still had an appetite. He stepped over some sleeping bodies, not wanting to interrupt the few moments of rest they managed to collect.

As he carefully placed his boot in an empty spot, a figure in front of him froze his step. In the flickering light, he recognized Les from under the brim of the hat. Stuck with legs wide apart and a hot metal bowl in hand, he waited for her to angle from his way. She stood firm.

The first words on his tongue formed a gruff order to move, but he held those back and eased his temper. "How did you get along out there?"

She stood stoic for a moment. Slowly, he saw her chin bob up and down. "All right, I guess." Her tone didn't hold the same spite he'd known since that day he discovered she wasn't a boy. With the heat building in his palm, he slowly pushed off with his back foot to get past this spot in the camp and her. When he managed a step, he glanced back.

"Well, just stay close to the herd," he offered as parting advice.

She kept looking at his face but remained silent. Without a nod or a smile, she kept walking and disappeared into the darkness. He had a minor urge to call to her and ask more, but he was surrounded by drovers looking to him as the leader. It wouldn't do for him to be coddling to a young girl. He looked back toward the fire.

The nearest empty spot was next to his father. He settled on a log, balancing the bowl. Jack finished his meal and curled his coat collar around the back of his neck. "I think you were right."

Jody looked to his pa, then the stew. " 'Bout what?"

"About suspecting this cookie of not knowing his business."

Jody picked up his spoon and dipped into the stew. About to put it in his mouth, he asked, "Why you say that?"

Jack exhaled. "Worst food I've had in twenty-seven years."

Jody held his spoon stiff, then dropped it in the bowl. He put the dish to the ground. A chuckle occurred to him. "Might be that long since you've tasted other cooking besides Ma's."

Jack nodded. "That could be."

Jody inhaled deep, glancing at the half moon. He shook his head. "What else is going to go wrong?"

"Don't know, son," said Jack. "But we can't let it fret the others. They're counting on us to fix it."

Once more his father's advice had stirred his mind in a different direction. If matters were worst on the first day, they'd have to improve as a few more wore on. As he pondered, a rider reined in from the dark. A few moments later he saw it was Penelope. Her tall frame walked straight into the camp, carrying her saddle and removing her hat to show her braided blonde hair in a pair of tails. She strode straight for her bedroll. Even with the advice on the stew, Jody thought it peculiar she wouldn't be hungry. "Get you something to eat, Penelope?"

She shook her head. "I just want to get my share of shut-eye before my turn."

Her manner worried Jody. He turned to Jack. "She going out alone to nighthawk?"

Jack shrugged. "She's a big gal. Her daddy said she was as good as any hand he'd had."

"But she's still a girl," Jody replied.

"And," Penelope spoke in a loud tone. "If any of you come near my bedroll thinking you're going to get a chance to poke your pecker in me," she warned drawing a carving knife from her belt, "I'll cut it off and roast it for jerky." She continued on her way and settled just off in the dark.

Jody turned again to his pa. Jack shrugged once more and shook his head. "Must be her time."

11

DESPITE RIDING THE front flank, Jody couldn't help look back to be sure the drive was still following. The second day hadn't started much better than the first. Having been on Frank Pearl's drive the year before, he learned the value of rising an hour before daylight to get the sleep out of the eye, the bacon and biscuits down the gullet, and the saddle on the ponies about the time the sun rose to get the cows in the mood to move without much minutes wasted.

He hadn't taken into account the sun being lazy. However, the late winter morning wasn't as early as the ones in June. At least a good hour or more was lost just waiting on the light. The time could've been better spent pushing beeves across prairie, and once all were out of their bedrolls and awake enough to ride, it took more than needed just to get them headed in the proper direction.

Now, as he gauged the sun near in the center of the sky, he had to take some comfort that he was a good day ahead of yesterday's start. With each second considered, he boldly anticipated getting in ten miles minimum before the day was gone.

About the moment he faced straight, distant shouts twisted him back in the saddle. He squinted to the south. Some dust not from his own herd rose high enough to be seen. He steered about to get a better look. When he recognized the sight of a set of horns and then two, he nudged his mount to a trot.

As Jody rode by, Enos and Marvin slowed their pace, watching him pass. He waved them to continue for fear of suffering another lapse in progress. Once convinced they'd obey his stern motion, he resumed the way to the new discovery. Upon approach, he saw what appeared to be at least a dozen lead cows but no riders to keep them bunched. A few more straggled behind the first bunch, then a few more. Jody rode around the front flank and hollered them into form. A few minutes was all he needed to get them to follow the initial dozen.

As he kept riding the outer flank, more and more steers appeared over a rise. Finally, as he grouped them tighter, he saw Danny Cochran doing his best to huddle cows into a single direction. Jody rode out to help.

"Good to see you, Dann—Dan," he greeted while concentrating on keeping the cows from slipping further into a clutch of trees. "Didn't know you were coming."

Danny, the same youthful gleam on his face that Jody remembered from many years past, came alongside. "Been riding all night to catch up. You wouldn't believe the trouble it was finding them in the dark. Didn't think we'd catch you this quick."

The mention poked the sore spot in Jody's gut. "But it's good to see you."

When Jody was satisfied most of the steers would follow the ones in front of them, he stopped his horse. Danny did the same. The first thought was to explain why the drive hadn't gotten very far, but an instant's consideration stopped that flow of words to stem his own excuses. Instead, he decided to talk about their addition to the herd. "Seems a heap more than you expected."

The comment didn't have the intended effect on Danny's face. "Yeah," he answered with a nod. About the moment he was to explain, the cousin Tucker came cutting through the herd, scattering the bunch of cows Jody had just formed. "We just seemed to find more and more of them in the hills."

Tucker rode up next to Danny. "We going to stop to eat?" he asked Danny, who turned to Jody.

When Jody pointed in the distance, he saw Jack riding their way. "No, we ain't stopping. The chuck wagon is two or three miles ahead." He huffed a breath. "At least I hope so."

Jack slowed his horse and nodded. "Been a long time, Danny."

Jody noticed the disappointment on Danny's face. "It's Dan now."

Jack nodded, then looked to Tucker. "I heard you came up with a lot more head than you first thought."

The information appeared not an item Tucker wanted shared. He first peered at his cousin, then struggled to come up with an answer. "Just shows you don't know what's out there until you go looking for it, is all," Tucker said with a shrug.

"Any of them sick?" asked Jack. Both cousins shook their heads. "In that case," Jack continued. "We're awful glad to have you."

The pounding of hooves turned Jody to the north. Enos and Marvin approached. The son held a more pleasant face than his father. "It's darn good to see you," Enos said as he reined in. Marvin slowed his horse in a milder fashion. His caution also showed while eyeing the stranger cousin.

As head of the drive, Jody thought it his duty to be sure all knew the other. "Dan, you know Enos Adair and his pa Marvin. And you two know Dan. This here is Dan's cousin from near the border. Tucker." He paused. "What'd you say your last name is?"

It took more than a moment before the answer. "Winston."

"That's it," Jody said with a nod. "Anyways. These boys are joining our drive."

"Where'd you get all these cattle?" Marvin asked in an unfriendly tone. Jody had thought the same, but didn't think it time to start a squabble. However, it was Jack who was quicker with the right words once more.

"I'm sure they've got a few mavericks, but that ain't a matter to be settled while they're scattering before us."

Jody recognized his pa's tactic. There was a different time to be worried about others' stock. In fact, the more he thought, a different worry entered his head. "Speaking of that, who is driving the herd with all you here?" When each face looked to other with an expression of blame in the same manner as to who broke wind, Jody shook his head. "You left it to those Mexican boys and Penelope, with Les alone with the remuda? Two Mex and two girls," he paused again to shake his head.

"Fellows, we got a long way to go just to get out of Texas. We ain't doing it sitting here a yammering."

Brilliant light irritated his eyes. His mind swirling back to the desert, Rance opened them to discover that, instead of dead in the sand, he slumbered in a soft bed butted against a beautiful woman. He breathed relief.

Feeling a need to pay some gratuity, he gently pressed his lips to her cheek. It was enough to elicit a contented smile from her face. She rolled onto her back and while propped on an elbow he admired her bare front before she restored her modesty with the sheet.

"Good morning," Avis said groggily.

Rance squinted into the daylight beaming through the far window. "I'd say it may be more appropriate to welcome the afternoon." His masculine urges tempted him to begin this day as he had ended the previous. As he leaned closer, she apparently sensed his intentions and stopped him with the point of a finger.

"What is that?" she asked.

He peeked at where she touched. The scar on his shoulder was a painful memory. However, he instantly saw it as a reason she should comply with his plans for an encore. "Oh, that. That, my dear, is a wound I suffered while . . . while," he had to come with a better reason than the truth, "defending the honor of a woman."

A full moment passed before she cracked a grin of disbelief. "A woman?"

"Of course," he said, feigning insult. "I was put in a difficult position." As he thought more, a mix of the truth actually held appeal. "A young damsel had incurred a tainted reputation as one not faithful to her vows of marriage. It was a terrible stain on her name, and I felt compelled to stand good for her."

"Uh-huh," she hummed with a hint of doubt. "And, let me guess. You somehow were part of this 'tainted reputation' and played a part in breaking her vows?"

Rance rolled his eyes to the angled wood planks above. "Well, of course, we met."

"Uh-huh," she baited him to continue.

Her enticing smell distracted him. He didn't care to spend any more energy dreaming up a lie. He was lying naked next to a gorgeous naked woman. "You know, this is really not the point of the story."

"How would I know? It's your story."

The truth was much easier to recall. "A man named Colton Schuyler tried to kill me," he said, sliding his elbow in order to creep even closer to her. "His aim was off slightly. Thank God." His lips were within an inch of hers.

"Was that her husband?"

He shook his head but didn't stop his advance. "No." Before he could swoon her with a kiss, she asked another question.

"Well, who was he?"

Her interest in his past and disinterest in his presence forced him stop. He propped his elbow once again. "How can you be a professional in the games of chance and not know Colton Schuyler?"

Avis shrugged.

"He was renowned as the best player on the Mississippi. The legend was that no one beat his play. Until I did. A defeat he took completely too personal."

"So he tried to kill you because you cheated him at cards?"

Now he didn't feign insult. "No. He was hired by Hiram Schaefer to kill me. And why do you think I cheated him?"

"Because you look like you would have." While his pride took a blow, she pulled the sheet closer to her chin and appeared enamored of his history but not him. "Hiram Schaefer? I've heard of that name."

"He's the owner of the Eastern Pacific Railroad," Rance muttered as his ego healed.

"How would you know him? Did you cheat him at cards, too?"

"Of course not," Rance replied, disturbed by her persistence in believing him a cheat. "I coupled with his wife."

Avis's eyes widened. Rance wasn't confident with her capturing an amorous mood anymore.

"You coupled with his wife?" She eyed him from scalp to chest. "Did you seduce her? In her own bed? Took her against her will?" Her tone not only held a hint of curiosity but a pinch of jealousy. Rance decided to exploit her yearning to know.

He held his tongue, assuming a posture of thought. The truth was all too easy to expound. "Miriam Schaefer is a beautiful red-haired Southern lady of social distinction." Rance saw Avis's lips straighten. "Of course, she doesn't hold a candle next to your luminance."

Avis rolled her eyes at the ceiling.

"Anyway," Rance resumed, grunting his throat clear, edging that elbow an inch lower, "she is also twenty-five years younger than her husband. A fact she made plain to me," he grunted again, "as well as her intent on satisfying her primal desires that the old boy apparently wasn't able to." He projected his face toward her. "So, since she was overwhelmed by her bodily needs, she used her feminine wiles to capture me in her private railcar."

Avis slowly nodded, staring deeply into his eyes. "And?"

"And." Rance inhaled. "I found myself a prisoner to her demands. It was she that forced herself upon me."

"Forced herself." The tone was one of doubt.

"It's the truth," Rance said as a plea for vindication. "She practically . . . in fact, she did undress me. Stripped my trousers with the strength of a coal mining brute. She knew what she wanted and proceeded in getting exactly what she had to have."

His internal pacing distracted, he needed to get back on track.

"You know to what I'm referring. The irresistible power of attraction between a man and woman." He began his descent toward her once more. "Whether planned or not, the undeniable call we all must heed, as old as the world itself. Futile to resist what has been ordained by the laws of nature, the one act that every heart on the planet seeks out." He puckered his lips to meet hers.

Avis placed her finger in front of her mouth. "So, this railroad tycoon hired this Colton fellow to kill you? And so he shot you but missed and hit you in the shoulder? How funny."

Rance stood his ground. "Funny? The man nearly ended

my life. A life that, by the way, has included you since his attempt to snuff it out." He carefully inhaled and exhaled. "My dear, I'm in a sort of distress here." He cocked his head to direct her notice farther down the sheets.

She apparently got his meaning. "Oh." She forced an insincere grin. "I'm not that kind of woman. I don't have men in my bed."

Rance peered about the mattress and surroundings as if being alerted that this was all a dream. Finally, he arched a brow at her.

"Well, not for that. Not now."

Perplexed, Rance propped the elbow to tower over her. "I beg your pardon? Wasn't that you . . . here . . . last night . . . oomph oomph?"

She wiggled her head as a sign of being caught in her womanly deceit. "Well," she said with the same whine usually used by innocent children. "I had to do something to keep you here last night."

12

"WHAT!?" RANCE NOW propped himself at arm's length. Never had he been so insulted. Never so deceived. He'd been violated. "Are you saying this was all an act? That you really weren't overwhelmed? The attraction didn't stir your innermost urges?"

Avis again wiggled her head. "Well, it was nice."

"Nice?" He threw aside the sheets that bound him to the mattress. Her flesh exposed, she cradled the tangled bundle as cover while he stepped over her. "I have never been so mistreated by the female of the species," he said, collecting his clothes from the floor. "And believe me. There have been numerous such instances." Shaking out the trousers, he stepped into the legs. "That wasn't you kissing me? Pressing your lips against mine at the door?"

"I told you. If you made too much noise, then the landlady would send me out into the street."

Rance grabbed his shirt. "My bet is there is no old lady downstairs. That is all a made-up story so you could keep me here as an experiment. Evidently, I failed." He bobbed his head while buttoning. "Well, there's always a first time for everything."

"It's not like that," Avis said. She stammered, "I did want you to stay last night. And not just for the obvious reason."

"Obvious reason?" He dug the shirttail into the waist. "To which obvious reason are you referring?"

Avis once more wiggled her head, then bobbed her eyebrows. Rance took it as a description for the interlude.

"Then why else?"

Her hesitation to reply only fueled the fire ravaging his pride. Even if he didn't want to admit it, apparently her review of his skill as a lover didn't meet muster. He went to the door. As he passed the open window, the two figures from the previous night now leaned against the awning post at the corner building. In an instant, all her ploys became clear. He looked back at her. "Those men that stopped by the saloon door are standing at the corner."

The news sent her out of the bed, waddling like a duck to maintain the grip on the sheets trailing between her legs and not trip. As soon as she peered through the glass, she crouched behind him. "Don't go. Please." She looked up at him. "We can go back to the bed if you want. Just don't go."

Extortion for pleasure wasn't his manner. He shook his head, then resumed the view out the window. "Who are they?"

"They're Farnsworth's gunmen," she answered with a crackle to her voice. Further notice saw she shook from her knees to her chin as if she bathed in an icy river. In as comforting a manner as possible, he wrapped his arm around her shoulder. She huddled against his ribs. Another glance down below noticed the men's constant but distracted observation of the upstairs room. Rance edged both himself and Avis from their sight line.

"So, who is Farnsworth, and why would he send gunmen after you?"

She looked up at him. "Clyde Farnsworth is a no-good cattle rustler. He shot a lawyer named Willoughby nearly a week ago in the Raven. It was only me and Sam that was in there. He told both of us to keep quiet about what happened. I've seen those two walking around ever since."

Rance put his hands on her shoulders to try to calm her. "And where is Farnsworth? And why is Sam not up here with us?"

She took a breath of frustration. "Farnsworth is in jail. Arrested by some Texas Rangers when they heard the news. They're keeping him in the old Presidio until the circuit judge comes to town later this week. Sam is one of Farnsworth's friends. He's going to say what Clyde tells him. I don't know if I even trust him no more."

Even though he now found himself in one more feud that didn't include him, Rance knew he had to help. He took a confident pose. "I am here. Nothing is going to happen to you." He pecked her forehead, then went to retrieve both gun belts and pistols.

"What are you doing? You're not leaving, are you?"

"We can't stay up here forever," he said, strapping on the belts. "I'm just going to have a little look around. Let them know that you have a man in your life now. Get some food and bring it back."

"But I have some food," she said, going to the table and pulling out a drawer. "I have some saltines I've been saving for a stormy night."

He checked the loads on the .44 and the pepperbox, then snugged them into their holsters. He grabbed his coat and slid his arms inside. Once dressed, he again placed his palms on her shoulders. "Now, don't you worry. I won't be gone long. You just latch the door behind me, and I'll return before you know it." Once more he kissed her forehead. As he turned for the door, she put her hand to his jaw and faced him back to her. With the passion of a long love, she kissed him, dropping the sheets on the floor.

"Remember," she whispered, "this is what you've got to come back to."

A deep breath was needed to steady his pulse and remind him what he planned to do only a minute before. He nodded and winked, then went to the door. He opened it, with one long glimpse back at her, then stepped out on the landing. A second didn't pass before he heard the clack of the latch bolted behind him.

He stepped down the staircase with some caution. The two at the corner now stood straight when he reached the bottom. The best play was to beam confidence. As he approached, he kept a friendly grin so as not spark confrontation. Yet he didn't want to cower from their glares. He walked to the boardwalk that they flanked, stepped between them, and proceeded toward the center of the town.

He knew to expect their boots pounding the planks behind him and walked unalarmed at their near presence. From one boardwalk and onto another he proceeded straight ahead, pretending to admire the dusty streets bathed in cloudless sun. The withered trees that garnished the corners of the street showed little sign of the coming spring. The townsfolk, however, seemed to notice him as he strolled, or the two which followed.

Retracing the only path he knew about the town, he soon found the Raven. Since it had been a good week since his last taste of spirits, he slowed while approaching the door and turned quickly inside.

A few patrons sat at the tables; however, Avis's was left barren. He didn't know if it was out of respect or to distance themselves from any site that may be in the line of fire at any moment. He went to the bar where Sam silently approached him.

"I'll have your best whiskey, my man."

Sam turned and grabbed the nearest bottle, wrenched the cork free, then grabbed a glass, blew out the dust, and poured. Rance forced a friendly grin at the lack of hygiene. Once the glass sat full, Rance reached into his pocket. The sole feel of cloth without metal alarmed him; however, he kept the confident smile, even when he realized that the two dollars were in the overalls now sprawled on Avis's floor.

He took a deep breath. "I . . ." he paused, hoping some excuse for his lack of money to pay would occur to him. "I prefer to settle my debts at the end of my stay in your establishment."

Sam angled his shoulders enough to point at the sign hanging over the mirror: Pay Before You Drink; or It Will Leak Out When We Shoot You.

Rance gulped. "I see," he replied. "Perhaps you are unaware, but I am a dear friend of young Miss McFadden. I am sure she will vouch for my credit." Sam appeared unswayed. About the time he was certain he wouldn't taste a drop, he heard a voice from behind.

"Rance Cash?"

He froze. His right hand lay flat on the bar. If he were to just try to draw the .44, he would take a slug in the back before he touched the grip. He peered into the mirror. One of the gunmen slowly approached. With each step, Rance raced in his mind where this man could have come up with his name. He didn't appear familiar, though the many towns where he had left plenty of empty pockets may now cost him his life. With the gunman so close that Rance could easily reach him with an extended hand, he chose instead to turn and smile.

"Yes?"

The loud slap of a coin on the bar forced a flinch. "Let me buy you a drink, sir."

As Sam swiped the coin from the bar, Rance stood in utter surprise. "What a considerate gesture." He extended his hand. "Who do I owe?"

"Lucky Bob Swenson," was the answer with a gap-toothed smile. "Pleased to meet you." The other gunman came near. "This here is Nate Hopkins. Nasty Nate, we call him."

Rance shook hands with his newest acquaintance. "A pleasure, I'm sure." Rance picked up the shot and raised it as a toast as Sam filled two more glasses. Once all were full, he eyed the amber liquid. "To law and order." Before he could take a breath, he swigged the whiskey. The bite wasn't strong, a sign of being watered down. However, the aftertaste rose up his throat, and he dispelled it through his nose for a temporary warmth. He didn't expect any such feeling from his new company.

"I am afraid you have the advantage on me, Mr. Swenson. I don't seem to recall where I might have enjoyed your company prior to this moment." The swirl of words almost went unanswered.

The bewildered face lasted only a short time. "I ain't never met you before, if that's what you're a-meaning."

"Then," he said, peering into the man's eyes, "how is it that you know my name?"

The gap-toothed smile returned. "Well, that's what I want to talk to you about." He motioned for Sam to give them a full bottle. "What say you and Nate and me take a load off our legs and talk a spell." He took the bottle and tossed Sam the fare. Without a valid excuse to refuse, Rance pointed at the only open table in the place.

The three took their seats with Rance assuming Avis's

chair. Not only for sentimental value, but it also kept his back to the wall with a full view of the room and the door to the outside. "Now, what do you gentlemen have on your mind?"

Bob looked to Nate in a confused state, uncertain how to begin. Rance's confidence was growing.

"Well, you see, we both got an amigo of ours that's got himself in a spot of trouble. Me and Nate thought you could help him out of the spot."

Rance ran through his mind in what possible way he could help anyone. However, before he could jump to a known conclusion, he had to maintain the confidence of these men. "And who is your friend?"

"His name is Clyde Farnsworth. Clyde's a rancher. And he is a good man." Bob paused. "Most times he is. Sometimes he's a mite ornery when he's liquored up." The mention sent an alarm through Rance and apparently through Bob, because he then waved his hand. "Don't get me wrong. Ain't no more law-biding man than Clyde."

Despite Avis's opinion, Rance nodded. "Oh, I have no doubt, especially with you two fine gentlemen as his friends." The purpose for their conversation remained elusive. With high hopes he may walk out of the saloon rather than be carried, which at one time crossed his mind, he served himself from the bottle of rye. "But what do you want with me?"

"Well, sir, you being a lawyer and all, we . . ."

The rest of the words never made Rance's ears. "Ex—cuse me," he stuttered.

Bob repeated his speech. "You being a lawyer and all, we—"

"Hold on," Rance said, picking up the shot glass with a shaking hand. "You said lawyer. Why would you think I was a lawyer?"

Bob looked to Nate who then looked at Rance. "Folks in town said you told them you was a lawyer down on your luck until you drank that tonic that professor was selling." Nate shook his head. "If you'd ask me, I would have said that it was all a sideshow. But folks around here told of the effect it had on you. And now look at you. All dressed in your lawyer duds. I guess that professor fellow was telling the gospel truth."

Rance inhaled as he glanced at the ceiling. "All right," he

said with a pause. "I want to be sure I understand. You fellows heard I was a lawyer from the folks in the town. Due to a confession when I drank Professor Booker's tonic. And you think I can help your friend. And he is accused of . . . ?"

"Murder," Bob frankly answered. "Cold-blooded murder. They say he shot a man named Willoughby, right here in this room."

"And he did, didn't he?"

Both of the gunmen showed stern jaws. "No sir. It's a lie."

In his wildest delusions, Rance never imagined being in this spot. "Aren't there other lawyers in town more qualified? I believe I might have mentioned this to the professor. I haven't practiced law in such a long time, it would be like I never practiced at all."

"No sir," Bob again quickly replied. "The only lawyer we knew of was the man Willoughby, who Clyde shot."

Nate jabbed Bob's ribs. "Is falsely accused of shooting."

"And you men believe I am a competent lawyer, able to defend a man accused of murder in a court of law so to keep him from hanging?"

Bob arched a brow first at Rance, then at Nate, then back at Rance. He appeared to place his hand on his hip, a move Rance was familiar with gamblers about to settle a bet without funds. "Well," Bob said with a bit of surprise and spite in his voice, "you is a lawyer, ain't you? I sure hope we ain't been wasting our time with you."

13

RANCE NERVOUSLY CHUCKLED. "Of course."
He raised his hand to qualify the lie. "I must say, I'm not a
practicing trial attorney."

Bob leaned closer across the table. Rance watched the
hands, readying his own in case he had to trade lead with
these boys. "But you can still help us out, right?"

Rance's eyes darted to both of the men that sat between
him and the batwing doors. He wondered if he could make it
to the back door. They'd likely have him dead before he made
the alley. "Oh, I'm sure I can 'play it by ear,' as it is said."

Bob grinned. "Well, hot damn." He again extended his
hand, which Rance seemed forced by propriety to accept.
"Looks like we got us a real lawyer." The two rose from the
table, and for an instant Rance thought he'd been reprieved.
Just a few more minutes, and he could escape town. "Come
on," Bob said with a wave. "Let's go meet him."

Disappointment shrank Rance's face. "Meet who?"

Bob's gap-toothed grin was still in place. "Clyde. Who'd
you think? He's going to be a heap happier than he is right
now when he hears we found him a city lawyer."

With a nod, Rance repeated their expectation. "City
lawyer. Yes, won't it be a surprise." As they stood, Rance
knew he'd lingered as long as he could before appearing awkward and so rose from the chair reluctantly. With still some
thoughts of dashing out the back like a thief, the idea was
quickly quelled when they flanked both his shoulders and led
him out of the Raven.

The short walk across the town didn't give him inspiration of exactly how he would wriggle off this hook. While walking past the old mud-masoned buildings to the hurriedly hammered wood structures, he ran ideas through his mind as to how he might evade this predicament while pretending to listen to the two gunmen's conversation.

They steered him along one dusty street to another. With each turn, Rance grew more sure they'd seen through his game and were about to put a bullet in the back of his head. Despite that fear, it was about the time the sun dipped behind the mountains that they arrived at the jail.

A crusty, mud, square structure, it lay perched between trees growing near the foundation, no doubt to help the sinners inside from sunstroke. Iron bars filled all open windows. At the front, a brushy mustached officer of the law stood guard with repeater in hand and six-shooter strapped to his hip. Bob was first to make introductions.

"We're here to see Clyde."

The lawman shook his head. "No visitors after sundown."

Certain his fortunes had changed, Rance faced about. "What a shame. We'll have to come back tomorrow."

"No we ain't," Bob said rudely. He faced the badge-wearing guard. "This here is Clyde's lawyer. He can talk to him anytime he wants. That's the law, ain't it?"

"Not really," said Rance. "Sometimes you have to make an appointment." All eyes peered at him for the cowardly surrender of rights.

Finally the guard spoke. "You his lawyer?"

The decision to carry through with the act had come. He snapped his lapels flat and stepped from between the two gunmen. "Yes, I am. Ransom B. Cash," he paused and gulped. "Attorney at law."

The guard poked his nose about, swatting the sides of Rance's coat. "I'll have to have your weapons." Rance complied, with Bob appearing the most amazed at the big .44. Rance then handed over the pepperbox. The guard snickered.

Free of firearms, Rance felt a bit of relief that a representative of the law was the one holding them. The badge-wearing officer held all weapons, including the rifle in one hand, while slipping a key in the padlock that bolted the latch with the other hand. The thick-planked door creaked open. As Rance stepped past the guard, he heard another order. "Only the lawyer goes in." A glance behind showed the two friends of the defendant staying put at the threshold.

Bob waved him on. "Go ahead. Tell him we sent you."

With that endorsement, Rance turned to the dim interior. He squinted at the arched ceiling for any lamps. None were present. In the rear of the small room he saw a single side of the wall barred off as a cell. Not only was he to meet a murderer for the first time, but he cursed the fact it had to be dark, too.

"Pardon me, sir. You are Mr. Farnsworth?"

"Who the hell are you?" was the booming reply.

Rance grunted his throat. "I am . . . I am your attorney."

A short pause ensued. The dark, silhouetted figure sat slumped against the wall. "My what?"

Another throat-clearing grunt was needed. "Your lawyer." Perhaps he was going about this all wrong. He stepped closer to the bars. "I am sorry. Your friends sent me to represent you. Ransom B. Cash is my name."

Like a tiger in the circus, the figure lunged for the bars. Rance froze. The meager light allowed for the sight of the towering brute. Reddish stringy hair pointed in all directions except the top of the bald scalp. Thick, bushy whiskers covered the face and chin from any sign of skin. Hazel eyes seemed lit with fire. "You any good?"

Rance proposed in his mind what his chances of living if he were to give any less than a positive answer. He choked out his reply. "The best."

"Damn well better be," came out along with a wad of spit to the floor. "When are you going to get me out here?"

Reason was likely beyond comprehension. "Well, I've just now been advised of the case. I am confident I can arrange some kind of bail." He caught himself believing his tale. "However, it will take time. Normally, there is a judge in matters of murder trials. And I think it is his decision as to whether to allow you to leave these confines."

"What the hell are you talking about!? Are you saying that I got to stay in here until the judge comes to town? That's not for two more days. I've been here two as it is. If you can't get me out, what good are you?"

Rance caught himself before he laughed aloud. "I am the one to try to keep them from hanging you."

"They ain't hanging me."

"No, I believe you are mistaken." His brave argument stopped the towering brute from returning to the dark. "Killing a man is a hanging offense in this state, as it is in many others. And since you are in here, it is only I that can set you free. So, Mr. Farnsworth, I suggest you be patient, since your next alternative is to spend the rest of your existence in the fiery blazes of the place you so often call upon. I hope I made my meaning clear?"

Shocked the words flowed so freely, Rance had to bite his tongue to keep from apologizing. One grunt to the friends outside from this man, and he could be dragged by horses through the cactus. Instead, he watched as the man he was now about to attempt to stand next to in a court of law slowly came to the bars.

"Sounds like I got me a lawyer that got's some sand." A small grin cracked Farnsworth's face. "I'll do what you say. Just get me out of here."

Rance finally inhaled. When he let out the breath, he nodded. "I'll do what I can." He faced about, stepping slowly to keep from banging into the walls. "We'll speak again, Mr. Farnsworth." Rance found the door, rapped his knuckles on it, and it soon opened. When he emerged in the dusk, he saw the two gunmen waiting.

"Did he take to you?" asked Bob.

Rance shrugged. "We set a tone between each other."

Bob slapped his hands in celebration. "I knew it. I said to myself, there's a man that knows what he's doing."

Rance could only smile and cock his head.

"You know what we ought to do? We should go over to the Raven and finish that bottle and maybe play a little cards. Sort of relax a bit now that all is going to turn out fine."

The invitation appeared heaven-sent. "You're asking me to a game of cards?"

"Why sure," said Bob. "Have you ever played?"

Rance smiled. "I have enjoyed a few games. Of course, when I wasn't involved in a case." He took a step forward with the gunmen. "You know, I think all just might turn out all right, like you said."

Despite the ache to his back, Jody took a moment to rein in and gaze at the sight behind him. Not long before, he sat in the saddle certain that the foolish notion of driving cattle in late winter would likely never get this far. Now, the vision before him turned his mind full circle.

The herd had formed in a tight bunch, and the unseasoned drovers appeared able to keep them that way. Although they hadn't traveled far, for being just the second day, prospects were looking up for a successful trip.

A glance to the right showed the lone fire of the camp struck by Sanderson. Hopefully he'd found a spot with fresh water for man and bovine alike. For the last mile Jody joined in whooping and hollering at steers to keep them on course for the camp. Another glance showed only an hour at best remained of the light. In that time they had to find suitable grass for the herd to fuel itself for the next day. The same was true for those on two legs.

As they circled the cows to keep them from straying, they found a creek, which was just what they needed to wash the dust from their tongues. Once convinced his help was no longer needed, Jody rode to the camp. When he arrived, he smelled the aroma of bread baking and stew meat boiling. Nothing appeared out of place.

"Smells mighty good," he said, dismounting and uncinching the saddle.

Sanderson grinned at the compliment while walking to the kettle to stir his stew. As he did, Jody couldn't help but notice the Cheyenne woman toting wood for the fire from the surrounding trees on the bank of the creek. Their eyes met, and for an instant, Jody stood still. The woman called Dorothy did the same.

There was something about her eyes that said much more than her voice could ever sound out. After more than a time proper to be staring at another man's woman, Jody inhaled and averted his eyes from her.

Soon, the rest of the drovers gradually assembled in the camp. Sanderson, with his wife beside him, began doling out helpings on the tin plates. Feeling a need to allow the others to eat before him, Jody found a moment to find the wad of chaw in his pocket and bite off a chunk.

About the moment came for the first spit, he noticed all eyes staring at him. Confused as to their interest, he peeked at his clothes to see if he'd been splattered with dung or some other reason of ridicule. Once he saw their heads bob to the side, he realized he wasn't the source of interest. He glanced over his shoulder.

In the dimming light a figure of a horse stood a few hundred yards away, but there was no rider. An instant later, he choked on the spittle and spat out the wad. It was his pa's mount.

Like a shot, he ran for his own horse despite no saddle, and leapt onto its back. With a grip of the mane he kicked at the flanks and forced a gallop for the short distance. A yank on the mane with same force as the reins reared the horse, but Jody hung on to the mane to keep from being thrown. Once the animal put four hooves on the ground, Jody slid off its back and ran to Jack's horse. In an instant he saw his pa lying prone on the ground.

"Pa!" he yelled. With no answer, he knelt at Jack's side. When he rolled the shoulder over, never was he so glad to have caused enough pain for Jack to shriek. "You're alive," he muttered to himself but loud enough for Jack's ears.

"Just barely," replied Jack.

"What did you go on and do to yourself?"

Jack's anguished eyes directed Jody's notice farther down the body to see the blood-soaked pant leg. "You get shot or something?"

"No," Jack groaned. "Rattler spooked my horse. Threw me off crooked and snapped my leg. I'm sure of it. Had to keep hold of the stirrup to have it drag me at least a mile."

The description stole Jody's breath. Despite being thrown himself many times, he always got up. Now, his father's agonized posture squeezed his own insides. He put his hands above the injury. The motion was met with even more groans.

He heard riders approaching from the camp but didn't turn away from Jack. Soon, Sanderson was kneeling alongside carrying a leather bag. With the touch of a doctor, he turned the leg without mercy for Jack's pained cries. Jody knew it was for the best but couldn't keep from cringing. Sanderson took a knife and cut the pant leg to see the wound.

"Bone poked clear through the skin. It will have to be cleaned and bandaged before it gets infected, set, then put in a splint." The cook faced about to his Indian woman. "Fetch long enough branches sturdy enough to keep this leg from moving." With the order, the woman was off into the dark. Sanderson faced back at Jack. "We're going have to put this bone back in place. Going to hurt plumb awful."

Jack nodded at the plan between gasps of air.

"We're going to need to get him back home," Sanderson said. The words dimmed Jody's hopes. All the visions he'd had were now gone. Jack waved for his son to come closer.

"You need to go on without me."

"What?" Jody thought the idea foolish. "How can we do that? Without you to tell us where to go?"

Jack smiled. "You know your way about this land." His breathing appeared more labored. "The Pecos is not but twenty miles from here. You can make it in two days if you keep them moving."

"But we got to get you back home."

Jack nodded. "I can make it. You just keep driving them."

Jody shook his head. "You can't ride like that. All the jostling will cause you to lose blood and kill you."

A grimace shrank the smile. "I've been tending to myself before you were born. I think I know what's best."

"You can't go alone," Sanderson said. "Your son is right. If you keep bleeding, you'll never see your home again." The cook faced Jody. "We'll need to send someone with him. Pull him on a travois."

"No," Jack argued between gulps of pain. "You can't spare a man 'cause of me."

"Afraid we got no choice, Mr. Barnes," Sanderson said in a

calm but firm tone. He looked to Jody now as the leader needing to make the decision. In spite of not wanting to put on those boots, he now had to make a choice that would affect more than just his pa. He nodded when he was sure.

"I'll send Alejandro with you. He knows the way. You'll be safe."

Jack shook his head with fury. "No. You can't lose a seasoned vaquero. You'll need him on this drive. Don't let the others down due to me."

Jody's mind swirled. Once more, his father's wisdom conflicted with his own. And he knew Jack was right. But who could he afford to lose? Slowly he angled his head up. All the needs for such a chore appeared in the figure before him. He stared Les in the eye.

"I'll go," said Marvin Adair. All eyes were drawn to the next-oldest drover. "I'll get him home, Jody. Besides, all this riding is a heap more than I planned. This is a task for a younger man than me." Jody peeked at Jack. A small grin creased his lips. The best choice appeared to come without Jody having to say a word.

"Good," Sanderson said. "Now, we can't move him until I set this bone. Some of you get torches so I can see what I'm doing, and some clean water. And maybe some rawhide to have him chew on. This ain't going to be easy for you, Mr. Barnes."

As the rest mounted to return to camp, Jody knelt near his father. "They're all going to count on you, son. Make me proud." Jody nodded, and as Sanderson began his mending, he stood and took one more glance at the remaining member of the drive still there.

Les kept her stare at him and pierced his soul right through to his boots.

14

RANCE SLOWLY CLIMBED the wooden stair-
case. He winced at the early morning dawn. With just enough
energy, he reached the top landing and rapped on the door.
Seconds seemed like hours. Finally, a robed Avis peeked between the curtains, and locks snapped free. She opened the
door and yanked him inside.

As soon as she could slam the door behind him, she
wrapped her arms around his neck and kissed him long and
lovingly. He couldn't help but return the passion. At last, she
released the kiss, but only for a moment, kissing him between
each inquiry.

"Did they hurt you? Did they nearly kill you? I was so
afraid. I was sure they would kill you. I didn't get a wink of
sleep. I was expecting them at my door any minute."

Despite enjoying the onslaught of affection, Rance needed
to explain, and to sleep. He gently held her arms. "It wasn't as
bad as all that."

"What did they do?"

"Well," he said easing away from her. Despite the thin
robe's outline to her feminine form, a shape he preferred at the
moment was the horizontal plane of the mattress. "They did
follow me to the Raven."

"The Raven? Why did you go there?"

He shrugged. "It was the only place I knew certain how to
get to. By the way, your friend Sam is no friend of mine."

"Not really mine neither," she sneered. "So, tell me what
happened. You left here nearly eighteen hours ago. I watched

every minute pass," she said while he sat on the edge of the bed and took off his boots. She climbed onto the bed on all fours like a child awaiting a gift.

Figuring he didn't have the strength to uphold the suspense, he decided to announce his new position. "My dear, you are looking at Clyde Farnsworth's new lawyer."

Avis took a moment to first look at him, then at the door, then back at him. "Where?"

"Me," he said.

"You?" Her response came with wide eyes.

Rance nodded. "I cannot believe it myself. But," he paused to heave a breath. "They were very persuasive, if you know what I mean."

Avis shook her head. "Let me get this straight. You went down to the Raven, and they told you to become Clyde's lawyer?"

"Something like that." He groaned as he arched his back.

"Are you some lawyer?"

He shook his head. "No. But I have been in a few poker games with some back in New Orleans. It can't be that hard."

With a burp of a chuckle, Avis dipped her eyes to the wood floor. "So, you are planning to be a murderer's lawyer. The murderer that saw me see him commit the crime?"

Her words came a little too fast for his bleary mind. He nodded. "Yes, I think so. I'm sorry, my dear, but I have been playing cards with two of his gunmen for nearly twelve hours. I need some rest." He turned to her. "Can't you let me get some sleep, and then I'll tell you all about it?" He closed his eyes and puckered for a last kiss before bed.

The next sensation was a hard slap to the cheek.

"What are you doing?" she growled. She hopped off the bed and proceeded to shed the robe from behind a partition. "You're going to defend a man that wants me dead? A killer and a thief. I thought you and I really had something there. Now you go on and let them bully you into being his lawyer. Got to hand it to you, Rance Cash. You really know how to get a girl going in one direction then veer off into another."

Rance's head was still spinning. He rubbed his cheek as he rose from the bed. "Where are you going?"

"I got to leave this town," she said, slipping her arms through a chemise. "Since it won't be long before they use you to get to me. You think they didn't notice you coming out of my room? Won't be long before they see through you and come after me."

Rance stood at the partition. "I think you're being a bit too rash."

"Rash?" Another chuckle came after the word. "Ain't being nothing but sane. A woman's got to learn to get along for herself was what my mammy always said. No place proves that more than here out West."

"Avis," he said, poking his head over the partition at risk of receiving another slap for seeing what may yet be covered. "Believe me, I did all I could to get out of it. But once I saw and talked with Farnsworth, I got a sense he could be dealt with." Once he finished, he was glad to see the woman skirted from neck to ankles.

She finished buttoning her collar. "What do you mean?"

"I mean, I had words with him. He tried to size me up, and I put him in his place. After that, he said I had sand. I'm fairly certain it was meant as a compliment."

She tilted her head in surprise. "He did?"

"Yes, he did," he replied pointedly. "So, don't you see? I can manipulate him any way I want."

"Hah," she scoffed. "He'll manipulate you by getting me to get so near to put a bullet in my back." So certain of that fear, she marched for the door. Rance followed quickly and braced his arm to keep the door from opening.

"Listen to me," he said, twisting her about, his hands palming her shoulders. "Do you think I would let anything like that happen to you? Of course not. I'd rather die myself than see one hair," he paused long enough to plant a kiss on her forehead, "harmed on this pretty little head."

Slowly her face went from the headstrong pout to worried surrender. "Do you really think so? I'm gambling my life by staying in El Paso."

"Don't you worry," he said. "When Rance Cash makes a promise, he sees it through." He looked deep into her eyes. "Now, you don't think I would take a risk when the stakes included you, do you? Besides, if you were to leave, I as the defense counsel would have to subpoena you," he kissed her lips, "and have you kept under lock and key," he kissed her again, each time sensing her attentiveness to his advances, "right here in this room. So, you see, I would be your jailer. And as a hostile witness for the defense," he gave her a long-lasting kiss, "you would have to do everything I ask."

She pushed away from his hold. "I guess it is better if I stay. As long as you put it that way."

"Of course," he assured her, softly seizing her once more by the shoulders. "What I'll do is do the best job I know how in order to get him convicted," he kissed her lips, "jailed," he kissed again, "and hung by the neck until dead." He attempted to finish the point with one long-lasting kiss that would finally get him into the bed and some rest after a short interlude.

She turned her cheek to him. "What if I have to testify?"

The realistic possibility interrupted his amorous intentions. "Well, then I guess you'll have to tell what you know."

She wrenched away from his grasp. "That's what I thought. As soon as I tell the court that I was sitting at that table and saw Clyde shoot Willoughby right in the head, Clyde will send those gunmen after me." He approached her to again try to calm her fears, but she evaded him. "No. Your sweet talk ain't going to get you any closer to me."

Exhausted, Rance needed to find the right words to settle the matter and finally get some sleep. "Avis, I just told you what is the easiest of plans. You tell the judge what you saw. I will do nothing to interfere. When the judge hears your testimony, he'll have to find Farnsworth guilty and send him off to be hanged. What could be simpler?"

When she didn't argue, he knew he'd made a point. He took a step closer to her, and she responded with a step away from him. He sagged his shoulders, but an instant's second thought convinced him it was for the best. If he could just settle her nerves, then maybe he could get some sleep.

"Listen. I know you're nervous. I would be, too. But, trust me, this is the best situation we could hope for. If you were to leave town now, then he'd have a chance to hunt you down and do you ill. This way, with you in town, he can't send any of his men on any evil errands without arousing suspicion. Not even

Clyde is that dumb, and believe me, I've met the man. He is no scholar."

The more he spoke, the more sense he made even to himself, which seldom was his intent. Resigned to the fact that the only activity to occur in the bed was himself sleeping, he returned to the edge of the mattress. Avis remained silent. It appeared she stood in the throes of deep contemplation. So he wouldn't have to sleep with one eye open, which he never mastered, he needed to make one last assurance to be certain she wouldn't sneak off in the middle of the day.

So to be as casual as possible, he unbuttoned his shirt. "I understand the judge will be here in two days. I would think it might take him a day to begin the trial. So, in three days, we have enough time to gauge our next move. And, since you are a player, I know you know how to gauge the situation."

At last, a smile creased her face. She nodded as she approached him. "All right, Rance Cash. I'll trust your instinct this far. But if I see any of those men coming at me, I'm off faster than a tumbleweed in a stiff wind. But, for now, I've got to make a living." She shook her finger in a motion of recollection. "Didn't you say you were playing cards all night?" Her tone sounded concerned.

"Yes, I did. And I am exhausted. So, I'll thank you in advance to allow me at least a few hours of rest."

"And did you win?" The tone now sounded curious.

"Are you joking? With those gunmen?" He reached into his pocket and displayed his winnings, spreading the greenbacks like a hand of cards. "Of course, I had to carry them for some time. Especially since I am going to be surrounded by them until all this is over."

Avis showed a contented smile, then snatched the bills from his hand. "That will do."

With his mouth ajar, she turned for the door. "But that was my money."

As she tucked the money inside her front, she spoke over her shoulder. "I'd say considering what's happened over the last day, this money belongs to me."

Disappointed at the remark, he couldn't help but voice his objection. "You said you weren't that type of woman."

Avis opened the door. "I'm not," she said facing him. "This is for the rent on the bed."

Les flanked the remuda from the stream. She didn't want to lose track of the herd. If she did, the longer she'd be in the saddle and the worse the wear on her backside. It hadn't been but nine months since she joined the return trip from Abilene. At times, she thought the time to be years instead of months. The constant bumping astride a horse reminded her it hadn't been that long.

Once she got the horses far enough away from the stream, she eyed Lone Star. The racehorse had mixed well with the saddle ponies. Not having been gelded, she'd been told he might get too close to the mares or even smell wild mustang fillies and bolt for the hills. If he were to be lost, then so would her chances of getting back to Abilene.

As she pushed farther out in the prairie, she spotted Penelope chasing a stray. Since the horses kept to themselves, Les thought she could help round up the steer. She rode out to the far end of the stray's path to head it off and push it back to Penelope. When her plan worked, Penelope approached without a smile. "Thought you were to keep to the horses."

"I saw you needed help," Les explained.

"I don't need no help," Penelope barked back like a dog. "Especially no girl's help." She angled her horse behind the stray and chased it back toward the herd.

Les was not going to let that remark stand. "What do you think you are?"

The comment stopped the cowgal. She reined around and came back at Les. "I ain't no girl. But I am a woman. And I can do any work a man can and most things even better. So, don't think you can do the work that I can. Or even help me. I don't need no help."

"What crawled up your behind? I was trying to do a good thing. Ever since you been on this drive you've been sassing anybody gets close to you."

The blonde girl started to speak, stopped, then started again. "You ain't been through what I been through. Be glad for that." The jangle of metal approaching turned both their heads back to the herd. The chuck wagon slowly passed by with the Indian woman riding bareback alongside. It took several seconds for them to make their way. All during that time, Les kept watching the squaw.

"She has eyes on Jody, you know."

Penelope's remark pulled Les's attention from the woman. "How you know that?"

Penelope shook her head. "Plain to see. Every time she's around him, she can't keep from staring at him."

Les tried to deny the suspicion, but deep down she held the same one. She didn't let Penelope know that. "I don't see it."

"Then you're blind." She pointed at the woman. "She's of a savage people. Of a mind of getting what she wants. If you have some kind of plans for Jody, then you better hurry. That woman there is wanting him, too. Might even get him. Likely thinks about him most of the time. Hell, she ain't wearing nothing under them skins. Without no saddle, she's brushing it against that horse right now."

"Penelope!" Les shouted. "Why don't you mind your own business and shut your filthy mouth."

The blonde didn't take to the order. "I'm just telling you. I seen how you and Jody are. You've been living in his house. What's wrong? Ain't been bedded by him yet?"

Les slid off the paint. Her heart beat against her chest. Even though Penelope was bigger and a little older, she wasn't going to take talk about Jody or the Barnes family. "I told you to hush your mouth. Are you going to do it?"

Penelope smirked. "Or what?"

Les had backed herself into a corner with the dare. She charged at Penelope, clutching at her chaps and pulling the blonde girl off her mount. Penelope knocked Les down with a punch to the gut, but Les kept hold of the big gal's clothes and dragged her to the ground. Grunting and sneering, Les pushed with all her strength to keep Penelope from pummeling her face. But Penelope was a strong woman and ripped free from Les's grasp. She leaned back and clenched a fist. Les flinched, expecting the punch to crash into her face. Between the slits in her eyes, she saw Penelopes's arm yanked backward, spilling the cowgal off her.

Jody now stood above them both. "What's got into both of you!?" With a firm arm, he kept Penelope from attacking Les, all the while keeping Les away with just the point of a finger. "Whatever it is, I want you two to shake hands and forget about it. I've got a thousand cows to be thinking about. I can't worry about whether you two are having some girl fight."

Penelope spat the dust from her lips. "I handle my own business." She smacked her hat against her chaps and went to her horse. Jody faced from her to Les.

"Did you start this?" The question forced Les to jump to her feet. Her heart still pounded, and her breath heaved. As she saw the smirk still on Penelope's face, words would only betray her intent, so she was going to answer with action. Jody pushed her back. "Just simmer down." He looked over his shoulder as Penelope retrieved her mount. "Now, listen. I got to scout out what's up ahead." He looked to Les, then back at Penelope. "I can't spare Les. She's running the remuda. So, Penelope, you're coming with me." He backed away from Les, keeping his finger pointed like she was a trained dog.

Les watched as he backed his way to his mount, his face and eyes alight with dismay at her. Her breath still heaved but not from fatigue or fright. It was the sight of Jody and Penelope riding away. When they crested a small rise and disappeared, she sank to her knees and buried her face in her hands.

15

JODY RODE NEXT to Penelope for more than an hour, steam building between his ears over the trouble the girl had caused. A glance behind showed no sign of the herd. Ahead, there was little sign of water. He had to find some fairly soon. A distant hill looked like a good place to scan for what he wanted, but it was a distance away. He decided to pass the time by relieving some of the steam.

"Mind telling me what all that was about back there?"

The blonde girl only gave him a passive glare, then faced front. "Ain't nothing for you to be concerned. Haven't you heard? Women are the cause of what all ails men. If not for having a split tail there'd be a bounty on us like there is on coyotes and gophers."

Jody shook his head. "Why do you talk like that? What made you change?"

"I didn't change."

"The hell you didn't." His curiosity flowed faster than his head could censor. "The Penelope Pleasant I remember was a cute little girl. Always polite. Never without manners. She honored her ma and pa. Was the way all folks wanted their little lady to turn out to be. Now, to see you, I'd think you were raised in a barn with a bunch of ranch hands."

She only glanced at him. "You'd know how a bunch of ranch hands would turn out."

The remark confused him. "What's that mean?"

She shook her head. "Ain't nothing you can do about me, Jody. You ain't the first that's tried."

He didn't believe her. "Your pa proud of you this way?"

She scoffed. "Is now. I told him to leave well enough alone since I was doing his work and mine. When he saw it was true, he let me be. I don't have to answer to nobody now. I can do what I want, when I want."

The image of the little blonde girl in her Sunday best wouldn't leave his mind. "Well, I will say you do cut a fine figure as both drover and woman."

She glared at him with an arched brow. "What's your meaning? You been looking at me, getting some ideas in that head? Been thinking of trying to have a poke at me?"

He shook his head and smiled. "I've been looking. But I can't say for the reason that you're thinking. But it ain't like any man ain't going to notice what's poking out from that shirt, no matter how many calves you cut out to be branded."

She peeked at her front. "Don't do me no good. Ain't squatting no kids for them to suck on. I'd cut them off if it wouldn't hurt so bad."

He shook his head again. "See, there you go trying to talk your way into being a man. Ain't no man going to think better of you, neither way. A man is going to see you as a woman trying to be a man so bad, don't really look like one or the other. Or, he's going to see you as a fellow in the shape of a girl." When she shot an angry scowl at him, he held up his palm. "Sorry. A woman. A fully growed-up woman. But they ain't going to see you as nothing more than a woman." He hesitated his next words, but it might do some good. "Or, some freak. Like in those tent shows."

She stared straight. "Don't see why. If I can do the work of a man."

The reason was clear to him. "Take it from me. As one of those not split in the tail, that's the first matter come to mind when those less than square shoulders, a rounder rump, and bumpy chest comes ambling by. It don't matter what clothes you're a-wearing." Although he was glad he said it, it didn't show any intended effect on her face. However, she did turn to him after several moments.

"Don't appear to have done Les much good."

The mention stirred his gut. In an instant he realized what

the squabble between the females was about. "What'd you say to her?" he asked with a firm tone. The possibilities swirling in his head galled him more than Penelope's manner. The blonde remained silent for a moment. Jody wanted to insist on an answer but knew an ordered response might get him a hurried reply he didn't want to hear.

"If you don't know, then you're as blind as she is."

As the hill approached, he knew he'd only have a few seconds to learn more before he was distracted by his real duty. "All right. So, I'm blind. So, tell what I'm missing."

A grin broke Penelope's face. Then she shook her head. "One thing to be said about men. They won't never have the sight of a female. You don't know that that girl has been eyeing you, likely since you and she first ever laid eyes on each other?"

He wasn't so blind. However, no reason stood to admit it. "Les?"

"Yes. Les." Penelope repeated with frustration. "That girl has it bad, too. But, from what I seen, every time she eyes you, you ain't seeing the same thing."

Jody shook his head in bewilderment. He started this conversation with interest on why Penelope acted manly. Now, he was talking about his own matters. "I think you're seeing it wrong."

Penelope shrugged. "Don't matter to me. Ain't an affair that I want into." She paused as they ascended the hill. "But there may be someone else who wants in on the same stakes."

The comment fueled his curiosity. However, now at the top of the hill, he peered out on the plain to any scant signs of water. Nevertheless, it burned his gut to learn more. Penelope squinted in the distance.

"I don't see nothing."

Her observation pulled his attention back to the purpose of the travel. Certain as she was, he also saw only the dull, dusty reflection instead of a glistening one. If they should travel to another hill, the view might offer more.

"What is that?"

Penelope's question first had him look at her and then in the far direction she stared. In the distance appeared wooden buildings, some with more than one floor. "Looks to be some sort of town."

"Well, I didn't think it was some giant ant mound."

Her terse words distracted him only for a moment. He scanned for any other sign of civilization. When none appeared, he got a notion. "Seems any folks living out here got to have water. Even if from wells, its got to have a source not too far." He glanced behind. "We got time. Let's see if we can have somebody to tell us where there may be water." He nudged his horse, and she did the same.

As they approached the settlement, Jody noticed the sparse scrub dotting the plain. Even for the small herd, there wouldn't be much for them to graze on here. When they neared, a tune broke the silence. The closer they got, the louder the tune. Drums and fife filled the air to a marching cadence.

They steered toward a corral on the side of a livery. Confused, he listened to the tune, and the melody became familiar. It was a rebel song, one not heard in some time. As Penelope came alongside, Jody got ideas about leaving. However, the herd needed water, and he needed to find out where to get it.

A dusty street ran between several tall buildings. As the music became louder, he curiously scanned about. When he saw a sign with the town's name, he knew, although he was in the same state, he may not be among friends.

Robert E. Lee, Texas

He craned his neck to the right. Slowly, the townsfolk emerged from the angle, walking in parallel along the boardwalks as a band played the tune. When the four-man band could be seen, they wore uniforms in various shades of gray, some trimmed with gold piping. One of them was a color bearer holding a blue flag with a white star in the center waving from a wooden rod. Another bearer held the state Lone Star flag. As Jody watched, the refrain of the song was sung by all.

"Hurrah! Hurrah! For Southern rights, hurrah! Hurrah for the Bonnie Blue Flag that bears a single star!"

The drum beat out the beginnings of the next verse. With

each step closer, he noticed more and more folks, all of whom seemed to enjoy the show. During his attention to the parade, from the corner of his eye he saw Penelope wrap her right leg around the horn and fidget with her hands. When he took closer notice, she'd rolled a smoke and licked the paper, sealing it shut. She ran the paper through her lips and had a match struck against her boot with a fluid motion. Her familiarity with the habit appeared it wasn't her first time. However, in the center of a town that showed its attachment to old ways, he didn't think a female enjoying a vice reserved for menfolk was an example of respect. Nor did he want to stir up trouble with these people. He was needing a favor.

He reached over and pulled the smoke from her lips, wadding it in his hands, shaking it from his palm as the embers singed his skin. Jody scowled at her as she did him for his prudish action.

The band marched right in front of them. "Don't say nothing to rile these folks," he said. "Remember, this is their town. A heap more of them than us."

As the last bars of the of tune came about, the crowd assembled around them, finishing the lyrics in step with the music. Cheers erupted garnished with applause. As they hollered, a dapper-dressed man strode to the middle of the street and unfurled a scroll.

"On this date, March 2, 1870, we commemorate the ninth anniversary of our great state's redeclaration of independence from the allegiances previously sworn, and reaffirm our devout faith and belief in our sovereignty as a republic." Louder cheers, applause, and erratic gunfire peppered the air.

"What are they talking about?" asked Penelope.

Jody shook his head. "I ain't sure. But what I'm thinking is that they don't think the states war ever ended. Just the same, it ain't our place to set them straight. Be peaceful with them. We're only here to find out where there is water and nothing else."

The oration continued. "As veterans of the thirty-seventh Regiment, we stand ready to defend the rights of our sovereignty and repel all those who oppose those laws originally enacted to protect the citizens of the great state of Texas."

More cheers and gunfire followed.

Jody flinched at the shots. He looked to Penelope. "Remember what I told you." She sneered at his order. The assembly gathered in the center of the street, then dispersed in several directions. Jody saw it as his chance to get what he was wanting and leave. He dismounted and tethered the reins to a corral post. He drew the Remington revolver from his saddlebag and tucked it in his belt. "You stay put," he told Penelope while eyeing a likely source of information.

He walked along the boardwalk. Numerous men in his path appeared in a giddy frame of mind. Hopefully, he could use their condition to extract the information and leave without much fuss.

A man in dungarees gave the appearance of a farmer. "Beg pardon. Don't mean to stop your funning, but I'm wondering if you could help me out." The farmer seemed surprised by the inquiry. When Jody noticed more than one face showing the same concern, he took it as an unwelcome sign. It was then he decided the fewer words about a thousand head of beef a half day away the better. "I'm wanting to know where there's a water hole around here?"

The farmer slapped Jody's arm. "Follow me, son." As the farmer threaded his way through the mass, Jody thought about asking another person. However, he didn't want any offense taken, so decided to follow the man down the boardwalk. During the slow, single-step process, he hoped to see a map where he might gauge how far the water might be. When the man turned sharply into a open door, Jody found himself in the wrong place.

"Have a drink, son. It's a holiday."

Jody shook his head. "Sorry. My mistake. Not the kind of drinking I was meaning." Voices rose in song. Jody had heard "The Yellow Rose of Texas" enough in his life to know the words by heart. It appeared all about knew them, too.

Instead of singing, he politely tipped his hat to the man and left the small saloon in search of anyone who might share the location of water. A single brick building appeared an official source of information. He went across the street. He grabbed the knob. The door was locked. He noticed the sign in the window explained the reason for the closure was the observance of the holiday now being celebrated.

He faced about and searched for another possibility. When he saw an older short man of respectable dress, he went to him as the man crossed the street. "Beg pardon, sir," he said. The short gentleman stopped. "Was wondering if you might know where they might be a water hole hereabouts?"

At first, the man looked at him strangely. "What are you looking for one for?"

Jody inhaled while thinking up a suitable reason. "It's not just for me. I have some men returning to San Antone. We're needing to get our mounts some water." He tipped his head slightly. "Some of them fellows are needing a bath, too."

The older man appeared amused. "There's a hole about five miles out of town. A dug-up aquifer that's now a backed-up cistern. There's plenty there for a group of men and their horses."

"Obliged at the advice," Jody said with a nod. The short man headed in the direction of the drinking hall. Jody went back to the corral. During the walk, he hoped the amount of water at this place might be enough to quench the thirst of a thousand longhorns. Whether or not, he'd have to give it a try. Once beyond the tall buildings, he saw a welcome sight.

Clouds in the distance darkened. He stood for a moment, noticing a brisk breeze now coming from the north. Never was he so glad to recognize a storm. He went past the board-walk where the assembly gathered in numbers. Not interested in the celebration, he rounded the corner where he knew to find the corral. He stopped in his tracks. Only the pair of horses tethered to the post was there.

16

JODY FACED AROUND. Just when he got good news twice over, another problem blocked his path. He went to the street, turning his head from side to side, trying to spot Penelope's hat or maybe her blonde braids. He avoided the crowd, which only served to get in his way.

Across the street, he went from one end of a boardwalk to the other, peeking down the alleys. No one was there. He continued making his way to the center of town, thinking maybe she might have seen a shop with something pretty in a window. He stopped those thoughts when he remembered it was Penelope he sought.

As the wind blew a little stiffer, he had an urge to relieve his nature. The thought struck him, perhaps she had to heed the same call. But how would a woman do so in a strange town? Like being one or not, the female just couldn't find a wall of a building like some man. His search prevented him from paying a call to a fence post and resume looking for her.

He went farther down the street than he'd gone before, even when he asked about the water. However, he did not see much of any folks in that direction. They all seemed bent on cramming into the drinking hall where Jody was first lured.

His shoulders sagged. As he looked to the northwest, the clouds covered the sunlight. He was going to get wetter than he wanted when he started the day. If he headed back to the herd, he could oversee the huddling of the beeves so they didn't spook due to the storm. He could be doing a heap of things except what he was forced to do now.

Slowly, he started for the door of the drinking hall, hoping he wouldn't find what he had suspicioned. A crowd of men clogged the doorway. Jody pushed his way through. Over the heads of the mass he saw what he was looking for. Penelope, with a shot glass in her hand, stood at the bar.

Next to her was a burly fellow with a full set of whiskers. The fellow slapped two coins on the bar. "Four bits says you can't slug that one down like the first."

Jody rolled his eyes.

Penelope picked up the glass, brought it to eye level, then swigged in a single gulp. She exhaled in a wheeze between gritted teeth, then swiped the dribble with her sleeve. "Like I said. I can outdrink any man in this town."

"No you ain't," called out Jody over the crowd.

The burly man turned to look at him, then at Penelope. "That your man?"

She scoffed in her usual manner. "He ain't my man. He's got a little girl that's sweet on him. And a squaw, too." The crowd was awed at her brazen comment. "I ain't got no man and don't want one, neither."

Jody wedged himself between two men trying to get to the bar. "Penelope, I got what we came for. There's a storm brewing outside. Be here any minute. We need to leave. Now."

She slapped the bar. "I'll have another if you're buying." The burly man motioned, and the shot glass was soon full.

"Penelope!" Jody hollered, still unable to get through the mass.

"Jody Barnes, you ain't no kin to me and can't tell me what to do." In a defiant act, she picked up the glass and threw the shot down her throat. She wheezed again, then pointed her finger at the glass. The burly man picked up his and threw it down his throat. Soon, each of them kept picking up their full glasses, swigging liquor like it was a contest at a county fair.

After four shots that Jody personally saw, he gave thought to abandoning the girl to her own fate. A second thought convinced him it wasn't a choice he could live with. He pushed aside a man to get to the bar. The man took offense and pushed back.

"I'm trying to help my friend. She is a woman."

"Looks like she can handle her liquor, mister. Just stand back and keep your place."

Jody wasn't about to watch Penelope get drunk. Besides the trouble it would cause him getting her back to camp, they didn't have time before the storm hit. "I'm telling you to let me by." He pushed a bit more firmly but was met with equal resistance. As soon as he decided to rush through them, an arm from behind looped around his neck and dragged him backward. Hands pawed at his belt. He stiffened his arm against his gut to keep from losing the revolver. Through the maze of heads and hands he saw the burly man finish his drink and lurch toward Penelope.

"I like you, gal. How 'bout a kiss?"

Penelope pushed against his bearded face. The burly man appeared not to be denied. The more Penelope pushed, the rougher he got.

Jody had to help her. He swung punches in every direction. A few landed solid, but none were of a force needed to free him from the men. A few fists landed on his jaw. He clutched the revolver tighter. If he lost it, surely it would be used against him.

The burly fellow grabbed each side of Penelope's head like a melon and brought her face near his.

Jody kicked the closest fellow to him, then tripped the next one. He fired an elbow behind and felt it strike ribs. An instant later, the pressure around his neck eased. He kept swinging to clear the area around him about the time he saw the burly man pull Penelope's lips to his.

The burly man doubled over, stumbled, then fell back against the bar. Penelope stood, gritted teeth wheezing breath, eyes wide like a frightened cat, her right hand holding the carving knife. A quick glance at her drinking partner showed a bloody stain near his belly.

"She stabbed me!"

Penelope backed farther away, the crowd clearing her a path like she was a bull. "Ain't no man going to force his way on me," she yelled. "Are there more of you? Come on and try. I'll cut out your tongue." The burly man bled but didn't fall. His angry face now focused on her, and Penelope brandished the blade at him. "You want some more of me? Think you'll get to stick it inside me? Come on and show it." She held the knife high for all to see. Jody gripped the Remington. The burly man rushed at her. Penelope jabbed the knife at him, but he swiped it aside and punched her square in the jaw. Penelope fell back against the wood bar. The big man grabbed her neck with both hands.

"Turn her loose, or I'll put a bullet in you!" yelled Jody. He aimed the pistol at the big man, but soon two, then four barrels were pointed his way from the surrounding spectators. He didn't change his aim. "You might put lead in me," he said, pulling back the hammer. "But your friend is the first to get shot." He held his aim, peeking from side to side, alert for any motion of someone about to fire.

A blast from behind seized every nerve. "Everyone drop your weapons." Jody glanced behind and complied with the order. A man wearing a tin star walked into the bar with a double-barreled shotgun at his shoulder. "First one thinks he can beat me to the trigger is killing himself and five of those around him," said the lawman. He cautiously maneuvered to the side of the bar. "Mister, get your woman out of here and out of town. McPherson, you back away from that woman and get yourself to the doc."

Jody picked up his piece, tucked it in his belt, and went to Penelope. Before she slumped to the floor, he threw her unconscious body over his shoulder like a fresh kill. As quick as he could, he made his way for the door under the protection of the law.

"Mister," said the lawman. "Don't think this representative of this town. They're all law-abiding. We're all Southerners. Just a few forget they are gentlemen."

"I won't think badly of you. Just matters getting out of town, is all. I'll hold no grudge. Evening to you all." He backed away from the door. Rain pelted the street, turning it into a small river. Jody walked along the boardwalks, slopping through the mud in the alleys as he climbed on and off each one.

When he finally rounded the corner, he threw Penelope across her saddle, hat and all. He took the lariat from her saddle and looped it around her waist, then tied it off at the horn. The thick clouds had blocked most of the light. He didn't have time to search for her slicker. He mounted his horse and took the reins of hers. He steered about and headed back to the south in the dark torrent.

Les ran a rope from one tall tree to another. She didn't have much time. The clouds to the north were getting darker by the second. She tied it off as quick as she could. She had a dozen horses as her responsibility. If they scampered loose, she'd spend the night looking for them.

Once she encircled them with the rope from tree to tree, she ran to the canvas canopy put up by Sanderson. The wind was first to arrive, and it nearly took her hat off with her head still inside.

Tucker and Dan sat nearest the fire. The cookie came inside soon after to stoke the fire under the pot. "Coffee is all you're going to get tonight, boys. Better drink up. Looks like it's going to be a gully washer."

The news of no food didn't sit well with Tucker. "Damn," he said loudly, facing Dan. "I ain't ate but twice since I've been off on this fool chase. We'd eat better if we were on our own." Sanderson didn't appear pleased at the remark.

"Listen here, sonny. I've been cooking for drovers for ten years. Some nights are like this. By the time I can get the food to your plate it will stink worse then what comes out at the other end."

Les did her best to huddle as near the heat as possible and stay out of this argument.

"I'm hungry, is all," Tucker complained. "I was told we'd get fed three times a day, and that ain't been the truth."

Sanderson continued stoking the fire. "It'll do just to stay here and keep dry." His Indian woman came under the tent with more firewood about the time the rain hit the canvas with a fury.

"I wonder what happened to Jody?" asked Dan.

Les had the urge to explain but didn't want to answer more questions surely to follow.

Sanderson shrugged. "I guess he went to scout for water. He didn't say nothing to me." He looked out at the dirt quickly becoming mud. "Be hard to find your way back in this."

"Suppose he's lost?" proposed Tucker. "Then what will we do? Just sit here for days and still not eat?"

The words seemed to irk Sanderson. He shook the stoking stick at him the same way most folks would a finger. With each shake, embers blew in all directions. "You'd be best served not to think in those terms, sonny. No sir. Don't wish a man ill when there's a storm like this."

"I ain't wishing him ill. I'm just saying. I'm tired, hungry, I can't feel my toes. And I'm supposed to go out and nighthawk in this in two hours. A fellow has a right to some hot food." He turned to Dan, who nodded his head. "I tell you, we'd be better off on our own if we just took the cows we brung and took off without this bunch."

Sanderson poured some coffee in a tin and handed it to Tucker. "Drink this. It'll warm up those toes. Just keep your mouth shut and don't let none of that hot air inside you leak out. Think of that Adair kid and those Mexicans. They don't have what you have right now." The cookie looked at Les. "What about the remuda?"

"I got them circled up in them trees," she answered quickly, then reached for the cup Sanderson offered her.

"Good," he nodded. "Rain is one thing. An animal knows what that is. But if lightning starts flying, we're going to have to mount quick and keep those cows from stampeding. They won't know where they want to go, but they'll scatter looking for any place than where they was." He looked to his wife. "Is the wagon closed up?"

Dorothy only nodded.

Les peered long and hard at the Indian woman. If regular English was understood without benefit of pointing at what was needed, then it was likely to be spoken as well. Yet Les never heard a word come out of that mouth. It was almost like a cat hunting a mouse. You knew it could make a sound but didn't while it stalked prey.

Les recalled what Penelope said. Was this woman scheming to get at Jody? Maybe as some chore for her man, or to have him for herself? Despite the dark skin, it didn't hurt to look at her. Maybe Jody felt the same way?

With the hot tin in both hands, Les cupped it close to her nose, breathing in the steam. Part for comfort against the chilled wind, part to draw all she had inside a little closer.

17

A GUST NEARLY tore Jody from the saddle. He tilted his head for the hat's brim to shield his eyes. The drops came at him at a level nearly as flat as the ground, stinging his skin like thorns. Between squinted eyelids he peeked back at Penelope. She didn't move. Maybe it was for the better. There was less squabbling as to which way to head. Although, with it almost pitch-black, he wouldn't have minded some ideas as to where to go.

Even the horses whinnied complaints about the storm. Nevertheless, he steered to the south, or so he believed. The dark skies obscured the sun. The last he remembered, the clouds blew in from the northwest, so he tried to keep a course to the southwest.

Gales whistled through the leather bindings. Rain soaked every inch of him, from his head to his toes inside his boots. Concern for Penelope across the saddle kept turning his face into the harsh wind. The drops pelted his eyes, making it painful just to glance behind.

The force of the storm pushed his horse from its stride. A pull on the reins to right the course took all the strength one arm could muster. Keeping his head bowed in an attempt to keep clear his vision in the eerie blue darkness, he often shook his head to hurl the drops from blurring his eyes.

More and more shakes moved his arms about. The slick leather reins slipped from his grasp. When he leaned down the side of his mount to retrieve them, the other set slid through his right hand. A boom of thunder stopped his own horse, but

Penelope's reared, yanking the reins from Jody's hand, and scampered off into the dark.

The instant it bolted, Jody reined his mount around and kicked at its flanks. The dark swallowed the other horse. He kicked harder to make up the distance, but the slippery ground kept his own horse from making up any ground.

Not knowing where to go, he listened for the hooves pounding the ground. All he heard was the splash from his mount. Frantic, he spurred his horse, only to have it resist the command. The seconds lost to regain control over the animal cost him any chance of spotting the other horse in the dark.

"Penelope!"

The only reply was the howling wind. Jody set his horse to a gallop. The wet ground dipped. He clutched the reins. Water splashed over his boots. Not allowing the horse to stop, he again spurred its flanks. If he didn't find her, surely she'd be killed.

Arms pushing against the mane, boots standing in the stir-rups, Jody rode as if for his own life. A glimpse of white pulled his attention to the left. He yanked the reins in the di-rection in hopes the source was the girl's white shirt.

Faster his horse strode. Between the drops beating his cheeks and eyes, he saw the white image grow larger. It had to be her. Anxious to catch it, he swatted the horse with the reins. First twice right, once left.

Limbs shot at him. Then another. Suddenly he rode among trees, the white image barely visible. He ducked another limb and, for fear of being torn from the saddle, he drew the lariat from the leather loop. Maybe the next second would be his final chance to throw at the renegade horse.

As the white image dodged left then back right, he spun the lasso low so as not to catch on any brush. When he saw the shine off the rump, he tossed the lariat. The rope hit the hide of the horse, spooking it, veering it right. Reeling back the rope with one hand, he lost sight of the horse and heard a loud splash.

Jody reined in for a second to get the direction of the sound. Without being certain, he steered in the last direction he saw the white image. The ground steepened. He leaned back to keep from being thrown over the horn.

He clutched the reins as more water splashed his boots, and soon they submerged. In an instant, he recognized that he was in a river. This was the Pecos River. Even more worried, he called again.

"Penelope!"

Indecision pulled him left, right, back, and front. He reined the horse full about, but the swift current carried him downriver. She had to be gone. If he stayed much longer, he, too, would be swept under, horse and all. He pulled the horse to head to the shore where he might be able to see and gain footing in order to search. As he did, the white image flew by his eyes.

Reflex had him circle the loop overhead. A single snap of the wrist sent the knot flying. He couldn't see the target, but when he pulled, the resistance nearly yanked him from the saddle. In an instant, he wrapped the rope around the horn. Whinnies broke the air. It was the best sound a man could hear at the moment.

He again nudged the horse, but the slippery silt on the bottom wouldn't allow traction for his mount to pull. Not only was he fighting another horse's weight but the current as well.

The force drew him and the horse into deeper water. One kick then another wasn't enough for the horse to pull the load. As the water crept up his thigh and to his waist, he hadn't long to act before he wasn't going to escape.

He reeled in the rope with both hands. The single chance he had was to free her from the saddle. As he pulled, his own horse sought survival and struggled for the shore. He pulled with all his might, the hemp slipping from between his wet palms. With three more yanks, he saw the white image, but it was under the surface.

Once within arm's reach, he sank his hand beneath the churning water and grabbed cloth and skin. He jerked with all he had as high as possible. The dim light allowed the sight of those blonde braids hanging from the side of the head.

With one notion on his mind, he sank his hand to her waist. He felt the clasp of her pants, praying he would find the item needed. Finally, the wood handle filled his palm. He drew the knife and in a single motion sliced through the rope binding her to the saddle.

Before the current could sweep her away, he emptied both hands of all rope and wrapped his arms around Penelope. While still mounted, he used his thighs to straighten himself in the saddle and carried her to lie across his lap. With a kick, he sent the horse to the shore. Waves pounded their progress, but he was determined this was not to end now. Not tonight. Not after all he'd been through. He'd worked too hard and had not given up. He was going to live. All this drive was taken out on the horse's flanks.

Still in concentration, he felt the stiff jolt of hoof on rock. When the same was felt from one step to another, he soon braced against the gale chilling him to the bone. Atop the horse made him an easy target for the wind. He slid from the saddle and searched with one hand for a windbreak, all the while dragging Penelope with his right arm looped under her shoulders.

When his hand crashed into solid rock, he dropped to his knees. The immediate reward of calm breeze sank him further onto the sand. He dragged her close to him. He couldn't see, so he prodded with his nose in order to sense her breath. In fear she'd already died, he poked his nose against her face. The slightest of warmth steered him to her mouth. He turned her facedown and pulled her jaw open with his finger. Water lapped over his hand, and soon after warm air barely could be felt. She was alive.

Exhausted, he relaxed his own lungs. He took a deep breath, the first in maybe an hour, and lay on his back. He would only rest a moment, then be back on the way to the herd.

Dawn broke to a clear sky. Sunlight crept into Jody's eyes. His mind instantly wandered to the rushing water, and he sat up in a shot. The river had receded to just above the banks, leaving the ground caked with mud. Like a broom, the water had swept the land of its filth of limbs and some small trees and carried it to a new spot to rot. Jody nodded in realization of how close they came to being just such passengers on that trip.

A glance to the left showed Penelope prone on her belly, one cheek buried in the mire. He leaned closer, part in fear she'd died during the night. A closer look saw the nostrils flare. He, too, let out a breath.

Another glance spotted the horses farther up from the shore near a grove of bare cottonwoods. At least they wouldn't be walking back to the herd. He first nudged Penelope, but it took an outright shove to bring her back among the living. "Are you all right? We got to get out of here and back to the herd. Can you move?"

His questions went unanswered for several moments. With no sense repeating them, he saw her rouse her head, and so he decided to take her arm and rub some warmth into her skin through the wet clothes. It didn't take long before she commenced to flailing her arms and legs like a startled wildcat.

"Don't touch me! Let me go!" she blared with an angered tone. Eyes wide, she jumped off the ground to her feet in an instant. Jody stayed put so as not to get in a trade of punches. More than an instant was needed for her to scan about and recognize the surroundings. Between heaves of breath, she pawed at the mud on her shirt. The more frustration she showed when it wouldn't come off, the more plain it became it just wasn't a matter of the mud but of the wet clothes clinging to her front. Finally, while backing away, she crossed her arms, turned for the trees. It was time to pull back on her reins before she did something foolish.

"Penelope. Just simmer down," he said as he climbed to his feet, slipping on the muddy shore. "It's just me. Jody. I didn't mean nothing. We just need to get back to the herd." His words took time to slow her pace. Before she got to her mount, she gradually came to a stop, lowering her head in only one palm. As he came by her side he heard her sob, but when he came too close, she again backed away from him. "It's all right. Ain't nobody going to hurt you." The assurance didn't reflect in her reddened cheeks and eyes.

"How would you know?" she sniffled.

Her question stopped him. Bewildered, and certain she didn't have the drive to get on a horse, he took his own step back and sought what troubled her. "I reckon I don't."

The admission at least creased her lips in a slight grin, but it only lasted an instant. After standing for a few moments, she gazed him up and down. "Well, what were you looking at? When I was down in the mud? Were you thinking it?"

"What?" he replied arms wide. "I was thinking maybe you were dead. Or near it. And what I needed to do to keep it from being so."

In her common manner, she scoffed at the truth. "I bet that weren't all."

Jody shook his head in confusion. "We don't have time to stand here and play games. The herd is at least five miles yonder, or so I hope. I need to get back. If you're meaning to school me on the matter troubling you, then get to it." His firm tone seemed to seize her attention, yet she still faced away from him.

"Like you don't know?"

Still shaking his head, he steered his eyes to the ground. "No. But I'm fixing on standing here as long as needed to get this behind us."

The longer she stood, the thicker the clouds of mist from her mouth into the cold, moist air. Almost by the instant, the harder it got for her to inhale, then slowly her chin quivered, and eyes reddened. Tears quickly followed. Jody stood paralyzed. Unsure what was the proper manner to take, each idea was quickly dispelled from his mind, and so he stood five feet away from this girl he'd first known when they were little kids. Since she didn't want him close, he stood his ground and waited for the reason to come out.

With tears now streaming down her face, she sniffled her voice clear. "Do you know what it's like to have someone on you?"

His first notion came in words. "You mean like in a fight? Or just someone barking orders at you?"

She erupted for a single instant in a smile, but it vanished as fast. She inhaled deeper again. "Got you where you can't move? Can't do what you want? No matter how hard you're wanting, just can't move?"

Jody took a moment and couldn't recall such an instance. He shook his head. "Reckon not."

She tilted her head at the ground. "It ain't something I recommend." She wiped away a tear and sniffled once more.

When she strained to gulp, she spoke. "Long about three years ago, when my ma took sick and Pa, he had the ache of rheumatism, it fell to me to get the chores done around the place. And I did what I could. But there was only so much I could do. Can't feed the stock and chop firewood, and tend to the needs of the house all in the same day."

She sniffled once more. Jody listened without moving a muscle.

"My pa said he had found someone to help. Which was a good thing. We couldn't pay nobody. Couldn't hire no hands. But he found this fellow. Maynard was his name. Maynard Caldwell." She stuck on the name for a moment before she continued. "He was an older fellow. He looked more than thirty, but he said he was only twenty-three. And he was a mighty handsome fellow. Could fix the fences and patch the leaks in the roof, too. He did about all you needed done. I thought he was the one we'd been hoping for. All we paid was room and board. Said it was all he needed 'cause he was returning to Missouri. He'd come down to fight the war and defend Texas." Penelope looked at Jody. "But I think it was a lie. He didn't sound like he came from Missouri."

Jody took a deep breath, then nodded. "I think I heard of the man. Or least I heard what happened to him."

A cracking smile crumpled her face. "Did you? Did you know what he did before he left?" There was no call to guess at the answer. Still, Penelope seemed bent on telling, which as long as she did, then Jody was going to listen. "After a month of being there, when he got most things fixed up, he was going to teach me the ways a man does things. So I could know after he left how to do them." She took another long breath. "Now, he knew that I had a shine on him, and I didn't mind being with him. But he never showed me much back the same way."

She wiped another tear and stood straight.

"So, one day, the day he was planning on leaving, we went out to inspect the stock. I didn't know what we were going to look for, but he said it was important to make sure they weren't getting pestered by coyotes and the like." She paused. "We came up on this shack. Don't know for sure where we was, 'cause we didn't have no line shack on our place, but he knew where it was. He wanted look inside and told me to come along with him. And, I did, just to see what he was looking for."

She heaved heavier breaths, the clouds coming out her like a steam engine, each word followed by a plume.

"As soon I got inside, he shut the door. Slammed it. And he commenced to kissing me. At the very first, I didn't mind, but real quick I knew he was kissing me too hard and not for no love." Her pace of speech slowed. "And his hands pawed at my chest and places a man don't never touch. And I told him to stop, and that made him hurry even more. When I tried to push him away, he pushed at me, and before I knew how, I was down on the floor. That old dusty, cracked, vermin-ridden floor."

Now Jody took deep breaths, but she continued without much hesitation.

"And he kept me down there. And he ripped my dress to get at what he wanted. And took what a woman saves for the man she marries as my ma told me when I was a little girl. All the time, he kept saying he was going to show me how it is to be a man, and how I should act like a man, and not tell nobody." As the last words came from her mouth, she sat back onto the ground, her eyes and mouth without signs of life, as if in a daze. Finally, she looked to Jody. "And I never did. I acted the man from then on. Since I was in no kind of mind to ever look at a man the same. And I knew no man would look at me the same as before. At least, no man that would want to marry me."

Jody took a step closer, but slowly. He didn't want to spook her into any thoughts like before. Unsure what to say, all he could do was share what he knew. "Penelope, I'm sorry for the trouble that man caused you. I can see now why you may act the part of a man, but it ain't going to spite him." Still unsure, he inhaled deep and recited what he heard. "Penelope, Maynard Caldwell is dead. He got what was coming to him. He robbed a few places around here. I heard he rode with a gang of thieves, and the law was after them. They found him stabbed over in east Texas, out in the forests there. Said they found him under a tree with a wound clean through the heart."

Penelope slowly looked to Jody, her mouth no longer quivering, her eyes still red, but no more tears flowed. She nodded and spoke in a authoritative tone as if she knew more than just hearing the same story.

"I know."

18

RANCE SEARCHED HIS soul for confidence. If he didn't gain some, that soul may be leaving the body inside of this day. However, since this was not a matter he'd prepared himself for in the past, he relied on what he knew and considered it all the same game. Instead of cards, words would have to be parlayed, or so he hoped. Still, he wished he had another day. The absence of Avis in bed that morning concerned him. He hadn't spent much time with her these last two days. However, she appeared busy when at her table, and he didn't want to interuppt her winning streak. When she wasn't at her table, he found himself on a run of his own, and all thoughts of stopping and finding her were lost in the competition.

Prepared or not, Rance walked to the Soccoro Mission, recalling when he first set eyes on the judge when debarking the Overland Stage the previous day. Portly fellow. Silas? He thought he heard that was the name. No matter. A deep breath was needed. Rance just had to keep his head. From everything he had understood about the crime, it was a clear case of murder, and if he did his job right, his client would be convicted and sent off to be executed.

His pace slowed. Something about that didn't ring true. Yet he sensed he was already late and resumed his pace toward the old Spanish church. As he neared, he recalled how the front facade and parapet resembled the Alamo, only this one appeared in better condition, perhaps due to the constant dry heat that permeated this town night and day.

Just as the old edifice had been restored, he, too, made

changes. He rubbed his bare chin. A shave in the morning always did more for his spirit. Also, the black coat and trousers were purchased with the winnings during his two days to prepare for the trial. He couldn't show up in court or a church wearing a dusty, wrinkled suit.

Within the morning's shadow of the building, his thoughts turned to Avis. The woman was terrified by the situation, and if he could manage to secure a guilty verdict, it should be almost certain he would receive rent-free lodging with all its benefits for at least the coming months. Maybe the summer?

The pair of wooden doors brought him to a halt. A deep breath later, he put his hand on the handle and pushed. The doors didn't move. Once more he pushed. The tall, heavy doors didn't move. He pushed harder. Same result. After he shoved with considerable effort, the door rattling loud enough that he thought the bell above would soon ring from the shaking, the doors shoved back. An elderly gentleman, hat in hand, had pushed one door outward, allowing easy entry into the church.

Rance stood, feeling a fool. How was he to know? Despite the embarrassment, he thanked the gentleman for the assistance and entered. The walls still radiated the heat from yesterday's baking, although it did allow for a cozy ambiance to ward off the morning's nip. Slowly, he approached the altar, passing by the full pews. It must have been the biggest attraction in town. The hurried preparations didn't mask the surroundings of a house of worship.

A desk was placed at the front. Two tables sat parallel within three feet of each other. A glance right had a spindly man with a bald scalp shuffling papers. Rance felt a bit naked. He hadn't brought any papers. Had he been told, he'd have gladly carried something with him. Despite the lack of documents, he confidently scanned the room, not exactly sure what he should be seeking. The Ranger who'd been at the Presidio sat near the table at the front. At the table to the left, Farnsworth sat in his unclean garb, with his two gunmen seated behind in the front pew. The only person he searched for, he couldn't find.

Rance stared at the sculpted image of Jesus on the cross. Somehow, it did seem a strange setting for a murder trial where a man's life hung in the balance. After careful thought of the circumstance, he shrugged and found his seat.

" 'Bout time," Farnsworth chided.

Rance grinned. "Never appear eager to proceed with a solemn occasion." The statement slowed the big thug's scowl. A loud call broke the silence of the church.

"All rise. The circuit court of the Southwest Territories and western Texas is now in session." The portly judge emerged from behind a drape and limped to the desk. "His Honor, Horace B. Silas, presiding." The judge stood at the desk for only an instant, picked up a gavel, and smacked the wood.

"Be seated," was the order. Rance sat and placed his hands on the table as if waiting for a show. The judge put on a set of spectacles and read a single paper. An instant later, he peered at Rance over the rim of the spectacles. "Before we begin, this court fines the defense counsel ten dollars for contempt. This proceeding was set to start at eight. Not . . ." he paused only long enough to draw a pocket watch and flip open the cover. "Eight forty-three."

It was no setback. Often Rance found himself behind in a game. It was the end of the game that mattered. He tried to hold back a smug grin. However, before he could respond, Judge Silas motioned with his fingers.

"Pay up."

The demand alarmed Rance. "What? Now?" The judge only nodded. Not comfortable with the dispensing of funds immediately, Rance rose and opened his coat. He drew out his wallet and pulled out the appropriate amount. When he placed it on the desk, the judge snapped it up with the speed of a riverboat player. The recognition did his heart good. Perhaps this man was a gambler in his own right. Rance nodded and grinned, then returned to his chair.

"Now that that is done," said the judge. "Attorneys will introduce themselves in the court for the official record."

The spindly man rose. "Francis W. Dalwood for the state of Texas, Your Honor." He sat down.

Rance peeked to the side to copy the protocol. He stood. "Ransom B. Cash." He froze, his tongue molding several words simultaneously. "In defense . . . of the defendant . . . for the crime which he is falsely accused . . ." Without any further ideas in his brain, he quickly returned to his seat.

Judge Silas again looked over the rim of his spectacles like a perturbed schoolmaster. "We'll enter that as a not guilty plea." He paused and peeked at his papers. "This is a murder trial. Due to the familiarity with the defendant by the local citizenry, a prejudice against said defendant can be supposed. As a result, this will be a verdict decided by the bench." He turned to Dalwood. "The state can make its case."

Dalwood stood, peeked at the papers on the table, then placed a hand on his lapel and began a long strut around the altar like a proud rooster.

"What is a man's life worth? Is it worth the due process that the law of the land provides? Of course it is. And this is the reason we are here today." He took the hand off the lapel and put it on his hip while the other was at arm's length, pointing toward Farnsworth. "This man took the life of an honest man. A sworn officer of the court. Horace Willoughby, despite his relentless representation of those who cannot speak for themselves, largely those who can't speak English in any form, and those who aren't aware of their legal rights, was a hardworking man of the people. This man before you today, with blatant disregard for another human being, shot Horace Willoughby in the head and so ended the life of that hardworking man."

Rance sensed the break was his cue to present his case. He rose and cleared his throat, preparing his speech, until Dalwood resumed his remarks to Rance's chagrin.

"The state will present overwhelming evidence as to the guilt of the defendant. We will show how in a careless display of respect for the law, that man, Clyde Farnsworth, pulled out his firearm and maliciously pointed it at Horace Willoughby on February 23 of this year in the Raven Saloon, firing a bullet into Willoughby's head. We hope the court will find the defendant guilty of this monstrous act and send him to the gallows where his maker will deal with him in a suitable manner. The man is guilty, and the state intends to prove it beyond all reasonable doubt according to statutes of the state of Texas."

Appearing out of breath, Dalwood marched back to his

chair. During the pause, all eyes focused on Rance. This was not a game with which he was accustomed. Judge Silas turned to him with his now customary peer.

"Mr. Cash, do you wish to make any opening remarks to the court?"

The wind in his lungs was at an all-time low. A glance at Farnsworth expected an unreasonable retort to the charges. Rance felt his heart beat through his chest, hoping something of any value to speak of would come into his mind. As a delay tactic, he stood and cleared his throat. Still nothing popped into his head. When faced with similar circumstances, he always relied on the gift of babbling while waiting for some profound words to come forth. There was no better time to recount any and all tangible and intangible reasonings he'd experienced.

As Jody and Penelope approached the herd, his heart beat a little slower. All during his absence, he feared there would be no herd and only the scattered remnants of a cattle drive. He kept his horse at a trot when he spotted Les guiding the remuda ahead of the steers.

"Good to see you all in one piece."

She didn't reflect his mood. Her eyes squinted while propping her head up enough to see under the wide brim. "Where you two been?" The question ended with a stare at the arriving Penelope.

Jody noticed. "We got stuck in the storm." He, too, glanced at Penelope, who showed neither smile nor grimace. "We found the Pecos. Not more than a few miles over that ridge. We can give the stock some rest and fill them with water as we drive them farther west."

"Farther west?" Les questioned.

"Yeah. I didn't see no grass to the east. Besides, there's a town there I'd as soon not stray close to. No telling what could happen if they spotted us."

Les again peered at Penelope. "Why is that?"

"Just take my word." He scanned as the herd emerged from over a small rise. "Where's Sanderson?"

"I don't know," Les answered shaking her head. "He had

breakfast ready long before sunup. He and that wife of his packed up quick and were gone before we even broke camp. Most of the fellows were still in their bedrolls trying to stay warm and dry."

Jody's curiosity was roused. "How did you all get through?"

Les looked about in a motion showing she didn't care much to answer. Finally, she shrugged. "We made it. Sanderson told all of us to hush up complaining and stay dry."

"Complaining?" asked Jody.

The subject earned another glance at Penelope. "Yeah," Les said. "That cousin, Tucker. He was running his mouth about taking their steers and setting off on their own. Sanderson talked him down, though. Told Tucker to keep all the hot air he was losing on the inside."

The remark encouraged Jody. "He did? Sanderson did?"

Les nodded, her eyes darting between Jody and Penelope. "Kept up most of the night, making sure everyone took their turn at nighthawk. Is why I thought it strange he'd be moving so early."

Although at first, Jody admitted the action seemed out of place, then he thought again aloud. "Likely looking for a better spot. Maybe might be some water. Can't cuss him for that." Jody scanned in all directions. "I hope he's heading where I'm thinking. If so, then we'll make good time today." He looked to Penelope. "Why don't you spread the word we're turning west to meet up with the Pecos. Tell them Mexicans to help on the flanks." He shrugged. "Might even rotate them back to drag. Spell Enos from eating dust."

The blonde girl nodded without one snarl. "I'll spell him." She nudged her horse and steered in the direction of the right flank. As Jody watched, he couldn't help but notice Les pay more than usual attention to her, then back at him.

"What you do to her?"

"Ah," Jody started, not wanting to repeat the story Penelope told. "She just had to get some mean out of her system. Took a while, but I think she was able to get it all out. Remind herself that under the dust and them chaps and dungarees, that she's still a girl." While he tried to skirt the exact details, he finally noticed the wide eyes on Les. "What?"

"Remind herself she's a girl, huh? You lend a hand to help remind her?"

Jody shook his head. "It ain't like that."

"I guess not," Les said with a curled lip. "How the two of you get so much mud on yourselves?"

The question wasn't an easy one to answer without telling more than he wanted. As he hesitated, he left his mouth open while deciding how to explain.

Les filled in her own words. "Sure seems like a long time to recall. Must be more than just the mud involved." She yanked around the reins of the paint.

Before he could call to her, she kicked the horse's flanks and galloped back to the remuda. He let out a deep breath and shook his head. Once again, he found himself at the displeasure of a female, not exactly sure how he got there. There didn't appear much good in him chasing after her to try to explain. Besides, the hurt feelings of a teenage girl wasn't reason to neglect his responsibilities as the trail boss.

He glanced over his shoulder. At the moment, he needed to find Sanderson and be certain the cookie was on the same desired course.

19

"MR. CASH? WE'RE still waiting."

Judge Silas's reminder brought Rance from out of the swirl of ideas. Many memories flooded into his brain, all of them very good, but they didn't bring exactly the point he thought needed. He glanced at Farnsworth. The big man lipped the words that brought back Rance's worst memory.

"Self-defense."

"Mr. Cash!"

The judge's shout spun him about on his heel like a private answering an officer. "My apologies, Your Honor." He pointed at his mouth. "Something caught in my throat."

"If there is further delay, I won't hesitate to have you removed. I run a tight court. Now, get on with your statement."

"Yes sir," Rance replied, taking a last glimpse about the crowd. Avis was nowhere to be seen. He shook the distraction from his mind and replaced it with the easiest event in his life to recall. "May it please the court, I wish to bring to its attention that this case is a mere matter of one man defending his own life. And that man is the defendant Clyde Farnsworth."

The daring approach brought a roll of the eyes from the prosecutor. Yet Rance was not deterred.

"That is right. Self-defense. The most basic of rights not only under the law but in all of nature. We intend to show how Mr. Willoughby's death, although tragic at the loss of life, was a necessity for Mr. Farnsworth's survival. After all, is one man's life not worth the same as all others?" Certain he had made a point, he wanted to end the speech before he lost himself in the part. "And so, as Mr. Dalwood will no doubt describe events that might look poorly upon my client, I will show how it was a regretful act but completely legal under the terms of the law." He marched back to the table and sat quickly. Farnsworth leaned closer.

"That was good. Sure you can prove it?"

Rance got the feel of the court in his mind, reminding him of many a poker game. When bluffing, never divulge your hand. "Trust me."

Farnsworth appeared satisfied.

"Very well," said Judge Silas. "Mr. Dalwood, call your first witness."

Dalwood stood. "Your Honor, the state calls Tom Baker." As soon as the name was said, the Ranger next to the judge went to the empty chair on the other side of the judge's table. Dalwood brought a Bible as he approached. The Ranger put his left hand on the book and raised his right hand. "Officer Baker, do you intend to tell the whole truth, so help you God?"

"I do."

"Please sit down, sir." Dalwood placed the Bible back on his table and took hold of his lapel once more. "Please state for the court your occupation, sir."

"I am a corporal in the Texas Rangers."

"Please state for the official record your experience of the night in question."

The Ranger looked around for a moment. "Wasn't much. Me and another Ranger were in the livery tending to our horses. I heard a shot and came into the center of town. A few folks were gabbing about a man being murdered. I went to where they pointed and saw this dead fellow sprawled on the floor, a bullet hole in his forehead. Seen this other fellow at the bar finishing his drink."

With a smug smile, Dalwood faced about. "And what did you do then?"

Baker shrugged. "I drew my piece and pointed it at the man at the bar. Told him to put his hands up. He looked surprised at me, but he didn't go for his weapons. I disarmed him and took him off to the Presidio. I sent word there was a murder.

Learned a day later the circuit judge was scheduled here anyway. Is about all there is."

Dalwood kept his smug grin aimed at Rance while asking the next question. "And did you see any weapon of any kind on the body?"

Baker shook his head. "No. Weren't none when we took him to the undertaker."

"So," Dalwood drew out the word. "It is an easy assumption that Horace Willoughby was unarmed?"

"Appeared so to me," Baker replied.

"Thank you, Corporal Baker." Dalwood looked to Rance. "Your witness."

Rance returned the smug grin. He didn't want to give Dalwood any confidence. He rose from the chair, but as soon as he stood straight, he eyed the Ranger and thought: What was he going to question? It seemed important to say something. However, what exactly was meant to be questioned eluded him. He began with the beginning. "Corporal Baker, did you actually see my client shoot the deceased?"

"Objection." Dalwood complained. "The witness has already stated he was not present in the saloon at the moment of the murder."

"I object," Rance replied.

"You can't object my objection," the spindly prosecutor protested.

"You can't call it a murder," Rance replied with a whiny tone. "It was self-defense."

"The man was shot to death. That's a murder. Why he was murdered is what we are deciding."

Rance wagged his head. "In terms of self-defense, we call it salvation of one's state of being, not murder."

"Order!" the gavel slamming uncountable times reverberated off the walls. "Gentlemen," Judge Silas stated firmly, "I won't have my court used for a contest for childish banter. Both of you have been warned. Any further behavior will land the offender in jail for the night." Silas looked at Baker. "We do have a jail, don't we?"

Baker nodded. "We got a room with bars."

"Good," Silas said, then slammed his gavel again. "Now,

I overrule the first objection made by the state. Get on with the answer."

Rance sneered at Dalwood, who snarled in return.

Baker shook his head. "No. I didn't see the shooting."

"So . . ." Rance drew out the word as long as Dalwood had. "It is assumable that the alleged crime was actually no crime at all. That it is purely circumstantial. As in not a fact." He knew he pressed his luck with the last point.

Silas slammed his gavel. "Mr. Cash, have you ever tried a case before?"

He quickly decided to reply. As long as he was bluffing, there was no reason to stop now. "Of course, Your Honor. My practice is a bit rusty, but I tried many cases in the great state of Louisiana."

"Louisiana? What part?"

Proudly, Rance replied. "New Orleans."

"New Or—leans?" Silas said with a smile.

When the judge stretched the name longer than usual, Rance knew he'd been called. "Yes . . . sir," he stammered.

"So, you must have tried cases in front of Eustace P. Longfellow?"

Rance gradually cocked his ear toward the judge. "Who?"

"Eustace P. Longfellow. The superior court judge in Orleans Parish? He's been on the bench there for over fifteen years, even during the occupation. I'm sure that if you have practiced law in New Orleans, you must have stood in his court. Am I right?"

Rance gulped. He eyed the judge and gauged which lie to pursue. Despite a rather delinquent childhood in the gambling halls along the wharf that gave him brushes with New Orleans constabulary, he'd never come across a mention of that name.

If he was to admit he was lying, he probably then would have to represent himself at his own trial. If he chose to say he knew this famous name, then surely there would be more questions as to height and weight and other characteristics which he likely couldn't guess. The more he matched stares with Silas, the longer he sensed he was matching wits as well. After all, he thought this man to be a player, and perhaps this was just another hand.

If he guessed wrong, it could cost him all credibility, if he really deserved any. Nonetheless, just as with a pair of jacks, one could never be sure if two kings awaited should they be called. With that in mind, he called.

"I don't believe I had the honor."

Silas leaned to the center of the table. "Are you saying you never heard of Justice Longfellow?"

There was no sense lying now. "No sir. I cannot say that I have."

"And you say that you were an attorney at law in New Orleans?"

Now, it made sense to lie. "I do indeed." It was time for Rance to call. "Perhaps, Your Honor, you'll share with us a landmark decision or famous case in which Judge Longfellow might have rendered a decision?"

Silas slowly receded from the table and leaned back in his chair. A distinct appearance of discontent gradually etched itself across the lips and brow of the judge. "At another time." Just when Rance's heart slowed a bit, Silas put his hand to his chin. "The reason I asked as to your legal experience, Mr. Cash, is the impression you are leaving me with that you have none. This is a capital trial. Circumstantial evidence is often more reliable than the testimony given by eyewitnesses. So the very comment you made that circumstantial evidence results in a verdict of not guilty is extremely disappointing as a member of the court for over twenty-three years. Especially since this is a decision to be rendered by the bench. There is no jury to be swayed by such a diversion. Therefore, I will tolerate no more theatrics. If I find that you are attempting to turn my court into some kind of sideshow in order to confuse the issue, I will have you jailed for contempt for at least the term of not only this trial, but while I am in El Paso. Do I make myself clear?"

Again, Rance gulped. He knew he had pushed a pinch too hard, but he also guessed he'd won the first hand. As long as he watched his words and paced himself for the duration, he might take the whole pot. "Completely, Your Honor."

"Very good," Silas looked to Dalwood. "Call your next witness. "I'm getting hungry."

Dalwood stood and called the name. "Sam Preston, to the stand." The double doors opened, and the Raven's barkeep marched to the altar and put his hand on the Bible. With the oath sworn, he sat in the chair as Dalwood strutted. "Mr. Preston, what is your occupation?"

"I tend bar at the Raven Saloon."

"And, sir, were you in the saloon at the time of Horace Willoughby's death?"

"I'm there every day."

Dalwood frowned. "Just answer the question as asked."

Sam shrugged. "Yes, I was."

"What did you witness, sir?"

Rance sensed Farnsworth breathe heavier. The big man's arms propped on the chair's, and he leaned closer to the table. Recalling what Avis had attested, Rance thought he knew what to expect.

"Clyde came in, and Willoughby followed," Sam said. "Willoughby, he was nagging Clyde real hard about some such affair."

When Sam stopped, Dalwood prodded him with finger motion and words. "And then what happened?"

Sam sat like a man confused by the obvious. He shrugged. "Well, that's about all I know. I heard a shot and smelled gunsmoke. When I opened my eyes, Willoughby was dead on the floor. Clyde said it was self-defense. I believed him."

"What!?" Dalwood shrieked. The assembled crowd buzzed. While Judge Silas pounded his gavel, Farnsworth chuckled and nudged Rance with his elbow.

"Order in this court, or I'll have it cleared," Silas shouted. Once the buzz subsided, Dalwood marched directly in front of Sam.

"I don't understand. You were in the room, and you didn't see the shooting?"

"That's all I seen," Sam stated simply. "I was pouring a shot. I can't be listening and watching what's going on at the tables. I got to account for every drop poured."

"So you're saying you didn't see the actual shooting? Is that right? You were in the room, and you didn't see the shooting?" Dalwood's repetition was too tempting.

"Objection, Your Honor," Rance said calmly, hand in the air. "I believe the witness has answered the question."

Silas peered at him over those rims. "Sustained." By only moving his eyeballs, the judge looked to Dalwood. "No need to keep asking the same question, Counselor."

Dalwood inhaled deeply and snorted in exhale. "Your Honor, I believe this witness is lying. I believe he is the friend of the defendant and is protecting the defendant with his testimony."

Rance darted his view to Silas, who again was completely motionless except for his lips. "That may be. However, unless you can show his intent to perjure himself, the witness has given his testimony. Get on with it."

Dalwood walked to his table and abruptly swiveled around. "Did you at any time see Willoughby with a weapon? Knife or gun?"

A long moment followed. Sam finally shook his head. "Like I said, I didn't see nothing."

"No more questions," said Dalwood.

Rance sensed some momentum and didn't want to stop it. "I have no need of this witness, Your Honor."

"Very well," Silas stated. "Do we have time for another witness before we break, Counselor?"

Dalwood stood straight. "Your Honor, I do have one more witness. One that I believe will prove the state's case."

"That wasn't my question, Counselor," Silas admonished. "How long will this take? I'm hungry."

Dalwood peeked at Rance. "I don't think this will take long, Judge."

Silas smacked his lips in disappointment. "All right. Go ahead. Call your witness."

Dalwood's smug grin grew, and his hand once again profoundly latched onto his lapel. "The state of Texas calls Miss Avis McFadden to the stand."

20

AS THE MORNING gave way to afternoon, so did the chill in the wind to the heat of the blazing sun. Jody reined in. While scanning in all directions for the chuck wagon, he removed the coat and secured it under the straps for the bedroll.

The quick temperature change parched his throat. He took his canteen for some relief. In taking a slug of water, a splash escaped his lips and dribbled down his chin and finally soaked a few spots on his shirt.

While chiding himself for his clumsy manner, he took notice the mud smeared along his front. It was an easy reminder of how the night ended and the day began. If he were to find Sanderson, the same likely questions that Les had would have to be confronted. Not anxious to repeat his lack of answers as he had with her, he decided he needed to clean himself up. As soon as the thought hit him, he turned to the wide river just a few yards away. He steered the horse to the water. As it dipped its head for a drink, he searched for a better spot to bathe than out in the flat open. Not uncommonly modest, he didn't want to be in the middle of scrubbing his backside when some nosy intruder or maybe some of the drovers might come along. The desire pushed him to nudge the horse farther upstream.

At a leisurely pace he kept a course along the shore, the encounter with Penelope on his mind. He reflected upon it with some relief. At least she wasn't as loco as he had thought at first. Her manly manner now seemed justified after telling her story. The longer he thought about it, the more he was thankful for the experience, despite nearly losing his life and hers in the storm. Even though she had learned the skills of a cowpoke to a decent level, he was far less comfortable with a girl acting the part of a man. Perhaps now that she told somebody, her ways may turn a bit more in favor of a female manner. As he let his mind wander, another example of a girl acting the part of a man came to the front.

Although Les never presented herself with the same conviction as Penelope, he never could get it out of his head that he always saw her as he did for the first time in Abilene. There he saw a kid, a boy, looking for the adventure of seeing new things, just as he had at the same age.

As they drove the remuda back to Texas, he developed a fondness for the kid, considering himself a mentoring influence. Even when they got to Fort Worth, he passed on some advice for a young man's first experience at bedding women. Now his heart burned a bit thinking how he must have sounded to that girl. He took a deep breath and blew it out.

Despite shaking his head, the memory of Les in those duds of a boy wouldn't leave his mind. The vision persisted, forcing him to wonder why. What was it about that gal?

Maybe it was more than a fondness? He shook his head harder. It couldn't be that. Despite the betrayal he felt when he discovered Les as a girl in such a brutal manner, the ridicule from those bandit brothers stung him deep in his gut. After almost nine months of that girl living in his home, that sting was still sore.

The sound of water trickling drew his attention. Flooded ground appeared in front. The runoff from the night's storm surged over the riverbank and now flowed over a small cliff's edge. Curiosity stirred him closer. When he came to the edge, he saw the water falling into a rocky ravine. From what Jody could see, it would be at least a day before the flow returned to the river, allowing for a brief but steady stream over the cliff.

The sight was appealing. He stopped the horse and took a peek at his soiled shirt. His gauge at the height of the cliff above the ravine was about as tall as a man. He recognized it as a wooden shower stall, just like the ones he'd seen in Abilene, only there wasn't a wooden stall to surround him here, but he also would get more than a single bucket of water over his head. He scanned about.

The plain was vacant in all directions. His modesty might have to suffer to take advantage of this temporary reprieve from the heat.

The tall wood doors opened. Like an entry for royalty, Avis stood in the doorway, adorned in a dark gown buttoned to the collar, no doubt chosen for the solemn occasion. Without further summons, she marched steadily down the aisle and to the altar.

Rance was frozen in place. She didn't even cast an eye in his direction when she passed. Dalwood followed her to the witness chair and presented the Good Book for her to place her palm.

"Do you swear to tell the whole truth, so help you God?"

Rance held his breath. Perhaps she could have a change of heart.

"I do," she answered.

His heart sank. A thousand thoughts swirled in his head. When Farnsworth nudged him again, he faced his client. A slight smug grin creased the big man's face. Rance perceived it as a question of assurance. In an instant, Rance realized the man had a notion Avis's testimony could be guaranteed to help the defense. Upon further thought, Rance had told her to speak the truth. However, now, since the case had turned in their favor, it was the woman's that could put a dagger to their hopes.

Dalwood placed the Bible on the table and went about his pompous routine. "Would you please state your name and occupation for the record?"

"Avis McFadden." She glanced at Rance, or so he thought. The apprehension on her face may have reflected facing Farnsworth. "I run the card game in the Raven Saloon."

"And Miss McFadden," Dalwood continued, "were you present in the Raven on the day in question?" The prosecutor turned to face the defense table. "The day Horace Willoughby was mur—killed?"

Once more Rance held his breath.

"Yes," she said with a nod.

His cheeks puffed from expelling the long-held air. He

closed his eyes for a moment in full knowledge of what she would say.

"Miss McFadden, would you please tell the court what you saw?"

Avis sat with shoulders huddled, a pose showing her reluctance to speak. Rance reclined in the chair, hand to his chin, wishing in some way to rescue her from her fate. Before any idea emerged in his head, she started speaking.

"Well, I was in the Raven playing a hand of solitaire. You see, this time of year, there ain't much going on in town, and I was just passing the time."

Her pause was quickly made short by Dalwood. "Please go on, Miss McFadden. We're all interested in what you have to say."

Again, she inhaled deeply. "Well, Clyde came in with Willoughby following right behind. Clyde being there wasn't uncommon. He came in pretty much every day. But Willoughby being there was not. He was a teetotaler and tried to start a temperance committee. So when I saw him, I figured there would be trouble."

Again she paused, and again Dalwood urged her on. "And what else did you witness?"

She needed another breath. Each time she inhaled, Rance lost his wind.

"Well, they were shouting at each other. Willoughby was touting some such about Clyde stealing cattle and other such things of the sort. Clyde, he went to get a shot at the bar." She hesitated, her eyes darting back and forth from Dalwood to Farnsworth and finally to Rance. "And all of sudden, there was a gunshot. I looked up, and I seen Willoughby lying on the floor bleeding from the head."

The crowd mumbled their awe. It couldn't be certain if it was just her description of the act or if it was her courage for speaking the truth against the local thug. Silas hammered his gavel.

"We will have order in this court." The loud command was enough to squelch the voices. "Go on, Counselor."

"So," Dalwood said with decided delight. "You admit you saw the defendant, the man sitting at the table, deliberately fire his weapon at the victim. Is that right, Miss McFadden?"

Avis didn't pause. "Yes."

More crowd-mumbling was met by more gavel-hammering. When the voices subsided, Silas's did not. "That's your last warning, folks. If we can't keep a civil environment for this trial, then we'll have to have it moved to Ysleta. Now, you wouldn't want that?"

Rance sensed an opportunity. "I move that the trial take place in Ysleta, Your Honor."

"Sit down, Mr. Cash," Silas admonished. The judge stared Rance back into the chair, then faced Dalwood. "Let's get on with this. My stomach is grumbling."

Dalwood seized the moment with his now-predictable posture, arched back, chin high, hand on that lapel. The man apparently was ready for a portrait to be painted at the drop of a hat. "Miss McFadden," he began, facing her, then pirouetted at Rance and Farnsworth with eyes shooting arrows at the both of them. "Did you at any time see the victim in this case possess any weapon of any kind, whether it be a gun or knife, or any item that it could be said the defendant was acting in self-preservation?" The last words came out as gasps of air.

Avis stared right at Rance, as if regretting the words that would destroy his case. "No."

Dalwood looked to the crowd. His pose was still struck, and he appeared waiting for another buzz to erupt. However, they obeyed the judge's order and remained silent, much to the prosecutor's apparent disappointment. With no applause in the future, Dalwood again faced Avis. "What happened after that?"

"Well, I was fairly frightened at the moment. It isn't often we get gunplay in the Raven. It's one reason I like it there instead of the other rowdy places in town or across the river. I looked to Clyde, and he appeared mad. Real mad. And I didn't want to do anything that might rile him."

Although she didn't pause, Dalwood didn't resist encouraging her. "Go on."

"He looked at me real long. I couldn't take my eyes off him, even though Willoughby was spread on the floor."

"Did he, the defendant, say anything to you?"

Avis looked to Rance. "He said that it was self-defense."

The crowd murmured, but when the judge picked up the

gavel, the sound subsided before he could pound it. He placed it back on the table.

Dalwood cocked his head at Avis and cupped his ear with his palm. "I'm sorry. Would you repeat that, Miss McFadden?"

Even though all ears heard it the first time, his question required her to repeat it. "Self-defense was what he called it."

Dalwood nodded, casting his smug grin at Rance. "Self-defense? Would you call it self-defense, Miss McFadden?"

Rance rose from the table. "I don't think she can say, can she, Judge?" Since he was standing and all eyes aimed right at him, he thought he needed to finish the point. "I mean, she ain't no judge," he paused, trying to think of a better word but didn't, "Judge."

Silas merely turned his head while still slumped in the chair. "She's got an opinion. I'll hear it."

Avis looked to Rance, then the judge, then at Dalwood, then at Farnsworth. She cleared her throat but not nearly as loud as a man. The act tore at Rance's heart. Here was an innocent woman just trying to do what was right, and he had put her up to testifying against a known man killer. Even if Farnsworth was convicted, there would be hard feelings over her testimony, and it couldn't be certain she would be safe the rest of her life.

Rance wanted to stand. Even if it meant another fine or a week in jail, he wanted to spare her from putting herself in a bad place. His legs remained pinned to the chair.

Avis shrugged. "I guess not."

Rance's heart stopped beating for an instant, then began to rapidly pound. As Dalwood retreated back to his chair, he passed by Rance with the smug grin firmly in place.

"Thank you, Miss McFadden," he said, staring at Rance. "Your witness."

Rance looked to the judge. Silas appeared stoic during the testimony. Without a jury to play to, Rance was forced into a corner. He had to find a reason to save Avis from herself, and it had to be legal.

21

RANCE STOOD. HIS eye caught Farnsworth's glare, expecting him to trounce the woman either with words or maybe with hands around the throat. He couldn't keep looking at this thug, and so he put his eyes on the lovely jewel sitting in the chair on the altar.

The stall tactic of straightening his coat of wrinkles gave him time to consider his approach. With dead silence in the old church, there were no distractions other than his own mind, considering what plans he would like to fulfill with her that very evening. However, that was at least one miracle away.

Without any particular strategy in mind, he decided to take a chance. Risk was his specialty. "Good morning, Miss McFadden."

She appeared aware of the need to maintain the ruse by an almost imperceptible smirk. "Morning," she answered.

At that point, his confidence soared. His mind again swirled with ideas, but rather than try to have her refute what she swore to moments before, he decided to explore what seemed yet uncertain.

"Miss McFadden, we have heard what you said you saw on the day in question. The matter that is unclear to me is, what do you recall was said in the saloon that day?"

The question startled Avis. Her curled brow seemed to reflect her confusion. Rance did his best to give her the confidence to answer with the truth.

"I don't know. Willoughby was spouting off at the mouth at

Clyde about stealing cattle. I don't remember Clyde saying nothing."

Rance slowly walked to the center, catching a glimpse of Dalwood, who also showed bewilderment. Yet Rance was determined to find out what he himself had not known. "Do you remember what Willoughby was saying? I mean, exactly what he was saying?"

Avis tilted her head. Rance was certain she didn't understand why she was being asked something that couldn't matter to getting Farnsworth convicted and hung. He tried his best to silently urge her to respond.

"Well, Willoughby said he wanted Clyde to promise to stop stealing cattle."

Chuckles came from the crowd. Silas picked up the gavel as a veiled threat, but it was enough to silence the noise.

"Yes," Rance continued. "I do recall you saying that. However, what else did he say?"

Her shoulders slumped like that of a child pouting over the burden of chores. She shook her head in a motion of searching for an answer. "He said something like, that he wasn't going to leave there until Clyde promised him to stop stealing cattle."

Rance stood straight and pointed his finger in the air. "So, he was not going to leave."

"Your Honor," came from the voice of Dalwood. Rance turned to face him. "Mr. Cash is trying to confuse the witness on matters that have no bearing. It isn't against the law for a man to stay in a saloon. Certainly no reason to be killed."

It was a fair point, and Rance had no response. He was searching for any reason, and it just had not occurred to him at the moment. When he looked to the judge, Silas smacked his lips.

"Mr. Cash, I am hungry, and it is nearing the noon hour. I would like very much to enjoy a nice meal that I have so enjoyed in the past in this town. You are keeping me from it. What is your point of these questions?"

When at any table, and a bluff was being challenged, it always served him to tout the circumstances if someone wanted to call his hand. "Judge, my client is on trial for his life. I beg the court's indulgence to attempt to explain his actions. Otherwise, we may never know the truth of the matter. You want to know the truth, don't you, Judge?"

By the reaction of Silas averting his eyes, Rance knew he had struck a chord. After only a moment, Silas nodded. "I'll give you a few more minutes."

More confidence now gave him the courage to continue. He looked to Avis and took a step closer. "Miss McFadden," he began, but his thoughts were interrupted as he neared those emerald eyes. Instead of the facts of the case, he couldn't resist asking about the secrets that intrigued him since he first saw her. "How did you get such a name?"

"Your Honor," Dalwood cried.

"Mr. Cash," Silas firmly spoke. "This is a court of law. Not a social gathering."

"I was just being polite to the witness, Judge. I wanted to put her at ease."

"I'd think he would have had time to find that out in their room," muttered Dalwood. Some hoots came from the crowd.

Silas slammed his gavel. "What did you say?"

"I said," Rance began, about to repeat his intentions, but Silas slammed the gavel once more.

"Not you." The judge pointed at Dalwood. "What did you say, Counselor?"

The spindly man now slightly slumped in his chair like a child who spoke in church. "I . . . I objected to his questions, Your Honor."

"No. No. Not that. You said something under your breath that set off a cackle from those behind you in the pews. I want to know what you said."

Dalwood gulped. Darting his eyes in each direction in an instant. Rose from his chair. "I only said, Your Honor," he spoke with knees shaking, "that these two should have found out such information . . . outside . . . of the court."

Rance looked to Dalwood, then to Avis. If he was to stay out of the middle, an innocent posture had to be assumed, and so he did, while stepping from between the two legal professionals.

"That wasn't all you said," Silas reminded. "Speak the whole truth, Mr. Dalwood."

Still with his knees shaking, the prosecutor pointed his finger at Rance. "That man has spent the last week in the room of that woman, Your Honor." His tone had the shrill of an adolescent schoolgirl with a smarmy hint of the village gossip. "The whole town has spoken of it. I just thought that if there were matters about each other, that they should have discussed them before they got in here."

Silas took off his spectacles and looked to Rance. "Is that true?"

Now Rance's shoulders slumped. He felt certain he would be on the same gallows as Farnsworth. "Ah . . . I . . ." he peeked at Avis, "would not wish to impugn the reputation of the witness, Your Honor."

Silas looked to Avis, then at Rance. Although no words exchanged, the apparent discovery of the relationship between Rance and Avis slowly etched itself across his face. The judge reclined back in his chair and blew out a long sigh. "Am I never going to get to eat?" He quickly leaned forward in the chair and put his spectacles back on. "Gentlemen, am I to understand that defense counsel has had . . ." he paused while peeking to Avis in the witness chair. "A familiar association with the state's witness?"

Since the judge's stare seemed focused on Dalwood, Rance thought it best to allow the prosecutor to respond and keep his own mouth shut. Dalwood, still standing, looked to Avis, then at Rance, then at Silas. "Your Honor, I must admit that it is the talk of the town that these two have known each other in more than just as a witness and lawyer. In other words, Judge Silas, they have been cohabiting for the last week."

Silas faced Rance. "And do you deny this?"

With only a slight peek at Avis, Rance stood proudly, hoping to present a facade of chivalry. He sensed, however, that this was a better diversion than any he could have attempted during cross-examination. He slowly shrugged. "As I mentioned, Your Honor. I don't think it appropriate to respond in a public forum to a matter that should be private."

Silas shook his head in exasperation. "You're a lawyer and did not think it inappropriate for her to testify when she is a . . . dear friend with you?"

"Sir," Rance said, hand now on his lapel, "had I been informed she would be called as a witness in this case, I gladly would have resigned."

Silas curled his lip. He shifted his eyes at Dalwood. "Did you give defense counsel a list of witnesses, Counselor?"

Dalwood swung his head from side to side, catching only glances of Avis, Rance, and the judge. "I . . . I did not know . . . that . . . they . . . until . . . I . . . he . . . was the . . ." He finished by shaking his head. "No, Your Honor."

Silas threw off his spectacles. "Well, that does it. The state has bungled this case."

"Your Honor," Dalwood protested with his hands on his hips.

"He's right, Counselor. You should have presented him a list of witnesses. Without that, he can not be held accountable, despite my dislike for his tactics." Silas shook his head. "I am not going to decide on a matter of a man's life on tainted testimony." He quickly faced Avis. "No offense meant."

Avis only bobbed her head as the judge continued.

"Therefore, I have to dismiss the testimony of this witness." He looked to Dalwood. "Does the state have any other witnesses? Ones everyone is aware of?"

Dalwood, his face still in shock, mouth ajar, still turning his head in short spurts like a rooster, answered, "No, Your Honor. The state has no more witnesses."

Silas peered over his spectacles at Rance. "Does the defense have any witnesses it wishes to call?"

Rance, his mind in a daze over the last few seconds, couldn't bring a single thought to his lips except the truth. "No, sir. I don't know anything further to add."

With a single bob of the head, Judge Silas picked up his gavel. "Very well. Since I cannot consider the testimony of Miss McFadden, I rule there is insufficient evidence to convict the defendant on the charge of murder. Although I have personal reasons to hold all of you in contempt, especially you, Mr. Cash," he said with a leer, "I am forced by law to dismiss this case and set the defendant free." He slammed the gavel on the table. "Now, I am going to get something to eat. You have won the case, Mr. Cash."

Rance stood, dumbfounded. "I did?" He watched the judge rise and walk behind the drape from where he had entered. Slowly Rance turned to Avis. She rose from her chair, and he wanted to go to her, but his arm was snatched by Farnsworth.

"Damn, you are a good lawyer," he said, patting Rance's shoulder with the gentle touch of a grizzly bear. "I didn't think you knew what you were doing. I wouldn't have given you a plug nickel for winning when that gal started talking. But I seen how you got her to say what you wanted." Another slap to the shoulder cleared Rance's head.

Just as he had stumbled into a legal loophole, he now realized the big thug apparently had more confidence that Rance manipulated the verdict than he himself. However, whenever prosperity smiles on a risk taker with a fortunate draw, there is no sense to reveal that it all wasn't skill. "You saw that, did you?"

"Hell, yes," Farnsworth replied. His eyes diverted from Rance to the prosecutor. Rance looked over his shoulder. With a sneer firmly in place, the spindly man packed up all his papers and tucked them under his arm. As he walked up the aisle to leave the church, Rance sensed his client still held a grudge by the motion to follow the genuine lawyer.

"Don't," said Rance, putting his palm to the big man's chest. "He was only doing his job."

Farnsworth snarled. "Yeah, well, when a man's job is trying to swing me at the end of a rope, I don't cotton to the notion that he didn't have choices in the matter."

Rance now felt the role of a lion tamer. He didn't have a whip in hand, so instead he had to use his wits. "No, you don't understand," he said with a wink. "He was doing his job." A quick recollection of the events reminded him this bonanza was brought forth from Dalwood's sniping comment. "It was he that set our plan in motion." He winked again and bobbed his head to the side where the judge once sat.

Gradually, Farnsworth's grimace faded and was replaced by a wide smile. Again, he pounded Rance's shoulder. "Damn, you are smart. I'd never thought of that, getting the lawyer against you to work for you."

Rance saw no reason to disagree. "Rather smart of me, don't you think?"

"I say so," Farnsworth replied. "Let's go over to the Raven and have a drink."

Rance's attention was drawn to the now-empty witness chair. However, he didn't want to anger his new admirer. "Tell you what," he said, his hand still in place on Farnsworth's chest. "I'll join you later. Right now, I need to pay my respects to our star witness."

Farnsworth looked to the empty chair. He winked at Rance. "Tell her I don't hold no grudge."

Rance smiled. "I'll do just that," he said while retreating toward the door. "As soon as I find her."

22

JODY RELISHED THE splash of water on his face, over his shoulders, and down his body. Not only did the stream wash away the grime and mud, but it revived his skin and weary muscles. As he breathed between the gaps of the cascade, he let not only his body rest but also his mind.

Too often on the trip he had concerned himself with just about every detail. He'd been raised that way, to be sure the job got done and done right. During Frank Pearl's drive the previous spring and summer, he watched and learned how this job got done.

Early rising, long days in the saddle, constant watch over the herd, always making sure how far it was to the next waterhole, and keeping an eye on the sky so as to not get surprised by the weather. Stampedes not only were dangerous, they could cost you half the herd either charging off a cliff or just scattering in every direction.

So much bad could happen it didn't leave much room for any good. That only happened if you made it all the way to the market. They weren't even halfway to the halfway point. There was a heap of problems blowing in the wind just looking for a spot to take root. Only way to keep them from becoming big trouble was to stomp them out like a small fire. To do that, everybody on the drive had to watch and make it known if they spotted trouble. It was his job to see that it got stomped out.

Jody knew this likely was the last time he'd get a chance to get clean and clear his mind. He just stood, letting the cold water crash onto his scalp, rubbing his hands on his sides to spread the cleaning. His eyes closed, soaking in the relief while stretching his arms across his chest to reach the opposing back of his ribs.

While his chilled hands ran over his body, a warm one came around his waist. In one instant, his mind wondered what that could be, and in the next, he felt fingers touch about his man spot. A thrill shot through his spine, sending a tingle through his senses and making his heart skip a beat.

He twisted about. Through the waterfall he saw the Indian woman standing straight, her arm still outstretched, the mist beading up in her braids and face. "Mrs. Sanderson? Dorothy? What are you doing?" Jody backed away, using both hands to cover himself the best he could. A few steps showed how slippery the rocks were to bare feet. Not wanting to fall and crack open his skull, he backed into the cliff wall, peeking between his squinting eyelids.

"Your horse," she said in fairly understandable English. "Not worry. I come alone. I gather firewood for the food fire. He not know I here."

"I know you're here! You ought not be, neither." Jody frantically bobbed his head in all directions. "You ought to leave now. It wouldn't do for you and me to be seen. Not me . . . and you being a man's wife."

Her face soured. "I not his wife. Not his woman. I . . ." she hesitated, her face aimed at the rocks. "Captive. Like the black ones."

The notion concerned Jody. "You mean like a slave?"

She nodded. "I given moons ago to him for blankets and tobacco by the tribe. They took me. My people."

"Took from your family?" The practice was known throughout Texas. Different tribes stole horses and people to do the their work. "Why would they give such a good woman away?" he asked while trying to see her face through the falls.

"I hold spirits. They saw as bad spirits." She looked deeply to him. "Name Seota'e. Ghost woman. I say the words of whites. I shame to the tribe. They stand the real people. The whites not. When I speak white words, they afraid. They traded me for goods white man gives."

Jody shook his head. "People can't own people, no matter what color they are. It's what the war was about. Mr. Lincoln seen to it."

She stood there in the same place, her shoulders huddled from the chilly water, but she showed no discomfort, no irritation, no pain. "Not way of real people. If not want ghost woman, the tribe can take, trade. Kill."

"That can't happen. I ain't going to let it happen. I'll tell Sanderson to set you free if you want to go."

"He not. He laugh."

"Then he'll have to find another drive while you stay with me . . . I mean, with us."

She shook her head like the notion scared her worse than Sanderson. "No. It not way. He find me. Take me. Kill you."

Jody dismissed the idea with the shake of his head. "He ain't going to kill nobody. I got a dozen people around me that will back me up. Can't a single man do much against twelve."

"No," she replied shaking her head. "He not one. He many."

The remark didn't make sense. "What? How you mean?"

"He one man, many man. They take cattle. He tell many man, come, take yours."

The news spread Jody's arms wide in panic. "Rustlers? He's with a bunch of rustlers? Where? Where are they?"

"Not know. But later, on the trail they come. I see them. They come, many man."

"I got to get back to the herd." He took a cautious step to go back through the falls, but the woman didn't budge from her spot. "You're going to have to move. My clothes are on the other side of you."

She nodded, her face still etched with the same expression as telling about the rustlers. "I know. You not speak now to him. He close now. He bring them not now. When he not close, they come."

"You think it best if I just do nothing?" he complained.

"Wait. Follow him. See they come. You see them best."

Unsure if he truly understood what she was saying, he stood next to the falls. "You're thinking that I should follow him, see him talking to these rustlers, then deal with them."

As he spoke the notion, it seemed to make more sense. Still, he didn't like being away from the herd. Especially naked. The realization brought him back to standing in a waterfall without clothes next to an Indian woman. His suspicions rose. "Why you doing this? Why would you betray a man who feeds you and protects you?"

She pointed below Jody's waist. "I want your seed." She grabbed the sides of her buckskins and hiked them to her hips.

Jody faced away and recovered himself the best he could. He didn't want to even think of what she was looking like, or he'd have more on his hands to cover. "Don't do that."

"You not want?"

He couldn't imagine her. After all, he was a man, and he had bedded a woman or two in the cow towns. But this wasn't the way he wanted one. Not now. Especially not to spawn any kids. In another instant, he thought of her shame of the tribe and tried to ease his refusal. He reminded himself, even though she was Cheyenne, she still had a heart. He tried to think of her as a lady.

"It ain't like you're not a pretty woman. I am sure you're a catch for a man. Most men. I can't speak how it is for your tribe, but in my upbringing, it ain't proper." Her desire still confused him. "Why would you want that, anyway?"

When she didn't immediately answer, he gradually snuck a peek. The buckskin dress had returned to drape her hips. He peered into her eyes. Sadness sank her head to stare at the rocks. "Your seed make me your woman. He not keep me when I your woman."

In some way, he thought it a compliment, but he still stood confused and put his front in the cold water to help him concentrate on his question. "Why me?"

"You are chief," she said raising her eyes to meet his. "You leader of people. Seed bring son of chief. Me mother of chief son."

He read her face as sincere in the notion but still shook his head. "Don't work that way. Not in the white world. I ain't no chief. I may tell some drovers what to do, but that don't make me no chief. No leader other than someone just pointing the way to the next waterhole." His explanation didn't appear to stir any difference in her face. He decided to speak from his heart. "I ain't in the custom of giving away no kids of mine. Even the ones that I likely will never see. I'm obliged of your thinking me a leader, but a man has to take more care in who he takes as a woman, a wife. It ain't just a matter of coupling." He looked to the waterfall. As he took a breath, his first inner thought came out of his mouth before he even finished forming it in his head. "It's supposed to mean more than that."

His refusal dipped her head once more.

Besides not wanting to hurt her feelings, he needed to be sure that she still might help him ward off attack. "I am in need of your help. If you do, I'll help you get what you want. A place with some proper folks. A man that will take better care of you. I'll find you another chief." A whip of wind reminded him he was soaking wet in bare skin. "Now, if you don't mind, I'm going to come across the waterfall and take my clothes."

She turned and walked back on the rocks, clearing the small ledge for him to follow. He still had to get to his clothes and likely would have to put them on with her watching. However, the embarrassment couldn't have been worse than what he'd already been through. Modesty lost, any further delay for the sake of propriety would cost him time away from the herd.

Rance left the church at first with cautious steps, wishing not to be seen, then quickening his pace toward the Raven. When he walked along the boardwalk, women stared at him, but not with the usual tempted eye, but with more of a scourge. When he saw their reaction, he feared Avis would think of him the same way. As he arrived at the saloon, the doors were shut. Sam apparently had not arrived, and Rance didn't think Avis would come in through the back door. He ran to the next likely place.

Around two corners, he strode through the alley and flew up the stairs. "Avis!" he yelled, rapping his knuckles on the door. "Avis, let me in." He kept knocking, increasing the intensity with each second the door remained locked. "I'll stay out here all night." He needed a greater threat. "I'll wake the lady downstairs. I'll go and pound on her door."

The latch clicked. He opened the door, removing his hat.

He'd need all his charm to win this hand. As he went inside, she held dresses on hangers and took them to a leather case opened on the bed. "Going somewhere?"

"Leaving. I don't give me a rabbit's chances in a snake pit in this town no more."

He needed to relieve her concerns. Two steps in her direction forced her to twist about, the single-shot pistol steadily aimed straight at his heart. Rance stopped in his tracks. "One more, and I'll shoot you sure. Don't try any of your tricks on me. I'm through with you and this backstabbing town."

Rance opened his arms like a beggar. "You don't understand. It's all fine." He pointed at the window. "Farnsworth thinks you're in on it."

"In on what?"

"The verdict. The decision."

She cocked the hammer. "You got me in a mess, Rance Cash. I sat in that chair and told what I knew. You told me it would get him jailed and hung. Then you play a trick and get him set free. I don't trust Clyde. And I don't trust you."

He chuckled. "You don't understand. He wants to buy you a drink. He's waiting at the Raven. Right now." He lifted his knee to take a step, but stopped when she gripped the pistol with both hands. "Remember the last time you held a gun on me."

"That ain't going to happen this time. I'll shoot you dead."

He pointed at the floor. "You'll get her mad."

Avis shook her head. "Won't make much difference. I'm leaving."

If her stance couldn't be swayed, then maybe the consequence of it could. "If you shoot me, then who'll defend you in court? Remember, I'm the only lawyer in El Paso."

"It would be self-defense. Or haven't you heard about it? It's real popular. Lots of folks are claiming it."

He dropped his arms to his sides. "Then go ahead. Shoot. I don't want to have to live with a guilty heart." She closed an eye in a pose of taking aim. If he was to make his plea clear, it had to be quick. "I didn't play any tricks. In fact, I was concerned about you. I knew that if Clyde got convicted, then he might very well hold you accountable. So I had to do what I could to get him freed. It wasn't me that decided it. It was that damn prosecutor. And the judge. Luck, pure and simple. You know about luck, don't you." He snapped his fingers and pointed at her. "You're in the luck business, aren't you?"

Avis opened her eye. "Luck is for suckers."

Rance took one careful step. "Yes, but it makes winners of all of us in the trade. People believe in it, and they flock to the cards for a chance to make it all come true." He took another step. "Maybe there is something to it." Another step led to another. One more put the barrel to his chest. "So, if you want to strike at me, then put that bullet through my heart." He looked deeply into her eyes. "Because you'll do the same if you leave me now."

When he saw tears well in her eyes, he gently took the pistol from her hand and wrapped his other arm around her. "Don't worry, my dear. We have a bright future. And time now to celebrate."

He kissed her lips. She responded by increasing its passion. Only when they parted for an instant, did she surrender her firm stance with a mumble.

"You bastard."

23

JODY GALLOPED OVER the rise. When he saw the sprawling herd, he breathed a sigh of relief and slowed his lathered horse. A moment's realization saw the cows spreading in all directions. Despite seeing the answer to his hurriedly said prayers, the whole drive was breaking apart before his eyes. He kicked at the mount to scamper down the incline.

While approaching, he hollered and whistled to force strays back to the center. As he gathered one then another, he came upon young Enos. "Circle them back toward the middle," he yelled. The kid replied only with a nod. Jody rode off to block the path of three more. Arriving in front of them, the horse stopped the two cows and a calf. When they veered to the right, Jody steered his mount left with just a tap of boot toe. His horse jumped left and back right, dancing to the lead of the cows until they no longer desired to escape the herd and reversed their path.

Jody nudged the horse's flank to charge and scurry the strays back to the center. Once they were on their way, he looked for more trouble. He soon found it. Quickly, he reined right and rode to aid Tucker wrangle a bulge of steers from the mass. Again, Jody hollered and whistled, distracting the beeves. Like chickens in the street, they turned tail and ran back to the middle.

"Where you been?" Tucker angrily shouted.

"Been looking for water," Jody answered, riding past. "We're going to set them over that rise. The whole ground is flooded. It will make for a good camp. Spread the word."

When he left, there was still a scowl on the border stranger's face, but Jody couldn't let that stop him from passing to the next drover. He soon found Dan and was met with the same temper. He knew they had reason to fuss. Too much of his time had been spent on worrying about too many things. As he swung around the rear, he saw Penelope with the bandanna over her nose. Her face covered in dust, he expected to hear the same complaints.

"Keep them moving into the center. We'll take them over that rise and bed them down in the next two hours."

She only nodded without a word. He took it as a good sign. At least it was one less battle to fight. He expected at least one more as he came upon the remuda.

Les was having a hard time keeping the horses in a group. Jody came along to shepherd a couple back into the fold. When he saw her, he barely could make out her face under the slouched brim. "How you been?" he asked, regretting the question the moment he uttered it.

Instead, she replied in a civil tone. "They've been wanting to scatter ever since the wind kicked up."

"Yeah," he said. "Likely smelling some others from miles away." He moved alongside. "Listen. I heard some news I don't want you to tell anyone." The announcement turned her head to him. "I heard we might run into some . . ." he hesitated, not wanting to spook her worse than the wind did the horses. However, since his pa was gone, if there was anyone in this outfit that he could trust, it was her. "We might run into some rustlers."

Her eyes widened, and her mouth fell open. "Rustlers? How? When? Where? How you find out?"

About to tell the whole story, he again stopped with his jaw ajar. A second thought considered that he might have to tell more of the situation than needed to be said. "Don't worry yourself over that. Just do what I say when the time comes."

"Do what?"

Jody glanced ahead. He saw the outriders once more lose control of the point. "I ain't got time to tell you everything. Just keep a watchful eye and mouth shut about it." Before he kicked his mount, he looked back at her worried features.

"Don't fret too much. You do as I say, and it will all turn out fine. I'm counting on you."

The afternoon sun beamed through the front window. Rance propped himself on his elbow, dragging his finger along the contours on her bare top. During the gentle play, a thought struck him. "You know, you never answered my question."

She looked at him, puzzled by the inquiry. "Which one was that?"

"Where did you get that name?"

She grinned. "Why would that interest you?"

He waggled his brow. "I've always been fascinated with beginnings."

A deep sigh later, she relented. "My father was a Scottish merchant. He was in the sugar cane market, always traveling to the source of where it was grown and where it could be. He was from a long line of rich folks who wanted to get richer. He was in South America when he found my mother. She worked stripping the cane. The story she didn't tell me was the truth. She made it sound like my father saved her from the fields, took her in, and made her a home." Avis took a long breath and slowly let it out. "But what he really did was put her to work that didn't spoil her looks for him to gawk at. She stayed inside his house there and tended to him hand and foot. I came along a short time after that."

When he sensed the story pained her, Rance tried to change the subject, but she continued without his encouragement.

"He was a Catholic. Not a reputation for a dignified gentleman to have a baseborn daughter running around his feet. So he put me in my mother's arms and the two of us on a ship for the States. When we got to Galveston, she took sick. Not many folks wanted to help her, but she did get a job doing what she knew how, tending to the needs of rich white folk. She always told me to remember where I come from. And I still do, even now, ten years after she died."

It didn't seem the end of the story. "How did you get here?"

She curled the end of her lip. "A fellow like you. Handsome man. A man name of John P. Curtis told me he would take me to California where he was going to make his fortune." She shrugged. "Convinced me, since I didn't care to wait on the rich folks like my mother, so I followed him." Avis raised her hand to the roof. "This is as far as we got. He up and left me in the middle of the night, no note, no word on where he ended up. I learned playing cards from watching the men in the saloons. When a table opened up, I took it, and haven't left since."

The spiteful but proud words brought a smile to Rance's face. "So you are a survivor. Good for you. And now you have all this," he said, pointing his palm to the ceiling. She again sneered at the remark. A moment later, she turned the tables.

"And what about you?"

Rance wagged his head, not desiring to divulge his own past, but since he had learned all her warts, he decided to play fair. "I'm from New Orleans. My mother was a Creole from a French line. She was a dressmaker, so she claimed, but she made her money hustling cards. Quite good at it, too. My dear father was more the wandering spirit, which is where I may have inherited the trait. He was a salesman, peddling women's undergarments made in Northern factories from Southern cotton. He, too, always wanted to find riches elsewhere. And it always seemed like it was waiting just in the next town or state."

When Avis bobbed her brow for him to continue, he shrugged, figuring it was the least he owed her. "Like you, I suspect a different story, but my mother told me they fell in love and were married in a traditional ceremony, although I haven't found anyone to swear to the fact. I believe they became more involved in the modeling of his samples than merely merchant and tradesman. Despite their love, my father soon left my mother to seek his fortune. She was smarter than to follow him. It was rumored that he was found in a married woman's boudoir somewhere in Alabama. We never heard exactly his fate, but I know he must have lived the life of a happy man."

"How do you know he's dead?"

"I don't," he admitted. "As a matter of fact, I like to believe he's still out there. Someday, I'd like to meet up with him and compare certain experiences," said Rance, sneaking closer to her for a kiss.

She put a finger to his puckered lips. "Don't get any ideas. I ain't going to make the same mistakes as my mother. If I'm going to get out of here, it will be on my own."

Her pride intrigued him. "Why do you say that?"

"If there's anything I've learned, you can't depend on no man to solve your own problems."

Her philosophy was well-founded. He himself had left a few ladies where he found them. However, her spite challenged him to up the stakes. "I'll tell you what," he said, resuming his finger's play. "What if I were to make good on our plans together?"

She arched a brow. "And just what do you have in mind?"

"Maybe," he said with a nod, "we can find our destiny. Travel to the more refined destinations of the West. Maybe even California. I've heard there's some easy marks there. I think we could clean up in a town like San Francisco."

Initially, he expected to overcome more doubt, but she didn't scoff at his offer. "Don't play with me, Rance Cash."

In an instant, he added up his life. A regular companion, especially one in the same trade, might make for a less risky existence. "I'm not playing," he answered in a solemn tone. "I think we could make it work."

She didn't smile nor frown. A long, thoughtful expression creased her face, and as each second passed, he found himself more concerned with the decision. What if she called his bluff? Or was it really a bluff? In all his life, he had made many offers but seldom spoken sincerely. Finally, as she propped her head on the pillow to face him, his heart skipped a beat. Despite the many risks he'd taken, this one stopped his breath the longest.

"I won't follow you," she said. His heart fell in his chest. "But," she added. "I may be right next to you."

The reply started his heart again. He embraced her and sealed the deal with a kiss. "We'll make such a good team." They celebrated in each other's arms. When he kissed her again, he felt her passion for the idea. The warmth of her soul passed through her skin into his.

He didn't want to leave her side, but as the many ideas ran through his mind, he recalled another recent offer. Before they could embark on a life together, certain necessities had to be secured. "I hate to even say this, but I have to leave."

Her arms instantly fell away from him. "What?"

He wanted to reassure her, but he had little skill in such matters. "I have to go, but I won't be long. Farnsworth wants me to have a drink with him."

"You no-good son of a bitch," Avis said, covering her top and rolling away from him.

"Believe me, I hate to even think of it. But if we are to make good with any dreams of finding a new life, it will take money. Somehow, I think it's waiting for me down in that saloon. Why don't you come with me?"

Apparently, the suggestion was an even greater outrage. She wrapped herself in the sheets and left the bed. "I wouldn't be caught dead in the same room as Clyde Farnsworth. Don't you remember, I was the one who said he killed a man?"

"Yes, but he thinks it was all a charade. A game. He told me he held no grudge against you. Come with me. The way those gunmen play poker, we'll have enough money to travel to California in style."

"No thanks," she answered from behind the partition. "I'd as soon make it there without his blood money."

The pious standard seemed out of place. "Now you're worried about where all the money you win at cards comes from? Please, let's be reasonable. Think of it as some sort of retribution for the sad souls who lost it in the first place."

He thought the point a fresh outlook. She sneered at him from the side of the partition. He rose from the bed.

"Come with me, Avis," he pleaded. "It will appear that you were in on the game in court. I'm sure he believes that."

She emerged from the partition in a blue, stiff-collared dress. "I may keep a heap of unrightly habits," she said, still buttoning the back of the dress. "But one thing I am not going to do is go down to have a drink with that man, holding a glass in toast of him getting away with killing a man. Besides, with enough liquor in him, he might just change his mind about me."

"I can't see that," said Rance shaking his head.

She dropped her arms to her side. "It's more than that you can't see, Rance Cash." She picked a hat from a peg on the wall. When she got to the door, she turned to him. "I got to tend to some errands myself." She paused, taking a breath. "If you're here when I get back, maybe I'll stick with you. If you're not, then I'll guess that you've changed your mind. There'll be no hard feelings."

He sensed a tear emerging from her eye, but the room was too dark to see clearly. When she opened the door and left without further words, Rance stood a man naked, not only without clothes, but without a shred of dignity. He had to prove her wrong, and the only way to do so was to travel to the Raven and win enough money for a train ride to San Francisco. Determined to succeed, he picked up his hat from the floor and put it on.

24

THE SKY APPEARED afire. Sunset reflected an orange glow upon the streaming clouds. Jody stood watching, wondering what awaited him to the west.

As the drovers joined the camp one by one, he turned to see Sanderson tending to the campfire. A glance at the Cheyenne woman gave Jody an uneasy gut. Unsure whether to confront the cook about the story told by the woman, he stood a man frozen in mind. He gazed around the camp. As soon as each one had their horse unsaddled, a quick path was made to the chuck wagon.

Jody poured himself some coffee and slowly walked to the line. The smell of salt pork and beans wafted to his nose. Supper wasn't on his mind. A neigh from behind turned him that way. Les walked in from the rear of the camp. While the others were busy grabbing a plate, he went to her. Before he spoke, the sight of Enos and Dan settling near the fire changed his plan.

"Get yourself a meal and find me over by the creek."

He went about the camp, questioning the boys about the day's drive, slapping their back for encouragement, doing his best to act the part of the trail boss. He knew he wasn't the best. Far from it, if forced to admit, but he was the only one to get these fellows and gals through to Colorado. When he saw Les from the corner of his eye standing at the wagon, he refilled his coffee and walked off into the twilight.

A spot near the shimmering water appeared the best. He sipped his coffee and found some time for a well-deserved chew. As he waited, he recalled the day's events. In the middle of the night, he thought his life was lost along with Penelope's. He'd thought it enough excitement for a mess of months, but then that Indian woman found him in the falls and told him a tale that surely meant for little sleep for the rest of the drive.

The rustle of legs swinging through the high weeds signaled Les's approach. When he saw the steam from her plate against the distant light of the campfire, he scanned around to see if anyone might have followed. He didn't want any panic to get about the camp.

"Find a spot," he said. She stood for a moment, appearing confused, then did as he ordered. She sipped at her coffee. He spat to the side.

"I don't want you to get scared."

She looked away from him. "I don't know why you'd say that. You just told me that we might meet up with some rustlers and all."

Her sassy mouth was actually a good sign. It showed she still had some fight in her; she definitely wasn't scared, least ways not of him, and it also took him a step back. "Good," he said nodding. "Glad to see that you ain't." He settled on the ground next to her. "I just wanted," he paused, thinking of the best way to say what was on his mind. "I wanted you to know that we might run right into trouble."

She put a spoon into her mouth, appearing not the least bit concerned. "Yeah, I know. You said that."

He sat, convinced she really didn't know. "Les, there will be men with guns most likely. They'll try to take the herd, and they won't care who or what gets in their way."

The mention of guns must have slowed her appetite. She dropped the spoon into the bowl. After a long spell of not speaking, she made up for it with some sparked words. "Well, what are you going to do about it?"

Jody spoke his mind. "I don't know," he replied shaking his head. He looked over at the camp. "None of them boys been away from their homes long nor far enough to know what it's like to be out in the open country. Besides the bandits and thieves, there is Comanches and a few bands of lawless Mexicans looking to take everything you got." He shook his head and spat in the grass. "Don't know if I can count on them to put up a fight."

"What about you?" she asked. "Not like you have done this except one time."

He took offense. "What you say? It was me that shot that man taking shots at you, don't you remember?"

"The way I heard it, he started shooting at you first." She casually took another bite.

"What difference does that make? I killed him, didn't I? And, if I recall correctly, it was me that stopped McClain from shooting you and Cash both."

"He wasn't going to shoot us. He was going to take Rance's money," she responded with a sniping tone.

He spat again. "Listen, girl, I done my share of riding and fighting—"

"Hush up, or they'll hear you." Her interruption only riled him more, but with a second's consideration, he agreed with her. He didn't want to attract more ears to what he was saying. "What I'm trying to say is, you'll need to take more care about your business. Be watchful. You need to tell me when you see something that ain't right."

She took a long time to take a swallow. He wasn't sure she really understood until she opened her mouth. "Lately haven't been seeing you. If I was to try and find you to tell you something, I wouldn't know where to ride."

Again, he had to agree. "I hear you. But, now I got two duties. One as the ramrod, to make sure the drive is moving at a steady pace, and as the trail boss, which has me looking for water."

"Sanderson can do that," she said, taking another bite. He spat again. He thought about a sip of coffee, but it was cold; the night air had stolen its warmth.

"Sanderson I ain't sure about."

"What's that mean?" she mumbled while chewing through the pork.

He grew tired of her questions. "It means, I think he may be part of who is trying to steal our cattle," he said through gritted teeth.

"Don't get your tone all mad at me," she said with her mouth full. "You're the one that wanted to talk to me."

"I'm doing it for your own good, Les." He shook his head and spat with the fury building in his mind. "I'm trying to make sure you ain't going to get hurt."

After the last spoonful, she finally swallowed. "I can take care of myself. I made it this far on my own."

"On your own? You'd still be in Kansas looking for someone to take you Texas if not for me and Smith. On your own: that's a laugh." He turned his head and spat. The clank of the spoon slammed into the tin bowl, and he turned his head to see her standing. "Where you going?"

"Back to the camp. I heard what you had to say."

As she turned, he feared her temper might loosen her senses and her mouth. "Wait. Don't go back and spark no fires in there."

"Ain't gunna," she said taking a step. He wasn't convinced. He rose and snatched her arm. She shook it loose faster than a crazed wildcat.

"What's got into you?" he asked in form of a command.

"I'll tell you what's got into me, Jody Barnes," she said, backing away. "I don't want to be around you no more."

The words pierced his gut worse than a knife's edge. He stood, wanting to chase after her, but held his ground. "Now you're talking fool."

Les shook her head. "No, I ain't. You ain't the same. Not the same as when I saw you first in Abilene." She stopped in her tracks and her voice crackled. "You don't smile anymore, Jody, like you did before. You don't laugh except when it's at me. Ever since them brothers stripped me of my pants, and you knew then I was a girl, I ain't been nothing but a bother to you. Never looked at me the same." She wiped her nose. "Before, you used to laugh and joke, and you played your mouth reed. Now, you're just nothing but mean. And you do it 'cause you got it in your head that it's making you a man." She shook her head. "Well, I ain't going to take to being treated like no Jonah. I joined this drive to get back home to Abilene. It was a mistake coming to Texas, and it's my fault for thinking I would like it here. But it's yours for making it so easy to decide."

Before he could say a word, she faced about and scampered

back to the camp. He knew there would be questions as to why a girl would come running to the others with a face full of tears. He sat back down to try to think of answers. While he pondered possible excuses, the only real thought in his mind was how true stood every word she said.

Rance considered stopping at the batwings but decided to make a confident entrance. He strode through the swinging doors with a bright gleam for all to see. When Farnsworth and friends saw him, a loud cheer erupted. It sent a tingle through his nerves. Before he got to the bar, a full shot glass was slapped into his palm.

"Here's to the best lawyer a man can get," said Farnsworth. Before Rance had a chance to reply, all those attending threw down their whiskey. He quickly copied the move for fear of seeming ungrateful. More cheers erupted, and the glasses were refilled.

One of the gunmen kicked out a chair for Rance to sit. He tipped his hat at the gesture and took his seat. Soon, his one-time client joined him at the table as well as three gunmen who Rance had not seen before.

"What took you so long?" asked Farnsworth. "We thought for a while that you weren't coming."

"Oh," Rance began with a confident boom. When a valid excuse didn't arise in his mind, he thought the truth might suffice, although at the last second he knew to censor the details. "I had an intimate appointment I had to remain faithful to." A long pause followed with puzzled faces on all. So as not spook the simple minds, he decided to speak simply. "A certain client desperately needed my counsel, should we say?" Only after a few more seconds did grunts turn to hoots.

Farnsworth slapped Rance on the back with slightly less force than to jar teeth loose. "You're one handy fellow." The big thug glanced at Avis's table. "Where is that gal?"

Rance thought the opportunity to enhance the legend of his virility might substitute for the actual truth. "Take it from me, boys. She's in no condition to meet society in her present state." He smiled when they did and couldn't resist one more comment. "Or walk."

When they laughed, he seldom had felt the confidence he

did in the room. Besides the need of a good cigar, which he
had none, he needed to feel a deck of cards at his fingertips.
"Maybe we should play a game in honor of the lady."

Farnsworth nodded. "Sounds like a good idea. But first,
there's a matter to settle." Rance's heart stopped. He bet
wrong this time, and it was going to cost him his life. The man
he helped set free was about to kill him. He was certain of it,
as the gunmen all wore smug smiles. Rance gulped, slowly
reaching for the pistols strapped to his waist. Farnsworth motioned in the direction behind Rance. In an instant, he thought
to turn and draw iron, but instead his hands were seized in
panic. Rance closed his eyes.

A pronounced crumple sounded in front of him. Slowly he
opened one eye. Not only was it a red carpetbag, but in few
moments he recognized it as the one stolen from him in San
Antonio by Rodney Sartain.

Farnsworth opened the bag and drew out a stack of bills.
He thumbed out five and slapped them in the middle of the
table. "A hundred dollars. Don't let it be said that I ain't grateful to those that help me."

Some giddy laughs forced a smile upon Rance's face, although he wasn't sure at first whether to be relieved for not
losing his life, excited at the surprise of being paid, or ecstatic
at having the prize of his quest being presented inches before
him. "How thoughtful of you, Clyde." He picked up the bills
and peeked inside the bag. The rapid view saw the stacks of
bills before Farnsworth snapped it shut. Rance offered an
apologetic smile for his curiosity. "What an unusual bag. May
I ask where you got it?"

Farnsworth shot a glance at one of his gunmen. Rance took
a breath in hopes he'd not sparked a change in the gleeful
mood. After a moment, a contented smile creased the thug's
lips. "Oh, we found a fellow that weren't needing it no more."
Some chuckles followed the subtle explanation. Rance recognized a bluff.

"Seems an item a man might miss."

"He ain't missing it now," was said from the surrounding
crowd. Guffaws showered the air. Even Farnsworth couldn't
keep a straight face. The thug rolled his wrist.

"Come on. Let's play cards. Give us a chance to win some of that hundred back."

A deck of cards was slapped on the table. Rance rubbed his chin and peeked about the room. The men who surrounded him appeared about the same skill at cards as he with a pistol. This was exactly the situation he envisioned before in Avis's room. However, one of the marks he planned on attending appeared absent. Rance picked up the cards and shuffled. "Where's Bob?"

"He's tending to business," replied Farnsworth, who then downed his shot and filled the glass. Rance continued to shuffle.

"Business?" The idea seemed peculiar. "At this hour?"

He dealt the cards when a reply again came from the mass. "He's scouting out what brung you that money." More chuckles spattered the air. Rance felt compelled to join but still sat curious as he took coins from his pocket for the ante.

"I'll open with five dollars. What business is that?"

"What business do you think?" came from one of the men at the table. In an instant, Rance knew the answer and didn't want to know any more. However, liquor and the need to brag brought more of the story from Farnsworth.

"Some fool is driving cattle along the Goodnight while we're sitting here. Can't nobody make it. Not this time of year. So, we thought we'd have a look. Heard they ain't nothing but a bunch of kids."

Rance peeked at his pair of jacks. "Kids? You mean like children?" More chuckles abounded. Farnsworth threw in ten dollars. Two other players called the bet.

"No," replied one of them. "Nothing much more than that. I heard they took two split tails with them."

"Something's got to keep them warm at night. Gets awful cold out there on the range." As drunken laughter rang in his ears, something spurred Rance to learn more.

"Women, huh. Who would take females on a cattle drive?"

"Some fool name of Barnes," Farnsworth answered, then motioned for a card. Rance's muscles froze. The thug slapped the table to awaken him from his trance. Rance finally complied, but his mind was miles away from the game.

"Ba . . . Barnes? From San Antonio? Jody Barnes?"

The men didn't show interest at Rance's inquiry. "I don't know. Don't care. Why, you know these folks?"

Instantly, Rance realized the danger of an admission. "What?" he responded with a gleam. "Of course not. I've just heard the name. I really don't know anyone there." He gulped. "Anyone need any more cards?"

He dealt those that motioned and did his best to play the hand. His heart pounded. He sat at a table where the fate of his friends had been decided. As he drew another jack, reflex had him reach for another coin to raise the pot. Instead, he folded the hand. He needed time to consider what to do. All that was on his mind were the visions of Les and Jody.

He had to do something. His only weapon was his skill with the cards. He had to find a reason for Farnsworth's attention to be drawn to him instead of attacking Jody's cattle drive. His eyes edged slowly at the bag full of money.

A determined march through the weeds brought Sanderson's attention to Les, the girl remuda driver. It was unclear what troubled her, but being a female a long way from home it likely could be anything. He turned his attention back to the cutting board while his mind wandered to another female. With a discreet glance, he eyed his Cheyenne woman.

The long days on the trail had worn into his old bones. She, being much younger than him, had taken up a better share of the cleanup duties, except for the last few days. In fact, recently she seemed in more of a hurry to snatch the plates from the drovers at the first hint they finished. After a quick rinse of the leavings, she stacked the plates and wandered off soon after, leaving him to strike the kettle.

The more he thought about it, the occasions he recalled losing sight of her, if forced to answer, he couldn't swear to know where she might have wandered. He chopped the onions a mite harder. The night had just begun, and surely these younger appetites would demand seconds. He needed to concentrate on his job.

Still, just like a struck match, the flame of suggestion wasn't about to go out easily. He couldn't help but notice earlier that very day it was mighty coincidental she and that kid ramrod came from the same direction not but an hour between one another, maybe less. He turned his attention about the camp. A quick count didn't make out that ramrod. The onions felt the wrath of his frustration.

Once more he looked at the woman. With her continual stoic lip, she made her rounds about the camp refilling the coffee tins. He looked to her eyes, which concentrated on the steaming brew. Then he watched the eyes of the drovers. Enos showed respectful appreciation at the courtesy, despite her heritage. It was the kid from down near Laredo who concentrated on her uncovered ankles. Sanderson chuckled to himself. The sight of a female's bare flesh was a rare sight and not something to take offense from some kid. When that kid's eyes glanced at Sanderson, the slight smile vanished instantly on both their faces. The cook made it clear that although he wasn't going to make a fuss over wandering eyes, as soon as a hand was extended in any attempt to sample the goods, the blade in his hand would be chopping more than onions.

Once confident the silent message was received, he resumed his work, but even though he stared at the board, he saw another image. Further thought on the matter had him recognize certain signs. He sensed the last few nights the woman rise from the bedroll in the middle of the night. In the state of grogginess, he reasoned she was tending to nature and needed the extra time to find a spot of suitable distance. Usually he was helped back to sleep with the aid of a few snorts taken before he bedded down to ease the pain of the day. However, in order to ease the qualms burdening his mind, he decided right there it might suit him to keep the cork in the jug.

25

JON SANDERSON ROLLED on his right side. Despite the yearn to get some shut-eye, he couldn't even if he wanted. A restless mind led to a restless gut, which twisted and turned each time he thought of the woman on his left. Doing his best to maintain the facade of slumber, he kept his eyes closed and ears tuned for the sound of the bedroll rustling.

The previous night he'd discovered himself alone when nature called, and he took her absence as a Cheyenne habit not to be concerned over. However, his notice of numerous occasions of the sort at odd times and the fact he couldn't see Jody Barnes all that well in the dark kept his mind swirling.

His dismay harkened memories of when he first set eyes on the woman. Toward the end of summer, he found her alone in the Indian nations. He accepted her tales of woe, spoken in reasonable tongue of the whites, of being sent adrift from her tribe on the charge of becoming too much like the whites. Even though he suspected there stood more to the tale, her need of food and shelter and his need for a warm female to sleep with overwhelmed any objection.

Up to the time of this cattle drive, she had given him no trouble. She accepted her duty as apprentice to his trade and caretaker to his loins without reservation. He thought it a fair barter. However, this was the first cow drive worked since their merger, and although he took confidence in her ability, the consistent surrounding of men, and young ones at that, might have been too much temptation.

With those ideas constantly banging the inside of his head,

he risked a careful glance over his shoulder. In the dimness he recognized a shape of wrinkled covers. Although not his usual habit of affection, he extended a hand, the excuse as a gesture of a loving pat if one needed to be explained. He reached his right arm a mite farther, but his fingers felt only the chill of the air.

Casually, he rolled slightly toward her. He patted, but didn't find anything but the hard ground. He sat up and turned. Despite the dark, his hands and fading eyesight discovered no woman sleeping next to him. With breath choked and ire rising, he peered out into the opaque prairie.

With three down for the night and only Farnsworth still playing, Rance rubbed his eyes, but for only a moment so as not to give a sign of fatigue. He focused his bleary eyes on the cards, peeking over them at the big man.

"Are you going to call the bet, or stare at them cards all night?" Farnsworth barked.

Rance once more examined the pair of threes with a jack and a six. He couldn't be too quick. For the last four hours, he'd played the others out of the game with ease but carried the thug Farnsworth so as not conclude the game too soon and have the carpetbag full of money leave the saloon. "I'll call," said Rance, slowly pushing the matching amount into the pot. "And raise fifty."

Farnsworth's eyes rolled. It was the third raise of the hand. In an act of frustration, Farnsworth threw in the fifty. "I call." He slapped the cards on the table. "Full house, ten high. What you got?"

The loss wasn't what disappointed. It was the amazing stamina of the big man after nearly a bottle of rye and half a bottle of tequila. Even Sam had given up for the night and locked the front door. Rance couldn't stall anymore and relented and placed his hand facedown. "Single pair."

With a chuckle, Farnsworth dragged the money to his side of the table. " 'Bout time. You took long enough to make up your mind. For some card player, you don't play with much sense."

Rance replied with a smile, "The race doesn't always go to the swiftest horse."

"Yeah," Farnsworth grumbled. "But at least he's got to run to stay in the race." He yawned. "I think I'm going to call it a night. Got to ride out in the morning."

Rance's eyes widened at the remark. "Are you sure? You could be on a winning streak." He displayed the fifty dollars he had left. "Don't you want to clean me out?"

"Hell, Cash, you act like you want to lose all that money I gave you."

Rance shrugged. "I am a sportsman. An incurable addiction to risk. What do you say?" He spread the bills out like a hand of cards.

Farnsworth just grinned. "No. I got to leave you with some money. I'd feel bad if you left here without a nickel after all you did for me."

The gratitude didn't swell Rance's pride. It was hard to accept from a man who contemplated ambushing Rance's friends. Instead, he suggested the first thing in his mind to keep the outlaw at the table. "Well, let's have a toast then. To your good fortune." He took the tequila bottle and poured himself a shot. The notion amused Farnsworth. The thug nodded with a tired but contented smile. Rance raised his glass. "To Texas."

Farnsworth picked up the bottle. "To Texas." Rance threw down the harsh liquor. Farnsworth raised the bottle spout to his lips. By the time Rance had wheezed away the burn from his palate, he saw bubbles through the green bottle. Gradually, the liquid funneled down the neck and spiraled down through the spout to the very last drop into Farnsworth's mouth. He swallowed and let out a loud belch.

Rance sat in awe. Not only did he witness enough alcohol consumed in one night to kill a circus elephant, he was stuck for any further suggestions to stop Farnsworth from leaving.

He stared into the big man's eyes. Slowly those eyeballs rolled over to white, presenting a ghostly appearance, sending Rance to the back of his chair. An instant later, the head of Clyde Farnsworth toppled like a tree felled by an ax, crashing onto the tabletop with the force of a sledgehammer.

Rance gradually scanned the room. Three henchmen and their leader lay about in drunken slumber. Cautiously, he stood, careful to not scoot the chair's legs across the wood floor, then after one more sure eye cast at each of the men, especially Farnsworth, Rance stealthily clutched the handle of the carpetbag, gently lifting it from around Farnsworth's arm.

He restrained his enthusiasm to peek inside, choosing instead to escape the room as soon as possible. With no time lost, he walked on his toes to the back hall and rear door. He opened the door. Only the brisk night air waited in the alley.

Out the door, he gently closed it behind him, just in case the cold might awaken the gang inside. Now, sensing time was in short supply, he ran through the alley and toward the street. As soon as he arrived, searching for means to leave town, a thought stopped him with the force of a bullet. Avis.

Rance took a step to leave, stopped, took a step back, stopped, then repeated the same motion, reclaiming the same ground for a half minute. What was he to do? He didn't want to leave the exotic beauty, but he had to make tracks in a hurry, and it might take too long to convince her to follow. He didn't have the luxury to argue with her. On the other hand, if he left her in El Paso after stealing Clyde Farnsworth's money, the thug's reputation might come to bear against her to get at him. After many a long, silent sigh, he decided he at least owed her a warning of what he'd done.

Like a shot, he turned for the building. He went into the alley and up the stairs. In the darkness, he tried to peek into the curtained windows. He risked a rap on the door. No answer. He looked down into the alley, expecting Farnsworth or one of the gunmen to come around the corner at any instant. He rapped again. Still no answer. Finally, he saw what appeared in the darkness to be a card stuck in the jamb.

He pulled it loose and angled it into the moonlight to see the best he could. It was the ace of spades. It was then he realized the message. It was a gambler's way to convey good luck, and good-bye.

He dropped the card. More than likely, she had waited for him for some hours to return, or at least he wanted to believe that story. Then she must have thought he wasn't coming back. At first disappointed she had beat him to the draw by leaving first, he realized that her timing couldn't have been

better. Perhaps she knew more about him than he really knew
about himself.

A second later, he stuck the card back into the jamb, only
upside down. It was his way of letting her know he had gotten
the message, that is, if she were to return to El Paso. However,
it was his turn to leave the border town.

He looked again to the street. He knew what awaited him
to the east, and he didn't care to find himself there again. He
looked behind. In the light, he saw the glistening of the Rio
Grande. Maybe it was time to give Mexico a try. All he'd
heard of that place was that it was full of thieves and cut-
throats, but how much worse could it be from what he'd witnessed in Texas? Standing there on the landing, he plotted his
course through the small villages and eventually to the impe-
rial palaces of Maximilian. All he needed was a swift steed to
carry him like the wind to riches beyond his wildest dreams.

She gently pulled back on the mane and listened. The stars
were the only guide over the rough ground. A call might be
heard by ears she did not care to waken. Through the brush,
she steered the remuda pony she snatched where her instincts
told her to go.

To the right were hills, but to the left the horizon flattened
and helped her discern a figure from the background of the
night sky. A whistle was the signal. Little time passed before
the message was returned. She slid off the horse and started at
first cautious, but soon she ran as she recognized the figure in
the dark.

Once in his arms, she hugged his waist, put her cheek to his
breast for only a moment, then pressed her lips to his as enjoyed in the white tradition. His face was rough with whiskers.
Dust caked his face and lips, but she ignored those to keep
him under her spell. With a whisper she spoke. "Long you
ride?"

He shook his head. "Couple of days."

She ran her hands along his ribs. "No food two days?" She
felt him jiggle with a chuckle.

"Had some jerky along the way. Don't fret about me. What
about the cows?"

She knew to expect the question. "No far. Two hills crossed."

"Good. I've got a place already picked out. It won't be long, and you'll be free from him." The words calmed her, but for only an instant.

"Free from who?" boomed a familiar voice from the dark. The man in front of her drew his gun. The noise would echo about the hills. She seized the arm with the gun and faced the direction of the booming voice.

"Jon."

"What are you doing out here, Dorothy? I found Barnes still asleep. Who is it you're with?"

The arm with the gun tried to pull free, but she clutched it firmly. "I alone," she said while patting the one with the gun's belt. Her fingers ran along his waist until she felt the recognizable shape of a hilt.

"Now, Dorothy, don't be playing any games. I may be old and don't see as well as when I was younger. But I do know you ain't talking to yourself out here. I heard a man's voice. I got the shotgun aimed, and don't want to hurt you. Step away from him."

The threat was real. The anger in Jon's words she'd heard before. In a casual manner, she pushed the arm with the gun down, then slowly started toward her husband. "I come to you." Despite the dark, she made out the buckskinned figure. Careful with each foot placement, she needed to calm him. "Only Cheyenne here. No other. Is good for you."

"Good for me? How you mean that? I don't suspect any other man meeting my wife in the middle of the night good for me. Now, you get close to me so I make sure I don't cut you in half like I'm about to do to your friend out here."

She increased her pace. Even if she and the other were out of the way, the blast from the gun would cause more harm. The cows might scatter and be lost. With stones stabbing the soles of her feet, she came near the man she claimed in the white tradition. "Jon, I here. No shotgun. No fire." His arm wagged in the air until his fingers touched her skin. She felt his grasp, and he yanked her toward him.

It was not the choice she intended when she left, but if she risked more chance of the guns firing, all she had come for might be lost. When Jon pulled her to his side, she ran her hands about his ribs. It was an easy target, but pain often caused cries. One could cause the same as gunfire.

"You all right?" asked Jon.

"Yes," she said, reaching near his mouth, sliding her hand across his beard. In an instant, she clutched the long hairs, giving her bearing as to how near his throat, running the edge of the knife across the skin, slicing into the flesh, wincing once warm blood spewed in her face. Gurgles told her she had found the mark. When she sensed Jon fall lifeless, she turned to the dark figure yards away. "He dead now. You come."

The figure approached and came to her side. An arm wrapped across her shoulders. "Don't worry. I know a place I can put him no one will find."

Jody sat in the saddle staring at the rolling plain from a hill-top. The midday sun lit up the cloudless sky. Over the last week since he'd been told of the rustlers, he tried to maintain a careful watch over every horizon for any sign of an attack. As they drove the herd now west of the Pecos River in order to pick up the Goodnight Trail, he risked leaving himself and the rest open for the pickings.

He dipped his head. He should have done more. He should have confronted Sanderson when he had the chance. Now, as he scanned the slope to the wide, scrub-filled valley, he put them out in the open, without a visible sign of water, and now without a cook.

He'd hoped to spot Sanderson from the high view, but only the sand and dust were visible along with the tall rock mountains in the far distance. He glanced behind. Dust in the air meant the herd wasn't more than an hour behind. He'd given thought of turning the whole drive back to home. However, he had to think of more than himself. These folks had invested their trust in him and his pa. If they went back, the disease could wipe out all they had. He couldn't let them down, even if he didn't know what to do next.

He steered about and rode back to the herd. As he approached, he wasn't sure exactly how to explain the fix that now surrounded them. He signaled Noe and Alejandro first to circle the steers, then went one by one to each of them to meet up at a spot overlooking the valley.

It took better than a half hour to get the beeves to settle in one place. He wouldn't have long to tell his tale. One by one, they filed into the makeshift camp with Jody in the center.

"What's going on?" asked Dan, reining his horse alongside his cousin.

"Get off your horses. Both of you." Jody tried to sound stern but not too forceful. When the cousins complied, Jody looked to the Mexicans, then Penelope dismounted and brushed herself off. Enos soon joined the group, looking quizzically to the others for a sign what this was all about. The last to join was Les, still with her hat pulled down close to her eyes.

With all assembled in front of him, Jody grunted his throat clear. "I don't want to take too long, but I feel a need to let y'all know what's happening." He needed another breath. "I found out that we're going to be expecting rustlers come and try to take the herd." A mix of voices stirred with all the typical questions he expected. He peeked to the side. The only voice he didn't hear was Les's.

"Simmer down," he yelled. A second later, the questions faded into the slight breeze. "About a week ago, that Indian woman came to me and told me that Sanderson was planning on leading rustlers here to steal the herd. I was plumb scared plenty, but I didn't want to get all y'all spooked until I could learn more. I'd been following the chuck wagon fairly close. I didn't see anybody nor any sign. But today I've been looking for Sanderson, and . . . and I haven't found him."

"What do you mean? You were following him. He's in a damn wagon. How could he get away?" Tucker complained.

"I was trying to help you out, too. I got a late start today. I got a late start many days. But today is the first day I ain't found him. I got to think he's left us on our own."

More grumbling only frustrated Jody. "Just hold off on that talk. It ain't going to help now. We ain't got water or food now, so spare as much water as you can until we find another creek."

"Well, how do you know it's true?" asked Tucker.

Jody arched a brow at him.

"I mean, she is Indian. You can't really trust them type."

At first ready to defend his conviction of the Cheyenne woman's story, a shred of doubt crept into the back of his mind, but he didn't want to share it. It would only lead to more uncertainty and maybe panic the rest. "I got to believe her. She ain't got no reason to lie about a thing like that."

"Indians got a reason to lie about anything," Tucker replied. "They hate white folk and will do what they can to keep us off the land."

Jody shook his head. "If she wanted that, she'd told us another story to get us to turn back."

"What worse story than rustlers?"

Penelope's question only brought more grumbling. It was time to take charge. "We ain't turning back. We come too far, and all of you have put up with eating a heap of dust for us only to go back and let those steers take sick." He paused to take a breath and speak his plan, which he hadn't really convinced himself was the best. "No, but I do have a notion about some Indians. I think if they were to come and take our cattle, it will be from the north. There's still Comanches roaming the plains up there. So I reckon we'll head west."

The idea seemed to stick for a moment. Then Noe the Mexican spoke his piece. *"Hay un poste lo base de El Capitan. El dueno es un hombre a quien le dian French. Esta como a medio dia de aqui. Yo Puedo ir a buscar ayuda."*

The rest of the bunch stayed silent, until an impatient Tucker voiced his ignorance. "What did he say?"

Jody knew, but Penelope spoke first.

"He said, there's a trading post a half day's ride from here at the base of El Capitan, that mountain off in the distance. Owned by a man named French. He knows the way. He can look for help."

"How do we know he ain't one of them?" Tucker complained.

"The same way I know you ain't one," Jody barked. "Seems you have a past of trading other people's property across the border." The loud accusation quieted the complaint as well as the others. Jody needed another breath. He couldn't spare a vaquero who knew how to move cows quick. But the idea was the best at the moment. Someone else needed to make the trip. Someone he could spare. He replied to Noe. *"No, no podria, tu eres muy valioso. Mandare a otro persona."* Once he knew Noe understood, Jody looked to Les.

26

A REPRIEVE FROM the Almighty came in the form of clouds layered in enough stock to block the sun's barrage. When relief came, Rance took the moment to stop and survey what lay in front of him. Pillars of crusted reddish stone stood like centuries-old sentries over the rock-laden land. The ground lay open and barren of any inhabitants. He quickly understood why.

A small valley below held green and brown scrub. Its only purpose he could imagine was to impede any progress he may be planning at that moment. A look to the left only showed more of the same: miles of massive inclines of rocks and brush illuminated in splotches of sunshine and shade. A glance behind soon discouraged any thought of retreat, and further gazes into any other distances only appeared the exact copy of the previous direction. He let out a sigh. He was lost.

His plan to conquer Mexico hadn't accounted on the odd turn that he couldn't find it. Another deep breath and a dip of the eyes reminded him of another compromise. Instead of a swift steed beneath him, he was forced to settle on this gray burro between his knees. Nearing the close of its second day, if his journey were to continue in the fashion it started, then death from thirst or starvation couldn't be long ahead of him. Perhaps it may even serve as a grand deliverance from being discovered alive and bearing a life filled with humiliation. At least he had the carpetbag packed with money reminding him why he'd put himself in this predicament.

While filling his head with self-pity, motion stirred Rance's attention to the right. Down in the valley, a single rider headed away across the scrub and sand. By the gait of the horse, his path appeared certain and direct. Perhaps this one could be one to follow? Despite likely several miles away and on a tall horse, Rance still gave chase to the thought of catching this rider on the burro. Why this man would be as far out in the desert, likely with a better reason than seeking fortune in Mexico, wasn't an immediate necessity to know.

About to kick at the burro, another distraction pulled Rance's eyes to the left. Closer than the single rider but barely discernible, he saw at first one, then a second followed by five more men on horseback all appearing during the same deep gasp. A patch of sunlight broke through the clouds and rolled across the valley, then the rocky hills, illuminating the riders for a few seconds. He didn't see shiny reflections of metal from any harnesses. The variety of hues both on the riders and the horses confused him initially. However, the longer he stared, the more he recognized the fact that he didn't recognize these fellows. Fairly confident he could read any man's intentions even from afar, it quickly became a sad reality that trait was based on cultures with which he was familiar. Once more he hadn't counted on the possibility on engaging those of indigenous standing. As the sunlight rolled up the hill and the warm rays resumed cooking him in the long coat, he squinted to concentrate on their faces. It wasn't until they proceeded up the same incline that he was atop that the fact he now faced armed Indian warriors hit him square in the eyes. The sunlight stopped moving and presented him like a spotlight on a stage. The first Indian pointed at Rance, and instantly all began riding at a gallop in his direction.

Heart pounding, eyes wide, Rance yanked the rope attached to the burro's bridle hard to the right and slapped its rump. Kicks to the flanks did nothing to hurry the lethargic animal beyond its short, choppy stride. Panicked glances behind showed the approaching warriors. Rance was lost in indecision as to stay astride the burro or hop off to run faster himself. If still mounted, the tactic may give him a chance to draw the .44 and fire in defense, but the jumpy steps of the burro bobbed the pistol from any firm grip.

Wild yells filled the air. Rance, expecting to be hit by an ar-
row or bullet in the next instant, closed his eyes to prepare for
the pain. The count of one second went by, then two, but only
the loud cries of war reached him. Finally, at the count of
three, he peeked open his left eye. The clouds separated to
show blue sky all the way to the horizon. The horizon ran all
the way beneath the hooves of the burro. The animal had
veered to the edge of the cliff and proceeded down the sheer
incline.

Every muscle seized in Rance's body. He couldn't move
his hand to secure the .44 nor swing his leg in attempt to leap
to solid ground. He no longer heard anything except the whir
of the air circling through his ears. Survival reflex leaned him
back so as not to tumble over the long ears of the burro.

Tossed and swayed left, right, up, and down, it was only his
legs locked around the animal's tiny girth that kept him from
crashing on the jagged rocks jutting from the cliff wall. Unknown to only nature and the burro how its sure step kept
them upright, Rance relieved his tense grip on the burro's
girth for an instant. The mistake sent him sliding across the
slick hide and over the side, landing with a thud just inches
from a stone sharpened by nature over a thousand years just to
lie there and split open his skull. Only an instant of thanks
could be given to his guardians of luck. His hearing returned.
The loud cries did also.

He scrambled behind a massive boulder, which gave him
only nominal cover from those about to swoop down and scalp
him. A long, deep breath was needed to steady his nerves.
Surely these savages wouldn't be distracted by sleight-of-hand
card tricks. His hands clutched the pistol handles. He had
come to the end of a long journey and was about to meet his
maker. He took another breath and prepared to do battle.

Gunshots rippled through his nerves but not his body. He
flinched as more blasts crackled through the air. Sensing there
was another battle going on, he poked his head around the
edge of the boulder to peer at the top of the cliff. With even
more gunfire erupting, he did the sane thing and tucked his
head back behind the stone shield. Like a storm, the cracks of
thunderous explosions slowly subsided to a few random bursts.

Uncertain exactly what fate awaited, he peeked once more. The grating of footsteps against the gravel stirred him to focus on the cliff above, where the sun now clearly shone. He squinted to sight a tall man with a broad sombrero standing on the top.

"You hurt, mister?"

Rance soaked up the familiar words of English like life-giving rain. Quickly, he stood up from the cover from the boulder, his apprehension lost in the relief of living just a few more seconds. "Bless you, sir. I am unhurt, thanks entirely to you."

No more than a few seconds passed before a rope was thrown his way. Rance grasped the line and prepared to climb, when he realized he had both hands free. He glanced at the pistols still holstered. A full second passed before he observed that the carpetbag full of money no longer was in sight.

His heart again pounded. Sweeping his head about in all directions didn't reveal its location. His heart pounded now through his chest. Behind the boulder? No. Just a few yards farther down the steep slope? No. On that miserable excuse of a mount, the burro? Long gone. His lungs choked up through his throat.

"Pull up, mister," came the call from above. "I don't want to be around if them Comanches decide they'd like another go."

At first, the need to find the bag seemed a reasonable excuse. An instant's thought later decided how smart it would be to alert these strangers to a bag full of money. His money. "Yes, of course," he answered politely, attempting to hide his paranoia. Without any cards to play, he went through with the request from his savior and pulled himself up the incline.

When he reached the top, he offered his hand in sincere gratitude. "I owe you a great debt, sir. Rance Cash is my name."

The one in the sombrero took the hand. "Robbie Escobar." The unaccented English was a surprise.

Motion to the right turned Rance's attention to three other riders approaching. "Am I to believe these are your friends?"

Robbie nodded. "We're part of the Hopper spread."

"Hopper spread?" inquired Rance.

"Maybe five miles over them hills," replied Robbie with a point in the appropriate direction. "Came out looking for strays when we heard them yelping. Figured someone was in trouble. We saw you chased down the side."

"And might I say none too soon, sir."

Robbie coiled his rope and tethered it back on his saddle. "This is no place to be. How come you're here?"

Now was the time for sleight of hand. "Oh, I was traveling. Trying to get back to friends I'd left in San Antonio."

"San Antonio? Awful long way on a burro."

"Yes, well," stammered Rance. "I had to make very late arrangements, let's say." He turned to peek down the side of the slope in desperate hopes of spotting the carpetbag.

"I hope you weren't fond of him."

The remark startled Rance. "How is that?"

"The burro. Comanches likely will have him for supper."

The idea panicked Rance further. The poor animal might have saved him, but that fate was the nature of the hostile place. His fear was more inclined toward finding the bag. And what would the Indians do with white man's paper money? Napkins perhaps?

Robbie continued, "We need to get back to the spread. Ain't no telling when they will come back."

Rance let out a sigh and forced a smile on his face. He couldn't show his hand about the bag. "Of course, you're right."

"I guess you can ride double with me," said Robbie with a motion for Rance to mount. One last peek behind was all he could afford. He stepped into the stirrup and took his place on the rump of Robbie's mount.

Les lugged her saddle off the paint. During the toil, she couldn't get Jody's face out of her head. Once he told her he needed her to make the trip to get help, she had mixed feelings. Part of her felt picked on. Just as in times past, he had told her in no soft terms what to do. It wasn't like she didn't want to help, but he held a tone like a parent scolding a child.

As she walked with a skip to her step, she reconsidered. Maybe he was sending her because he wanted someone he trusted. He did say once he was counting on her. Perhaps this was one of those times. Her talk with Greta came to mind. She had to find the good in this. Be less trouble and do what was asked. She nodded in silent agreement. She had to make it there and bring help. The whole drive was counting on her. She couldn't let them down.

While carrying the saddle through the remuda, each horse scampered from her path but one: the one with the white star on its forehead. As soon as she was told she needed to make time, there was only one animal she knew could run fast enough to cover the ground.

A rider approaching turned her head. Penelope reined in. "You needing any help?"

The offer came from a different person than the one that started the drive. "I can do it," Les replied in a terse voice. She wasn't forgetting the whipping she took from the bigger gal. Penelope dismounted.

"Here. Let me lend you a hand." The blonde girl soon took a grip on the saddle and took it from Les. "You going to ride this one? Ain't this that racing horse?"

"Lone Star is the name given to him. Not any of these can run as fast as he can." Les turned back for the paint to pull off the bridle. A neigh pulled her back to Penelope and Lone Star. The skittish horse moved away. Penelope dropped the saddle and quickly snatched the ear to stop the horse. "Stop that," Les ordered. She went to Lone Star and patted his neck. "He don't take to rough hands. He ain't like a saddle pony." Les rubbed her hands along his shoulders and back. "You have to think like the horse, is what Jody's always told me. Ain't normal to have something on its back. It's why they buck. Like a predator jumping on them."

She rubbed the horse's nose. Once she had the horse settled, she slowly picked up the saddle and blanket. With care, she flung the blanket across his back with no complaint from the horse. She knew then he was comfortable with her handling. The saddle took a little extra time than with the paint, but soon she had it cinched in place. A few more minutes were needed to put on the bridle.

Penelope picked up the bedroll. Les shook her head. "Ain't

taking it. He ain't used to the weight of this saddle. Can't have any more than me on him." The blonde girl showed her doubt. "I know what you're thinking, but I'll make it."

The big girl dipped her head. "Got something I need to say."

Les stopped and stood in front of her.

"I want to apologize for before. I wasn't of sound mind for a long time." She wagged her head side to side. "This ain't a thing I'm good at. But, I've been thinking. You're the only girl I know, now. You know these fellows. They don't know what goes on in a girl's mind. I just wanted to say that I'm sorry for snapping at you all the times I did." She pulled off her glove and offered her hand to Les. "I think I want to try to be friends."

Maybe this wasn't the same girl that started the drive. With a little apprehension, Les slowly took the hand, and they shook once. A moment later, Penelope leaned closer and wrapped her arms around Les in a hug.

"I ain't dead," Les said.

They both snickered.

Les nodded. "I know acting like a man ain't easy on the mind. I don't begrudge anything against you. Maybe when this is over, we can be friends."

Penelope inhaled, then nodded. "I think I'd like that."

Hooves pounding the ground turned their attention. Jody slowed his horse, looking at both of them with some bewilderment. "What's wrong?"

Les looked to Penelope. She shook her head.

Penelope's mean streak returned. "Ain't nothing you'd need be concerned."

Jody furrowed his brow in further confusion. "I just came to see if you got what you need. Be sure you take a full canteen."

Les picked hers from the ground and shook it. "Sounds near full."

He took his and tossed it to her. "Be sure you got enough." He dismounted and went to Les. Penelope took a step back.

"I guess I need to get back to the herd." She pointed at Les. "You get there and get back, you hear?"

Les smiled. "I plan on it." As Penelope mounted and rode off, Les looked to Jody. "I be going now."

"Wait," he said. "I can't say it right, but I wouldn't be sending you if I thought anything bad would come from it." Even though she nodded, he continued. "I mean, I want you to watch yourself. There's bad parts out there. Don't lose sight of what's ahead and behind."

She nodded her head to agree.

He kept talking. "Be watchful. Know where you are."

She nodded again.

"Don't want you—"

"Jody, I know what you're saying. I'll be careful. It ain't like I don't know that I got to be careful."

He shut his mouth and inhaled through his nose, snorting it out in frustration. "The real reason I'm wanting you to go is I don't want you around here when it gets bad here."

She didn't understand. "What you saying?"

He needed another breath. A moment later he put his hands on her shoulders. "I can't be thinking what's best for the herd. If there's shooting commencing, I don't want you around here." He inhaled once more. "I don't want anything happening to you, Les."

His words stopped her from thinking about the ride ahead. She didn't know how to answer. Unsure what to expect, he patted her shoulder as she had Lone Star. In an instant, all dreams of what might be meant vanished. A moment passed before she once more nodded. "I know. Don't want to be thinking what might happen to you." Torn between showing her feelings or keeping them silent, she forced herself to Lone Star and mounted. With just a glance down at Jody, she spoke quickly before any more words than what she wanted spilled out. "I'll bring help back as fast as I can."

The bouncing journey finally ended with sight of the ranch house. As the riders filed through the gate, Rance observed the surroundings. Even though large, the house appeared rather spartan. Gnarled posts supported an awning in front, shielding only a dirt entryway to the front door. Two windows on either side of the door showed dreary red cloth as drapes. Further inspection had rickety planks squared off some ten feet from the house. A pen on the far side in the opposite direction appeared to be the pig sty. All about the place showed only the isolation of being in the middle of desolate land. Nothing resembled the greenery seen in San Antonio.

Robbie stopped the horse. With a helping hand, Rance slid off the rump. He swiped sweat off his brow as he heard the door creak open. A gentleman with white hair, a pale shirt under suspenders, and dark gray pants tucked inside boots to the knee stepped from the interior.

Sensing he was in the presence of the host, Rance initiated the greeting. "Good day to you, sir. Rance Cash is my name."

Despite the features of an Anglo, the sun-baked face gave the man the appearance of his Mexican cowboys. When Rance offered his hand, the host slowly accepted the gesture with some apprehension. He looked to Robbie for an explanation.

"We found him being chased by Comanches. Lost the burro he was on, so we brought him here."

The host didn't appear pleased. Rance flashed his dusty gleam. "I am forever in your debt, sir, for having such trusted men in your employ and so to spare me from the wrath of the local savages." The words didn't bring about a smile.

"You were on a burro? Out here? With those clothes? Don't see many a man wearing long dress coats and a short-brimmed stove hat out here with stories of riding donkeys," the host drawled.

Rance peeked at his soiled attire. "Yes, well, I found myself at the mercy of the least available when I left El Paso."

"Why would you leave El Paso?"

The inquiry had the tone of the judge in court. Rance scrambled for an answer. "I . . . was . . ." he mumbled. Faces of Les and Jody popped into his head. "Anxious to see friends of mine."

The alibi appeared to suffice with the shake of the host's head. "Donald Hopper."

Relieved, Rance shook Hopper's hand with renewed vigor. "A great pleasure to make your acquaintance, Mr. Hopper. If not for your men, I fear I would be the main course at those savages' dinner tonight."

Hopper again didn't smile but rather shook his head. "Comanches aren't cannibals, Mr. Cash. They just don't like white folks crossing their land. With all the cows being driven across these hills, they see it as an insult. Must have mistook you for more of the same." Hopper looked to Robbie. "Once they're stirred up, they'll come calling on us."

Confused, Rance was more eager to leave the oppression of the heat than to seek further elaboration. "My regrets if that causes you any bother, sir." He took a step closer to the shade of the awning. The urge to recover the carpetbag wouldn't leave his mind. "If I could trouble you for a sip of clean water, I'll be on my way."

A long snorting huff served as a sign of acceptance to the offer. Hopper turned to the door. "Margaret."

Rance looked to the door, expecting the rancher's spouse to appear. He readied his hat to be tipped to a woman of similar age and white hair. Instead, what emerged from the door was an angel on loan from heaven. A fair-complected beauty of straight blonde hair flowing over her shoulders with a single braid draped to the side of her face to show her sky-blue eyes, the same color as her blouse blooming with her feminine form from beneath.

Rance's knees buckled. Caught by surprise, he came to his senses and snatched the hat from his head. "My, what an oasis for the eyes," he muttered. "So pleased to meet you, Mrs. Hopper."

"Margaret is my niece. She'll get you your water and maybe some food for along the way."

"That would be very gracious of you, Mr. Hopper." As Rance stepped in under the shade, he was followed by Hopper. Margaret went inside the house, inviting the way for Rance to continue. With the white-haired gentleman in very close proximity, Rance kept his hat in hand and waited patiently while observing the interior.

Just as with the exterior, the room was vacant of any luxuries. A single rocking chair sat in front of a dormant fireplace. A coal-burning stove sat against a wall. Two other sitting chairs were near the window. All of it appeared a very modest existence, but one that made sense, considering the remoteness of the dwelling.

To the right in a narrow alcove sat a short table with just two chairs. Evidently, the hands of the ranch took their meals elsewhere. The far wall of the alcove held a single closed door. Curious, Rance looked to the opposite wall of the building where another door stood. It was a flip of coin, but his intuition bet that the door in the alcove might be where the young niece, a woman nearer his age than not by his gauge, might sleep. He made note of the discovery just as Hopper approached him with hat in one hand and rifle in the other.

"Might I have a word with you?" asked the host. Rance nodded and stepped back under the awning. While speaking, Hopper opened the breech of the rifle and removed loaded shells from his pocket. "When the Comanches get riled like this, they tend to raid the local stock of the spreads around here. It isn't good practice to leave livestock unprotected. I'm needing to bring my cattle in closer to the ranch while I can, and Robbie will be taking his men to do the same." With the last word, Hopper snapped the breech shut. "Do you understand what I'm telling you?"

Rance showed his best face of comprehension. "Of course. Certainly seems prudent on your part."

"Prudent," Hopper repeated. "Now, there's a word I haven't heard in these parts for a while." He dipped his eyes and cleared his throat. "I'm a plain talker, Mr. Cash." He stared Rance dead in the eyes. "You'll do nothing but slow us down. That's the sole reason I'm leaving you here. If I come back here and find one hair out of place on my niece, you'll wish those Comanches did barbecue you on a spit. Are you following my meaning?"

Stuck with his mouth open, Rance ran the described scene through his mind. Convinced Hopper was a man of his word, Rance nodded. "Understood, sir. I am a gentleman of the South and would do nothing to compromise the reputation of your fair niece. You have my word." Rance extended his hand. Hopper gripped it and squeezed with a force capable of crushing iron. The rancher called to his men, and they all proceeded to mount horses and leave through the gate, but not without contemptuous stares from all the riders. He'd been left in the girl's charge under desperate conditions and knew he'd face the wrath of his saviors should he falter in that duty.

When he turned, he found Margaret standing in front of him with a cup of water. He gently took it from her delicate hand, brushing only slightly against her pristine finger. "Why, thank you, Miss Hopper. You are quite kind."

She stood in front of him for a moment's pause, then led him back inside through the open door. "You are very welcome, Mr. Cash. Although I don't share my uncle's name."

Rance took a sip, savoring the moisture on his parched lips. "Oh? My apologies for the mistake."

"None needed," she replied while slowly closing the door. "My uncle was widowed by my aunt's death. She was my mother's sister. Since I didn't have any family to keep me in the East, I came here to look after him." She latched the door shut.

He took another sip and was about to take another when courtesy caused him to ask, "So, how should I address you?" Then took the sip.

With her back against the door in a pose as a temptress sealing them both inside, she replied. "Hornblower."

Rance choked on the water, coughing it back in his mouth, but quick enough to keep it from dripping onto the wood floor. "Ho . . . Hornbl . . . Hornblower?"

Margaret took a step toward him. "Yes. Scottish, I believe, although our lineage is Irish. Not exactly sure how that came about." She was within a short arm's reach. "My family came over during the famine. I was born in Maine, but my family moved a great deal." The closer she got, the breathier her tone. "I always wanted to come west and see for myself if it were true about all the stories told."

"Told?" Rance squeaked, in part from the water still choking his voice. "About what?"

"Not what, Mr. Cash, whom. The stories about the men of the West. Stories about the men of Texas." She now stood just inches in front of him. Barely an effort would have to be made to bend down and taste those lips. However, the fire from an imagined open flame burned his face.

"I am from New Orleans," he softly replied while arching away.

Margaret peeked at his coat. "I should have guessed a man dressed in such hot clothes might not be from here. Would you like to remove them to cool down?"

The suggestion took him by surprise. "I'm afraid removing them might increase my temperature. My, it is hot in here, don't you think?" He gulped the rest of the water. Fighting every manly urge to accept this woman's enticing offer, he strained to change the subject. "Margaret. What a beautiful name. But you don't look like a Maggie. Maybe a Peg?" He snapped his fingers. "I know: Meg. Is that what they call you?"

The distraction seemed to be working. She took a step away from him. "No. My name is Margaret. My mother named me after a dear friend."

Like a lantern wick blown out, the woman's mood quickly changed. She stepped away from him, taking the cup from his hand, and walked to the stove. Whatever his words, they had a profound effect on her. "I apologize if I've offended you in any way. I just am very grateful for the salvation of your uncle's home and don't wish to . . ." He had to think of a word. "Smirch the gesture."

Margaret refilled the cup. "And just how would you do that?"

Her frank tone signaled an end to all facades. "By succumbing to my primal desires as a man and deflowering one of nature's blossoms."

She giggled. "Deflowering? Mr. Cash, I may have offered more than just a drink of water," she said, returning to give him the cup, "but the chance of deflowering has long since passed."

The revelation forced him to pause before he accepted the cup. "Again, I find myself mistaken."

"Oh, don't appear so coy, Mr. Cash. Although I might take exception for being considered a libertine, as I might mistake you by your manner, even though I seriously doubt it. I am a woman of twenty-seven years. Long past the respectful chaste age."

Again, he stood stunned at her candor. "Is that so? I am apparently uneducated in the formal upbringings of women of the East." The remark brought only a minor snicker from her lips. Yet, despite the unaccustomed banter between two unwed adults of similar age, he couldn't help wondering aloud, "A betrothed lover, perhaps?"

At first she faced away from him, then turned with a frank face. "No. There never was one."

About to drink, he lowered the cup from his lips. "Another unexpected discovery. How could you elude all the eligible men in the East, who no doubt would duel at risk of taking a bullet for the chance of making you their bride?"

She smiled. "There you go again with that manner. My, aren't you the sweet-tongued devil, Mr. Cash."

He shrugged in admission to her opinion. "I've had no complaints. And please call me Rance."

She faced the wall for a moment. "There were offers. But none I felt right about. I came to Texas in part to take care of my uncle, but also on the off chance I might find the right man to spend the rest of my life with." She turned to him. "A tall, dark, handsome man who might sweep me off my feet with proposals not necessarily of marriage, but of companionship. Where I could enjoy the rest of my years with someone with whom I share the same life's dreams. I think someday I might find him." She smiled again at Rance. "No offense meant, but you are not him."

He couldn't help but smile. "None taken." He watched as she took a broom from the corner. So intrigued by this woman's self-assurance, he thought to further his luck by proposing not an interlude but a business deal. "Margaret, are you one to look fortune in the eye and grasp at it?"

No doubt perplexed by the question, she stopped sweeping and turned her face to him at an angle. "And what would that entail?"

He inhaled, always a trusted tactic when stuck for a reasonable explanation, then honesty overwhelmed him. "Before I was rescued by Robbie and his boys from those savages, I had in my possession a rather important article."

She raised a wary brow. "Article?"

Although no one else stood in the room, he felt compelled to take a step closer if for no other reason than just to inhale the aroma of a woman. Her blue eyes sent his mind into a whirl. The urge to steal a kiss quickly faded with the image of roasting on a spit. He shook his head to clear away the image. "A small bag. I was carrying it when I was chased by the Indians. Somehow, I lost it in all the terror. It means a great deal to me. If you thought you could supply me with the use of a horse for only a few hours, I'd gladly make it worth your trouble.

Margaret first looked to the side and grinned, then focused on Rance. "And just how would you do that?"

With one more step, he closed the distance to her where they stood chest to chest. He leaned closer to those inviting lips. Even the risk of roasting wasn't enough to keep him from tasting those lips. "In the oldest manner by which men have always satisfied women." He paused as she closed her eyes and prepared for his kiss. However, with Rance Cash, the concern of lost money overruled all other priorities. "I'll pay you."

Margaret opened her eyes. "Pay me?"

"One hundred dollars. All you need do is to get me a horse." He thought his smile would seal the proposal.

She batted her blue eyes but more from the appearance of confusion than any of his flattery. "One hundred dollars? My, you know how to capture what a lonely girl in the wilds of Texas really wants."

Rance bobbed his head side to the side. "I figured a lonely woman in the wilds of Texas might be able to use the money to buy a new dress. Perhaps a whole trunk full of them. From the finest boutiques in New Orleans."

The idea registered with her bright smile. "And bribery, too. You are a charmer, Rance Cash."

He shrugged, an admission of guilt on all charges.

A few moments went by before Margaret gave her answer. "I'll tell you what I'll do. Since those are my uncle's horses, I don't feel I can just loan you one without properly escorting you on this search for your bag."

The counteroffer stunned him. "What?" The suggestion

sounded ridiculous, and so he grinned. "No time for levity, my dear. I just need the horse."

"Do you have the money? I mean right now?"

The demand also caught him by surprise. "What? Right now?" He stuttered for time and an answer, but he had neither. "Well, you see, part of the reason I am looking for the bag is to regain certain funds I am missing."

"Uh-huh," she replied with arched brows.

"So, you see, I don't have the money exactly here. Right now. You see. Don't you?"

She propped the broom against the wall. "You have only one chance to find your bag, Rance. And that's with me. Besides, a tenderfoot like you would only get lost all over again."

She made a good point, but he still had his doubts. "What about your uncle? He's expecting every hair on your head to be in proper order."

"My uncle won't be back for days. There's over eight thousand acres on this ranch holding more than three thousand head of cattle. Takes a long time to round them up. We'll be back long before they return." She went to the door, taking a wide sombrero from a peg. She reached for the latch, then turned to him. "Are you going to come?"

Les kept Lone Star at a steady pace. More than a mile on the trail, she sensed the horse huffing louder than normal. Not as stout as even the paint, the racehorse was used to short spurts and not carrying the same weight as now. She began rethinking her choice of the horse. However, it was her choice, and she was going to have to make the best of it.

The long grade made for an easy ride. Les only hoped it continued downhill until she made the trading post. The small bushes sprouted from the ground down the plain beneath her and ahead for as far as she could see. Prickly cactus stood the highest and was easy to avoid. More than once she glanced back to the herd, but the high plateau that she had left was gone from sight.

Despite chiding herself for looking, she rationalized she had to keep a bearing on where to send help. The thought hit her like falling headfirst on a stump. The herd was moving.

Where would they be by the time she could get back? The fear of losing them had her kick the horse. Like a bullet, the race-horse bolted. Memories of winning the race filled her head. The wind blew in her face from the speed.

Before she knew which way to head, Lone Star had charged down another valley. Tears watered her eyes. From her blurred vision she saw a mountain range emerge from the horizon. This had to be where they meant. She steered the horse in that direction.

The sun descending behind a far ridgeline made it hard for Rance to see. The reddish stone pillars in the distance regis-tered in his memory. "I think we're close," he yelled to her. A peek to the side showed Margaret close to his side. Allowing for the small amount of ground covered during his escape from Comanches, Rance gauged a spot near a sheer cliff as the one where he so nearly lost his life.

He reined in and pointed to the spot. Without further direc-tion, the woman dismounted from her sidesaddle without waiting for assistance, sombrero still tight on her head. Once afoot, Margaret loosened the chin cord and removed the hat, shaking loose her blond locks. The action was understand-able, due to the wide-brimmed hat's weight and its lack of ne-cessity with the setting sun. However, the sight of her blue eyes against the fading light stopped him in his tracks. It took a good four blinks before he remembered the purpose of their journey.

"What's wrong?" she asked, staring him straight in the eye.

He closed his mouth, and reflex had him smile. "Never mind." He turned his attention to the cliff. Focusing in the dim light made it hard for him to concentrate on any object as small as the bag must appear at that distance. Despite the dread of returning down the side of the cliff, he looked to Margaret and gave a halfhearted smile. "Do you know how to tie a knot?"

Soon she had the lariat cinched tight to the saddle horn of his horse. Rance spat into both palms and readied himself to rappel down the side. With great trepidation, he inched his heels closer to the edge. What was he doing? About to launch himself down the side of an escarpment with only a flimsy piece of hemp to spare him from crashing into jagged rocks hundreds of feet below. He needed confidence supplied other than his own. "You sure you know how to tie a knot?"

"My father was a sailor. He taught me how to tie off most anything. This is a rolling hitch. Believe me, it will hold you as long as you hold on to the rope."

Not completely sure, Rance accepted the opinion and slowly leaned backward. His weight against the saddle pulled his mount closer, sending him faster down the side than he desired. Before his view of the ground above was obscured by the edge, he saw Margaret pull the reins to steady the horse. The instant lack of slack snapped him about like a puppet. His arms nearly jerked clean from their sockets, he strained to keep his fingers wrapped around the rope. Both pistols fell lose from their holsters. He could do nothing to stop them from falling below.

"Are you all right?" her voice echoed from above.

"No," he replied with a shriek. "Move the horse closer to the edge." A few moments passed before he descended slowly but not far enough to feel his toes hit solid ground. "More," he shouted.

"That's all there is."

Her response sent a chill of terror through his spine. Reluctantly he peeked down. Certain the drop to the bottom was deeper than any sea, he evaluated his chances of survival if he released the rope. He knew he couldn't hold on much longer and decided to attempt a drop and perhaps roll his way to safety. The odds were good his legs might snap in half from the force, but he knew it was a short matter of time before his tired fingers gave him no choice. Counting off in his head, he squinted tightly and prepared for the impact. Reaching the count of three, then five, then ten, then fifteen, he opened his fingers.

Air rushed by his face after one entire second. Another passed before he could scream when finally his boots smashed into the gravel. In an instant, he thanked himself for misgauging the fall from hundreds of feet to a matter of just a few. Once the instant expired, gravity took hold of his uneven stance and sent him backward down the cliff wall. Tumbling like a clown in a circus, he came to rest as the loose gravel slowed his body more than the grade could propel it.

Once his mind reassured him he'd survived, pain took over. He yelled to relieve the agony, reaching behind himself to rub his aching back, stretching his legs to soothe his arches, and rolling his shoulders to stop the piercing edges of stones from pinching his nerves.

"Are you hurt?" Margaret shouted.

"I might be paralyzed."

"How can you be paralyzed if you're moving?" echoed down.

He was no doctor. "There may be a delay in its effect." Still wincing from the pain, he scanned about for any sign. Slowly he got on his feet and stumbled to stay on balance while gently making his way from rock to boulder, descending to where the ground leveled. Although dim, the evening light allowed him to peer into the scrub in hopes of spotting the red bag. Swatting at high brush, he stepped one long, slow stride at a time due to the pain in his leg. His last swipe at a high thorn-filled weed brought a low, threatening growl.

Rance froze. Despite the fading light, white daggerlike teeth filled his view. Some animal took exception to his approach. Reflex had him grab at the holster on his side, but it was as empty as the one on his right hip. He'd have to fight this beast barehanded. Unsure whether to attack in hopes of frightening it off or tempting it to charge at him, he stood locked in indecision. As the huffing, snorting growls filled the air, the faintest of rhythmic pounding slowly crept into his ears. Satisfied to stand his ground as the animal remained at the same distance, he concentrated on the approach of what he now recognized as the clop of horse hooves.

Summoning enough courage to take his eyes off the beast, he saw a rider in the light round the far side of the escarpment wall. A loud voice shouted, *"Hah!"* The beast ceased its growl and scampered off into the desert. Inhaling for the first time since he heard the growl, he had breath enough to speak.

"Where did you come from?" he asked Margaret.

"The slope is much gentler about a hundred feet farther up. I just rode down and heard that coyote growling."

"Coyote? Is that what that was? Not a bear or wolf? Mountain lion?" He saw her slide off the horse and shake her head.

"No. It was just a coyote. Usually afraid of all men," she said as she approached.

Rance took offense. "And what is that supposed to mean? The animal thought less of me?"

She ignored his masculine paranoia, sidestepping him to push the brush aside. Her shriek brought Rance out of his self-pity, lurching behind the brush to see the figure of a man prone on the sand. He pulled Margaret away and held her. After he was certain she was all right, he stepped through the brush to get a look at the corpse.

The arm had been gnawed, likely from the coyote making use of an easy meal. The grisly sight repelled him, but he did see the appearance of buckskin leather and the presence of a beard on the body. Before he could pull his eyes away, he saw the dark coloring under the beard, the same coloring as the gashes on the arm, only the throat wound appeared much cleaner.

"Looks like our friend here met with an unfortunate end at the hands of an enemy." His eyes were pulled to another white object closer to the rocks. The size of a feather, he picked up the small object, which his fingers sensed as hair with a faint feel of gum. In an instant, he recognized it as the disguise used by the man he knew by two names, one being Rodney Sartain. The mystery of how Farnsworth held the carpetbag seemed solved. "Poor Dudley," he muttered.

"What do you mean?"

Rance restrained her from viewing the body. "The throat appears slashed by a clean blade. Not something you get by an unfortunate fall. Maybe the Comanches found him."

"I don't think so. They would make a better example of anyone trespassing their land. They wouldn't hide a body under brush."

Margaret's opinion made Rance think. "Your uncle mentioned cattle being driven across this land. The Comanches taking exception to the intrusion. Maybe this fellow was one of those?"

She shrugged. "I don't know. My uncle normally considers anyone driving cattle around here to be rustlers."

As soon as she said the word, Rance knew who to suspect of the murder. Quickly, he recalled the rider previously seen and knew it had to be Bob. Rance took Margaret's arm. "We should leave here. It isn't safe. I know the kind of men who'd do this." They got to her horse. "Perhaps we can look for the bag in the morning."

She reached on the other side of her horse and presented the bag to him. "You mean this?"

Gratefully, he grabbed the bag and hugged it to his chest. "You found it."

"Yes. It was lying at the top of the cliff where the gentle grade began." She paused, looking at the top, then at him. "You wouldn't have dropped it there?"

Immediately, Rance reviewed the event in his head. The gentle grade likely was the course the burro took, and the bag must have fallen when it descended the side of what he saw as a rocky slope. He gently squeezed her hand. "Of course not."

The sun dipped to the west by the time she could get a good look at the mountains. Les had to smack the horse's rump to climb up the steep inclines and take a tight grip on the reins once she descended down the other side. Once she was in an arroyo, she used it as a trail to find an easier way to climb the next grade.

Atop a hill, she scanned about in search of the trading post. Long shadows cast by the tall rock mountain made it hard to see into the shaded slopes beneath it.

She steered toward the base of the mountain. A glance west served as a warning she only had few hours of light. Up and down two more hills, and she saw a structure in the shadows. By the time she came closer, the sun's light angled through the gaps in the mountains, illuminating the Texas flag, which snapped in the breeze. Les took a deep breath of relief. Surely, she had found it. This had to be it.

When she approached, she clearly saw the tall wood stockade wall and the tall roofed tower standing from the center. When she got to the wall, she rode about until she found the opening to the interior. When she entered, the ground held the

same scrub as the outer plain. The open windows were dark.
The sight brought her to scan about, and no one was present.

"Hello!"

No response pushed her further inside. The flag popping
drew her attention. It was tattered and faded. The sight struck
some fear in her. Either someone wasn't a good caretaker, or
there wasn't a caretaker at all.

She called again with the same result. Curiosity took her off
the saddle. She led Lone Star to the trough. It was dry. The disappointment took her wind. She'd traveled almost the whole
day and found nothing. How could she go back with news that
she found nobody?

"Mr. French!"

The desire to succeed drew her closer to the dark building.
She peeked into the shadowy interior. A table and some chairs
were overturned. There was no sign anyone had been here for
some time. Slowly, she garnered the courage to open the latch
and go inside.

Once she entered, the lack of light made it hard to see. With
the thought that just maybe this French fellow might be asleep
in a room in the back, she went farther, stumbling over a chair.
"I'm here from a cattle drive out of San Antonio. We're looking for help." Her words were more to comfort herself than really expecting someone to hear them. Still, she went around to
what appeared a bar. The wood was old and cracked by her
dim view. The bottles on the sagging shelf barely balanced at
the edge. She couldn't resist reaching for one, but the mere
touch of one dropped it from the side. She fumbled it between
her clumsy hands. The crash broke the silence.

She looked about. No one stood to hear the noise. Although
tempted to reach for another, she convinced herself it only
would meet the same result as the first. She went around the
bar and saw an opening to another room. The pitch-black interior kept her from entering.

"Mr. French, you in there?"

No answer stirred her curiosity, but she still didn't have
enough courage to go inside. In fact, her confidence in finding
anyone waned. Cold air emanating from the room pushed her
backward. A neigh faced her about.

A man stood in front of her.

Les screamed at the sudden fright. He snatched her arm.

"Who the hell are you?"

His voice was low and gruff. The outer light projected him in silhouette and didn't allow her to see his face. "You Mr. French?" She tried to pull away from him.

"Who's that?"

Her heart pounded. If he wasn't French, what was he doing here? "Who are you?"

He slapped her face. "Don't sass me, kid. What are you doing here? Better tell me, or I'll lop off your ears." His grip tightened. She couldn't pull away, and she couldn't see enough to slap at him. Her arm tingled from the crushing pressure of his grip. He shook her. "Tell me. Why are you here?"

If she was to survive, she had to tell the truth. "I'm part of a cattle drive out of San Antonio. We were in need of help. I was sent to fetch it."

He shook her again. "Help? Why you needing help?" He shook her again. Les was being yanked back and forth. She couldn't think. If she just told, maybe he'd let her loose.

"We was told we were about to get attacked by—"

The idea slammed into her head. He stopped the shaking. "Tell me, damn you."

She couldn't keep the answer from mumbling out of her mouth, although she thought he knew the answer. "Rustlers."

27

THE MORNING WAS near past done. Jody couldn't keep it out of his mind. He kept one eye on the steers and the other cast at the west. Les had been gone almost a whole day, and although it might be a reasonable time to gather enough help to be of any good, the thought of her being gone wouldn't stop gnawing at his gut.

He steered the drive directly west. The scrub didn't provide much for the cattle to graze, and it made more sense to head farther north. However, if they headed in a different direction, he might be making it hard for her to find them.

The choice bothered him so, his horse stopped and nearly reared from being ridden too close to a cliff. When Jody settled his mount, he knew he had to decide before he got someone or himself killed. And there was only one choice he had to make.

He reined about and rode at a gallop, whistling at each of the drovers to follow him. Confused, they did as he directed. They assembled at the outer right flank. Tucker and Dan each had their perturbed faces while the others were just interested in why they stopped.

"What is it this time?" asked Tucker. "We ain't going to get nowhere by stopping all the time."

Jody had enough. "Hush your mouth." With his stern voice still hovering over them, he didn't see a need to change. "It's been about a day. Les ain't back." He turned and pointed to the lower range leading to the far mountains. "I should have been able to see riders, and I ain't seen none." He faced them again and took a breath. "So I'm going to look for her." He looked into each of their faces, knowing what he had to say meant to them. "I know it's going to stall the drive with two of us gone, the remuda and all to tend to, it will just spread you too thin and it can't be helped. I shouldn't be long."

Tucker had another question. "What if you don't come back?"

"Didn't you hear him say hush your mouth?" Penelope yelled.

Jody looked to her. With her settling the tone for him, he continued. "I hope to be gone not longer than a day." He looked to Tucker. "But it has to be said. If I don't come back, I think y'all should head northeast. Maybe hook back up with the Chisholm. At least there's towns close by." He went to his horse and drew the repeating Henry rifle from his saddle scabbard. "I know y'all are aware of the money out there on the hoof. I don't have to tell you what desperate men might do to get their hands on a herd of Texas longhorns." He tossed the rifle to Penelope.

"Why does she get it?" Tucker complained.

"I know you have your own guns, that's why. Besides, this way I know it ain't going to end up in the den of Miss Hattie's Parlor House in San Angelo." He went to the saddle bag and pulled out two revolvers. The Remington he tucked into his belt. The short-barreled .45 Colt he walked over and presented to Enos. "You know how to use this?" He flipped it butt first.

The farm boy slowly took it. Once he inspected the load, he looked to Jody and nodded.

Satisfied, Jody went to his horse and mounted. He looked to his drovers. "Just keep them quiet. Weather should be good for the next day. When I get back, we'll make some tracks north." He reined about and slapped the horse's rump with the leather.

Rance came to a long, sloping mound with more than what was over the hill on his mind. He regretted his departure from Margaret. The possibilities of what could be wouldn't leave his mind. Back and forth raged the argument of whether the few days at the ranch without Uncle Donald and his boys could have been used to a better advantage. He recalled her smile upon payment of one hundred dollars and her lack of sorrow at his departure.

Despite her assessment of him as not exactly the epitome of the man she dreamed about, he wondered if he shouldn't have given her a chance to make a more informed decision. Certainly in the time allowed, he could have made a lasting impression not only on her mind but perhaps on other parts of her anatomy.

He crested the hill. The first sight to gaze upon was another long, sloping mound yet to be crossed. He slowed the horse and allowed his eyes to wander from the blue, cloudless sky to the base of the hill below him. Two people stood next to their horses.

He yanked the reins about and reversed his path. Once sure he was beyond their sight, he dismounted and crawled on knees and elbows back to the crest of the hill. He peeked over the edge to view the two not more than a few yards away. Immediately he recognized the figure of the man he knew as Bob. The other appeared to be a woman by her size and slight physique. Black hair in braids and the single piece of leather draping her body gave the appearance of an Indian of some kind.

Maybe she was a Comanche. Rance couldn't be sure. He knew little to nothing of the local tribes. Nervous she indeed may be part of the band that chased him, he scanned about in all directions. Not one sign of anyone. His concentration distracted, motion from the pair pulled his attention back to them to clearly see a friendly embrace. The next moment they were sharing a kiss with arms about the others' shoulders, ribs, and back. Clearly they hadn't just met.

The distance didn't give Rance a proper vantage point to judge the woman's beauty, but by Bob's passionate hold of her, she must be a stunning attraction. Whether it was the heat or the need to pursue the next step in their rendezvous, the couple separated and climbed aboard their respective horses. They rode together and headed what Rance believed to be east.

Unsure exactly what these two meant to each other, he couldn't help but draw a conclusion it had some bearing on that poor fellow the coyote found. Rance scratched his chin. Although certain the direction they rode off to was unlikely to be Mexico, he felt compelled to follow, at least just a little farther.

All during his ride over the hilly terrain he anticipated seeing Les bringing a bunch of riders so as to make a fool of him. As he got close to the tall rock mountains, he realized he'd be disappointed once more.

It took most of the day just to get near the base of the mountain. The one good sign as he approached was the green foliage. Although spotty, it would make for better grazing for the cows. This must be the best way to come.

Distracted by the fortunate discovery, he looked up and reined in immediately. Just before the shadow of the mountain stood a fortlike structure, with a lookout tower waving the Lone Star flag at the top. A concentrated second look showed no activity. However, the tall wall could be hiding what or who might be inside.

Jody found the opening and approached. "Hello in the fort!" Without a reply, he decided to ride in, but first he removed the Remington from his belt. Inside the yard, he saw the house in the center with the tower on top. The windows were dark, and he couldn't see anyone surrounding it. "I say, hello in the house. I need to talk to someone. Anyone around?" There was no reply.

He dismounted and came near the house, pistol poised in front to be sure he wouldn't be surprised. A peek inside the house showed only some old chairs and table turned on the side. Once more he called, but he only heard the echo. Not seeing any threat, he turned the latch and went inside. Stopping near the doorway, he saw a bar that looked to be long broken up for firewood, maybe for a cold winter long ago.

Jody proceeded farther, wondering if someone might be in the back room. As he took a step, hard steel crashed into his skull. Dazed, he tried to turn, but the blow disoriented his senses, sending a tingle through all his nerves. The dark room quickly grew darker.

A faint touch to his cheek roused his conscious mind. As soon as he blinked his eyes, the throb to his head closed them. When he tried to rise, it hurt worse. He let out an anguished grunt.

"Just stay still."

He knew the voice in an instant. He turned, ache and all, but his heart warmed to the notion. "Les?" The dark room didn't provide enough light to see clearly, but he saw her silhouette and sensed her kneeling over him. She leaned back into a single beam of light.

"It's me."

The relief of knowing she was alive sent his arm around her. He pulled her close, and she didn't seem to mind. "I thought you were a goner for a while."

"I could say the same about you. Especially when they brought you in here."

Her words stirred his curiosity. "Where are we?"

"I don't know." He could see her look about the room. "I know we ain't in the house no more. They've had me in here for the last two days. Gave me the canteens and haven't said a thing to me since."

Jody rose to sit up. The throb still pounded his head. He sensed the pain ease as he kept moving. She put her hands on his chest and back to steady his balance. It was a kind gesture. It made him think about her. "Are you all right? Are you hurt?"

She shook her head. "Nah. I ain't hurt."

He exhaled in a huff. "I never should have sent you. It wasn't a trip you should have made."

"You didn't know these men were here when you sent me. Ain't your fault." It took a moment, but they both laughed.

"And I was trying to keep you out of trouble." He looked about the small, square confines. "My pa used to talk about these places. This place must have been an old fort at one time. Probably to fight Indians, back in the early settler days. Keep the route open to New Mexico." The more he thought about it, the more certain he became. "This must be the redoubt. Where they would make a last stand if need be."

"Well," she said in a reflective voice, "it's a good place for us to be then."

Jody thought about more than just what she said. It was him that put them in this mess. But since he now had no weapon, it wasn't likely he was in a position to do anything about it. "I guess I really done it this time."

Les sat next to him. "Oh, you didn't do so bad. Can't all of us know all the answers to get out of trouble. Besides, you done a brave thing."

Her compliment confused him. "How's that?"

She didn't immediately answer. "Well, you did make it known about the disease killing the cows. And you made folks take notice. Got them to follow you. I know your pa had the name for them to count on, but it was you that got the fire lit for them to follow."

Jody sat confused. First Penelope seemed to change from a grumpy tomboy into a gentle puppy eager to please in the course of a single day. Now Les, who he'd known almost a year and had been not much less than a thorn in his side, was talking nice about him. With him in the same room. "Yeah, but look where it's got us. I thought heading west would put us in a better position to get to market. Get a good price for them beeves." He paused, thinking about the caution taught him on the return trip to Texas the previous year. "Old Smith wouldn't have made this mistake."

They both sat and let out gentle chuckles.

"Do you think about him?" Les asked. "Smith, I mean?

Jody had to confess to the truth. "Sometimes," he answered with a nod. "Especially when I see things go in the wrong way. I know what he would have said. He would have seen it coming and kept from making the mistake in the first place."

"Yeah, that is a fact," she replied. "But you have to think that he must have made those mistakes when he was young. Didn't learn it from no book. Not Smith."

Jody sat amused by the truth of that statement. "No. You are right. I don't even think he could read." They both sat on the floor without words for a long moment, until Les started grunting a laugh, which forced a smile on Jody's face. "What are you laughing at? Picked a peculiar time, don't you think?"

"I was just thinking," she said while giggling. "Can you see what would have been happening if Smith had been around when Penelope showed up?"

The thought burst him into laughter, too. The image in his head and what would have been the old man's reaction tickled him so much he couldn't stop nor could Les, until a noise from one of the walls ceased the laughter. Jody sat still, unsure if they both were to meet their end. He swung his arm to push Les behind him as a door opened. Through the entry came a silhouette. At first, Jody gulped, looking to identify the figure. When he couldn't make out the height and weight of a regular-sized man, he quickly recognized it as the stature of a female. An instant later, he saw the Cheyenne woman come into focus.

"What are you doing here?"

"I come. You leave."

"She's part of them," Les whispered.

Jody shushed her, then turned back to the woman. "Who are these men? Are they with Sanderson?"

The woman shook her head side to side. "He dead now."

The news pushed Jody to sit back. "Dead? How?"

"They kill him. He not one."

As before, Jody didn't understand all she meant, but he sensed she was telling him that Sanderson wasn't part of the rustlers. He couldn't be sure, and there were more questions he wanted to ask, but she went back to the door and waved at him. "Come now." Jody stood and pulled Les to her feet. The woman shook her head. "No. You." She pointed at Les. "Her not."

Jody glanced back at Les. "I ain't leaving her here."

"Two horses," she said holding a pair of fingers. "Three not."

"What about my horse? The one with the white star?" asked Les.

The woman shook her head. "Not here. Take from here."

"Lone Star?" Les whined in worry.

"Don't be fretting the horse," Jody told Les. "We got to think how we're going to get out of here." The notion of leaving Les stabbed at his gut, but it might be the only way to get him outside and enable him to get her out. But he wanted to know more. "How many are there? How many men? What do they want? Do they want the herd?"

Again, the woman shook her head. "Not now. Later." She dipped her head to the ground as she had before when she searched for a word. "Man they want. Other." She paused as another word stuck on her tongue. "Cash."

"Rance?" Jody and Les said in unison.

A nod confirmed the answer. "Cash take money. Boss money."

They drooped their shoulders. Again they spoke in unison while looking at each other. "Sounds like Rance."

"You here. He come."

The idea sank into Jody's head, but it was Les who spoke it. "They're keeping us here 'cause they think Rance is going to come after us."

"They tell all. Want him come." She backed into the door. "You now," she said pointing at Jody. He turned to face Les.

Les shook her head. "Don't leave me here."

"They kill Cash. Kill you."

Her voice from the shadows stirred Jody. He turned and put his hands on Les's shoulders. "Believe me, I think it's the only way. I ain't going to forget you're here, but if I don't leave, then I can't help neither of us."

"Jody," Les said on the verge of tears. "I'm scared. Don't do this. What is she to you? You to her?"

There was too much to tell. "I can't say now. But if she's going to help me, then it's going to help you." He took a step back, but he couldn't release his hands. At the end of their length, he snatched her to him and kissed her. He had wanted to for a long time, but not for this reason. He released her lips. "I will come back. I will find you. I will get you out of here." Before he lost any more time, he faced about and hurried out of the door.

28

THE CHEYENNE WOMAN led Jody from the door. Steps cut into the dirt led up to level ground. He scanned about quickly. The redoubt was a dugout with only the roof propped above the ground with a single pipe sticking out for air. He wanted to get a better look, but the woman pulled at his hand, and he followed in a crouch. Dusk gave them cover to move along the tall wood wall.

As she came near a gap in the stockade posts, she stopped and pointed. The gap was barely wide enough for her, but not him. He shook his head, she persisted. She angled her shoulders and slid between the posts. There wasn't a way he was going to fit. He glanced up. If he had the comfort of time or the use of a rope, he might be able to jump and pull himself to the other side. Without either, he couldn't use the gap to escape.

She silently urged him to go. He shook his head. Laughter brought his attention to the rear of house. A dim light shone through the window. He froze in place as the voices grew louder. The light brightened against the dust in the sand as a sign someone was leaving the house from the front. He only had seconds before he'd be spotted.

The woman's tug loosened his legs as they scurried around the far side of the house. The figure of a man emerged from the side they had just come from. As Jody moved out of sight, he saw the man head straight for the redoubt. He stopped again.

The woman yanked at his arm, but he stayed in place, paralyzed by the vision of the man about to discover he was missing and find Les alone. He wanted to go back. He wanted to protect the girl however he could, but the persistent Cheyenne dragged him farther to the side of the house. Finally, Jody saw the only good to come from it was to leave and seek a better chance to free Les.

As they got to the edge of the house near the front, he saw the yard in front was vacant. It wouldn't last for long. The woman crept to the front. She held him back. He tried to steady his breathing, but the sight of the man and what might happen to Les kept his heart pounding. He had to breathe hard to keep up.

"Hey! Come quick!"

The shouted alarm drew those inside out and around the far side of the house. Jody moved closer behind the woman. She took one step followed by another short one. Then she bolted, yanking his hand. He didn't know if he was about to be shot but went with her just the same. As they ran for the opening, he glanced over his shoulder to see the men all running the other way toward the redoubt.

"There they go!"

He faced forward and ran as fast his boots would let him. The Cheyenne woman was fleet of foot and stayed ahead of him. A gunshot crackled through the air. Jody felt no pain and kept running. Together, he and the Indian woman made it out the front and to the right. More gunfire rang out. He saw dust pop up in the plain but maintained the pace behind her. The short distance around the side of the stockade fence was completed, and they ran toward the outer rear of the fort.

His side ached. His legs ached from lifting them high to get over the scrub, but he kept the woman in sight just in front of him. Horses whinnying was a sure sign the men were mounting and would catch them on horseback. They had no chance to outrun horses. With the end of the fence in sight, he churned his arms to gain speed. He caught up with the woman as they turned the corner. He could hear the hooves pounding on the ground.

As much as he wanted to, he didn't slow. Through the dark, he saw his horse and another next to it, both saddled. When he came up to his mount, he leapt, sliding his boot into the left stirrup. He spanked its rump as he heard others coming around the corner. What about Les? He couldn't think.

With both hands on the horn, he hung on as the horse galloped. His weight on the side hindered its stride. A flash from one of the riders and a second later the boom of a blast ringing his ears, he righted himself in the saddle, kicking the animal to go faster.

From the corner of his eye he saw the woman also mounted, but he couldn't turn his head full round and maintain the speed. He lashed the reins against its rump. More shots ripped the air. He didn't feel any pain and as fast as his heart beat, he didn't know if he would.

They rode side by side. The gunmen were close behind. Jody kicked at the horse's flanks to gain speed. The dim shadow of the mountain ahead was the only marker he could steer for in hopes of finding an escape. The woman's horse pulled ahead. He smacked at his own's rump. A peek behind showed another flash and quickly a boom. He wasn't hit. Not yet. Their only chance was to hide in the rocks during the night. But it wasn't a good chance.

An outcropping caught his eye. Jody yelled at her. "This way!" He reined the mount toward what he hoped would lead to some cave or other shelter to hide. The grade steepened. He kicked at the horse's flanks. He saw the woman do so to her mount to keep the pace up the hill. Another peek showed nothing behind them in the darkness. He didn't want to be fooled. It was just too dark. He needed them to fire in order to see them.

The incline slowed the horses. Jody showed no mercy for the trouble. In seconds he knew he'd have to dismount and run for the first shelter. A shot was fired, only this one came from the front. He reined in the horse and slid off the saddle. He smacked the horse to flee, then lay against the rocks. He saw the gunmen below approach up the hill, but another shot from farther up the hill stopped them. In the dark, Jody couldn't see who was firing from above.

He lay still, edging his head to view down the slope. The dim light only afforded him shadows of men and horses at a stop at the base. A third shot rang from uphill. The pained whinny in the dark signaled the slug had found a mount.

"Let's get back. No telling how many are up there," was

barely audible. The muffled sound of hooves clacking against rock echoed to Jody's ears.

Every second he lay there seemed an hour. He held his breath to not give away his position. He heard steps against the loose pebbles approach from uphill.

"They're gone," said a familiar voice. Jody took a long breath and slowly got to his knees. While sucking in wind, he looked to the side on the ground. The outline of a figure against the sage drew him closer. It was the Indian woman.

He went to her side. When he touched her to help her up, his hands felt warm fluid. He put his palm to his face and sniffed. Blood had a recognizable scent.

Quickly he picked her up and rolled her into his arms. "Where are you hit?"

Her gurgled reply meant the wound had to be in the back. The caliber of the lead must have cut clean through her chest. She put a palm to his cheek. Although he couldn't see her face, he sensed her smile by the gentle touch. "I'm so sorry. Why'd you do this? Why'd you do this for me?"

"Make . . ." she strained. "My man."

He shook his head, and her body went limp. He clutched her close to his chest and whispered in her ear. "I can't say your given name, so forgive me. But, I thank you, Ghost Woman, for saving my life." He held her close until he heard the footsteps approach and was reminded who had fired from uphill. Jody gently put the Cheyenne woman back on the ground, then stood.

In the dim light he recognized the silhouette of the man he knew had fired the shots. When he gauged exactly where the man stood, he clenched his fist and landed a punch to the jaw. The silhouette slumped to the ground. The next words came with slurred speech. "Hello, Jody."

"You son of bitch," he replied. "What have you done now?"

"You mean besides saving your life?"

"You didn't save it, she did. By giving hers."

A pause ensued as the figure slowly got to his feet. "I'll give you that. But don't hold her in too high esteem. She was working with Clyde Farnsworth. He's a cattle rustler, and he came to steal your herd."

The words sounded like a lie, and this man was full of them. "Rance Cash, you spin one of your tales to save you from a whipping, and I'll beat you twice as hard."

"I'm telling you the truth."

Jody barely made out the features of the man he had befriended during the trip to Texas and in San Antonio. "One of Farnsworth's gunmen by the name of Bob left El Paso more than a week ago. When I heard they were planning on rustling a herd and I found out it was yours, well, I couldn't in good conscience let it happen without at least trying to warn you. I picked up Bob's trail maybe twenty miles from here, and I saw that woman with him. By the way they acted, I'd say they knew each other rather fondly, if you know what I mean."

The news stunned Jody. He looked back at the body. "It was her planning on stealing the cattle?"

"I guess so. She must have rode off on her own and sent word somehow back to El Paso. I found another body on the other side of this mountain. A white man with a beard wearing skins. You know who that might be?"

Jody needed more deep breaths. "I was told she was his wife."

"Well, I don't mean to speak ill of the woman, but she didn't appear a faithful spouse. I'd say they tricked that man just as they tricked you." Rance paused while Jody stared at the body. "I can't figure why she would help you out of there. But be thankful she did."

In an instant Jody recalled himself and that woman at the waterfall. "I know why." He tried to put it from his mind. Maybe her leaving Les there wasn't only because there were only two horses.

Rance continued, "When I came around this mountain, it was just when I saw you and the woman riding away. I'd say that was pretty good timing, don't you?"

Jody couldn't think about fortune. "They have Les."

"What?" Rance replied concerned. "She's in there?"

"Yeah." Jody turned and took a step back down the hill. "And I've got to go and get her out."

"Don't, Jody," Rance warned.

"I said I'm going back and get her out of there. I promised her I wouldn't forget she's there."

"There are at least six gunmen down in that fort. What chance do you have against them?"

Jody's gut boiled at the point made. He understood the odds. He just couldn't live with the result. "I ain't leaving her there," he said with gritted teeth. He held out his hand for the .44 Colt pistol. Rance flipped it butt first and gave it to him. "Should have always belonged with you in the first place. The thing makes me walk crooked."

"I ain't in a mood, Cash." He took another step down the slope.

"Well, are you in the mood to die? Because that's exactly what's going to happen." Jody stopped. "As soon as you show your face there, they're going to riddle you with lead long after you're dead. Especially when Bob realizes his woman caused you to escape. You've only got three shots left. There are six of them."

Jody faced Rance. "What are you saying?"

Rance took a seat on the rocks. "What I'm saying is we haven't a chance of getting her out of there with just the two of us. We're going to need help."

"All right," Jody replied, thinking of where he could get some help. "I got a half-dozen drovers just about a half day from here."

"Six?" Rance questioned. "It's going to take more than that. There's an army post two days from here."

"I ain't leaving Les in there for two days. You said it. They're riled now. They may take it out on her."

Rance's tone changed. "You have a point there. Well, it might work. But it will take time to get those drovers here."

The time needed only made Jody mad. "Then I'll go down there myself."

"No," Rance said without his usual swagger. "You shouldn't go. I'll go."

Jody faced in the gambler's direction. "And why should you go?"

"Because I have Farnsworth's money. It's really my money. The money I won from Don Pedro, you remember?

Well, that fellow Sartain, or Dudley, or whatever his true name is, stole it from me when I was distracted. You see—"

"Cash, I don't got time," Jody gritted.

"They killed him, Jody. They killed Sartain and took his money. When I saw the bag, I took it, thinking they would chase after me in Mexico. But, I don't know Mexico. So I came to warn you. You understand?"

Jody had heard ten times the babble he cared. He shook his head. "All I want to do is get Les out of there."

"Then I'll go. You see, Farnsworth won't kill me at first sight, like he would you. At least, he won't until he gets his money back." Rance came down the slope to stand in front of Jody. "We're going to get her out. But we're going to need a plan."

29

RANCE CASH WAS about to take his biggest risk, wagering his own life. And for such staggering stakes, he put the outcome squarely in someone else's hands.

The dawn's gentle breeze found him standing outside the fort's entrance. A small prompting was needed to get him walking and keep from facing about to the southeast. However, the game was all about timing. Many a time he had counted on another's play and others' lack thereof to muster an advantage. It was in his nature to take a chance. As he looked to the front, it was time to do just that.

He started up the hill that had concealed his presence and put himself in the game. With the stockade's opening firmly in view, he marched at a steady pace, wondering, hoping he'd calculated correctly. If someone in the house called the bluff too soon, he'd be an easy target to be shot dead before he could finish the play. Clearly in view of the house, he continued into the yard, unsure exactly when someone might call his opening ante. Past the absent gate and more than ten feet inside the yard, his answer came in the form of a rifle shot popping dust inches in front of his boots. He'd gotten the expected reaction.

The front door to the house opened, and out stepped Clyde Farnsworth. Rance inhaled the cool breeze. "Good morning, Clyde."

Two of the gunmen flanked the big man on the porch. "I did say you had sand as a lawyer," replied Farnsworth. "I guess that's all you got for brains. Where's my money?"

There was a point of order needed. "Well, you see, Clyde, that wasn't really your money."

At first there were chuckles, then outright guffaws. "Ain't my money, huh? It sure was back in El Paso. Why ain't it now?"

Rance needed time. "That's an interesting question. Actually, there's quite a story that goes along with it." He angled his shoulders to peek behind. The plain was empty. "You see, I was in this poker game in San Antonio, and just starting to win my money back when—"

Another shot pelted the dust.

"Don't want to hear all your babbling. Heard enough of it in that church and nearly got me hung." Farnsworth drew a revolver from his belt. "Now, tell me where the money is, and I might let you live. If you don't, I will find it myself and kill you for spite for making me have to ride a hundred miles just to come get it."

The reaction was anticipated. Another peek over his shoulder was needed just to satisfy the curiosity. Still empty. Rance faced forward. "Perhaps we can discuss this in a more dignified manner."

"I'm getting real tired of all your talk, gambler. Bring the money here, or I'll put you to the dust." He pointed above. "And the girl, too."

Rance's eyes rose to spot Les standing in the watchtower. Her hands appeared bound above her. His heart sank. In that moment he realized she was there because of him. However, to make it known she was a precious stake not to be bargained for would make her safety a matter of pride. One that the thug likely would continue to hold over his head, making her invaluable. He couldn't show his concern. "She's nothing to me. Don't hold me accountable for the trouble she's caused you. I'm just here to settle the issue of the money."

Farnsworth shot a glance in the direction above. "Then you won't mind if I let the boys have a little fun with her."

The ruse had to be maintained. Rance shrugged. "That shouldn't take long."

Les's heart, at first warmed at the sight of a familiar face, watched in horror. When she saw the most unlikely of people in the world to come to help, she hadn't figured that no-account gambler would have the gumption to stand in front of so many guns. For the first time in nearly three days, even more than when Jody was tossed in the same hole as her, she hadn't gotten her hopes up as much as when she saw Rance walk through the opening in the fence.

He had come to take up for her, and it almost brought tears to her eyes. Although she knew Rance Cash would not have shown his face if there weren't something in it for him, he also wasn't fool enough to not have a scheme in mind. And it had to include getting her out.

While hearing the exchange of words, she guessed his next move. When she heard her life was part of the deal, her hopes raised. Of course he would make her release most important. When she saw his reaction to the prospect of having men take advantage of her, it was all she could do to keep from yelling, and she just muttered the first word which came to mind: "Bastard."

Rance turned his view back to Farnsworth. If his plan were to proceed, he'd have to get closer. "You know, Clyde, I'm awfully exhausted from my trip here. May I come inside and take the load off my legs?"

It only took a moment for the big man to decide. He waved Rance on. "Sure. That way we can get a better look at you."

Rance accepted the invitation and went to the porch. However, when he climbed the steps, he discovered it came with conditions. One of the men pointed a pistol at him, and he raised his arms in reflex. While he looked Farnsworth straight in the eye, hands probed his person and soon his prized pepperbox pistol was presented for all to see.

"All he's got is this?" announced the gunman.

Farnsworth took the weapon with an arched brow. "This is all you brought? I'd thought you'd leave this to spare the weight. Where's the Walker Colt?"

Accustomed to ridicule for his attachment to the six-barreled cap-and-ball pistol with its unreliable reputation, he exhaled his answer. "Lost it. During the ride. That damn thing is so cumbersome, it must have slipped from the holster and I didn't notice it except for hours later when I wondered why I was enjoying the relief of its absence."

The gunmen and Farnsworth all peered at each other with confused faces. Rance couldn't decide if it was the reasoning behind the explanation or just his explanation itself. It was always a good tactic to seize the moment of the opponent's bafflement. "Let's go inside, shall we."

Jody crept closer. The fatigue of the all-night ride was wearing him down, but the importance of his role in the plan required it. He edged his head over the crest of the hill. The distance forced him to gulp. So much so, he slumped behind its cover.

When he suggested the idea it was only to say something, anything to make the notion of getting Les out of there sound reasonable. He knew they were outgunned both in weapons and men to shoot them. With all of Cash's reasons why he just couldn't go down to the fort and fight his way to her, the frustration forced the most loco of stunts into his brain.

Yet, as he edged another eye at the fort, he considered just exactly how he was going to get it done. The sun peeking over the eastern horizon meant the time was near. He just hoped the clouds kept their habit of staying away.

At a crouch he made his way back over the hills. In his mind too much time was lost just getting to where he needed to set the whole plan in motion. When he snuck over the last hill, he knelt in front of Enos, Penelope, Noe, and Dan, casting a quick eye at the sunrise.

"All right, it's almost time. When I give the whistle, we're going. Remember like I said. These are outlaws, and they're used to shooting and not caring what they're aiming at. Keep your heads down. I don't consider it a fair trade losing one of you for Les."

"I ain't scared," young Danny boldly stated. Jody thought the boast was made in part to make up for his lack of weapon in front of the rifle-toting Penelope.

Jody had seen brash talk lead to more reckless trouble in the cow towns. He stared Dan in the face. "Just keep out of the line of fire and try not to stain your drawers when the shooting commences." One more peek at the rising sun was all he could afford. He nodded at the drovers. "Y'all know what we're fixing to do. Let's get to doing it." Penelope, Enos, and Dan retreated, but Noe appeared still confused by all the commotion. Jody hoped pointing in the direction of the fort and his meager Spanish would suffice in order to convey the plan.

"Quando arribe el sol, vamos con las vacas ayi."

Rance uprighted a chair and calmly sat amid the thieves. Farnsworth followed him inside, still holding the pepperbox. The dim interior was barely illuminated by a kerosene lamp in the middle of a table. Rance couldn't determine if it would be a help or hindrance.

To project the image of confidence, he reclined in the chair, propping his head back. In a few moments, he felt his chin in the grasp of Bob, with a stiletto blade pressed against his throat. "I ought to open you up like a pig."

Despite his heart pounding, Rance remained motionless. If he was to survive, it would be due to his wits. "Is this how you treat all your houseguests? I thought we were drinking compadres, Bob."

Farnsworth chuckled. "You best be careful with Bob's temper, gambler. He took offense to his squaw running off with that cowboy to the hills. Found her shot in the back. Not a thing to do to a man's woman, even if she was a redskin."

Rance gulped. Admission to witnessing the act could spark a closer shave than desired. "First I've heard of it. What a terrible tragedy. Who was shooting behind her?"

Bob jerked Rance's chin farther back. "What are you saying?"

Rance felt the pinch of the blade's edge against his flesh. There was no sense antagonizing the man, so he chose to bring a greater threat into play. "If he kills me," Rance mumbled with his chin pressed against his upper jaw. "You'll never find that money, Clyde."

Although it took several moments, most of them Rance thought unnecessary, Farnsworth called off his dog. "Turn him loose, Bob." When the gunman didn't immediately comply, the thug's tone became loud and firm. "I said, turn him loose. He's right. I didn't come all the way out here just to avenge your heathen slut." Bob released Rance's chin and faced Farnsworth with the same angered face and point of the thin knife. For a moment, the big man seemed bent on enforcing his rank by aiming the pepperbox at Bob. Rance had to intercede.

"Don't kill him, Clyde," he said, exercising the cramps from his jaw. "I mean, there's no need for any bloodshed." He rubbed his own throat and checked for any sign he was too late with that proposal. "After all, we are all gentlemen, aren't we?" He looked to Bob. "Please accept my sincerest condolences for your loss." Without the arrival of the planned surprise, Rance needed to stall. "Of course, I didn't know the woman well. That is to say, I didn't know her at all. Despite that, let me express my sorrow over the discovery of her untimely passing." He took off his hat. "Should we pray, gentlemen?" He closed his eyes before they complained. "Heavenly father, please accept Bob's squaw into your pearly gates. We can only reflect on her life with the utmost respect. Even though we don't know the date of her birth, let us imagine the day she was born. Her mother—"

"That's enough!" Farnsworth yelled. "Quit your games, gambler. You tell me where the money is, or I'll stake you over an anthill. You'll be begging to give me the money, then." Farnsworth leveled the pepperbox at Rance's waist. "Or I may just see what kind of damage this thing can do to that which you claim so much pride to."

Les struggled against the rope around her wrists. Her knees ached from standing all night and her heart from the fright. She gulped back the tears. More than once she got her hopes up at escaping from this place only to be disappointed. So she decided to tug at her bonds despite the coarse twine rubbing into skin, resolved if she was to escape she could only rely on herself to get it done.

She pulled harder, but the knot wouldn't budge. The hemp cut into her skin, the pain adding to her maddening mood, causing her to lean back even farther. To use her weight to pull, she swung her leg backward, but her heel slammed into the wood wall of the small square, snapping a plank loose.

Despite all her efforts, she only made the loop shorter, cutting off the blood to her hands. She had to ease the knot and so stepped forward to the center of the tower. No matter how hard she tried, she was stuck there.

She closed her eyes. Memories of a simpler life she enjoyed in Abilene came to mind. The worst she had to fear there was having her knuckles rapped a few times from Miss Maggie for shirking her chores, a frequent offense. Still, she wasn't facing death. If only she could return to her room on the right at the top of the stairs. If only she hadn't left in the middle of the night, yearning to see Texas. She would give anything. She repeated the prayer over in her head.

She opened her eyes. The sight of what approached out of the glare of sun's light appeared the answer to the prayer.

Jody hollered at the steers, swatting each one he could hit with the lasso. At full gallop he drove the herd straight for the fort's entrance. He kicked his mount to gain speed. The longhorns needed to be driven not only past the gate but directly to the target. He left that duty to himself. If anyone was going to be shot at, he couldn't choose another to take the risk.

He rode alongside Brewster. The old bull had never run so fast, and it didn't take a smack on the rump. Maybe it was the freedom to roam free without being slowed by horse and man, maybe due to being the oldest he wanted to be at the front of the herd as a warning for the younger bulls to heed, or maybe because he was the orneriest son of a bitch with horns in the state of Texas.

Whichever, Jody's blood pumped more than a well pump. He let out a yell as he rode straight into the yard.

"Hot damn!" The yell from the gunman posted at the front door turned all heads his way. When the man ran to the rear of the house, Rance knew he had only seconds to react, get the prize he came for, and get out.

He jumped from the chair. Bob snatched his coat and jabbed the knife at him. Rance blocked the thrust, firing a knee into Bob's groin. As Bob collapsed, Rance seized the knife so as not to suffer further threat from the blade. He ran to the back room. A glance over his shoulder showed all eyes at the front. All of the men except one drew their weapons and fired at the stampede heading straight for the house. Farnsworth caught sight of Rance fleeing. The thug's first reaction was to raise the pistol in his hand and pull the trigger. Rance gulped, hoping he had loaded his gun as intended.

The pepperbox exploded. Farnsworth's right hand was a mess of blood, flesh, and fire. As Rance breathed a sigh of relief, he saw only horns charging. He ran to the back room amid the sounds of gunfire. Stairs dimly visible to his right drew his attention. Wood crashing and the structure shaking pushed him up the steps in a hurry.

Light outlined a square above him. He pushed, and the planks flipped up in the form of a hinged door. Les stood above him. He smiled. A hand clutched his shoulder, yanked him back, sending him tumbling back down the steps. When he got a good look at the man under him, it was Bob wrestling with him for the knife.

Rance took a punch to the jaw but freed an elbow to jam into his attacker's nose. The blow stunned Bob enough to release the grip. Rance turned to the front room. Cows filled his view, their horns and tails meshed together in too close quarters. One tumbled the table with the lantern. In an instant, fire spread over the floor. Now there were only seconds to get out.

He ran up the stairs and climbed into the watchtower. The stiletto blade still in his hand, he saw the rope binding her hands and angled the blade against it.

"What's going on down there?" asked Les.

"About to be the biggest barbecue in Texas history," he answered, slicing through the rope. The whole structure shifted backward. Rance reached for Les, but she was thrown to the far right of the tower. He nearly lost his balance but steadied it with a grasp of the wall. As smoke drifted up from the stairwell, Rance turned to find a way back down to the ground. Flames engulfed the outside of the house. Below, the cows madly scrambled about throughout the yard. Surrounded by flames, Rance didn't see a way that didn't involve getting burnt.

A shrill whistle drew his attention to the side. Jody rode to the side of the house swinging a lariat over his shoulder. Rance recognized the idea and nodded. Jody threw the lasso up to the tower. Rance caught it and secured the loop around one of the top beams, sliding the rope through the loop, then signaling Jody to pull. The rope stretched in a straight line.

A hand to Rance's shoulder jerked him about, and a fist crashed into his jaw, sending the knife to the floor. Sent nearly over the wall, Rance caught his balance, but Bob clutched Rance's throat, his enraged features a sign of his intent of crushing Rance's windpipe at the expense of his own life.

Hardly able to see through his squinted eyes, he felt the pressure from around his neck ease, and Bob collapsed to the floor. Les stood behind, coughing from the smoke, dropping the wood plank in her hands.

The next moment the house could crumble from the flames. Rance spat the saliva from his throat and grabbed at the stiff rope. He took off his coat and hung it over the rope. He turned to Les, left hand extended to her.

"Let's go!"

Les leapt into his arms, clamping her legs around his waist. Rance kicked off the crumbling tower wall and clutched the coat. As gravity propelled them to the ground, a whir from the friction against the coat silenced all other noise. In an instant, the speed blew air against his face; that, with Les's squeeze to hang on for dear life, robbed him of breath.

Jody, mounted on a horse, neared at a velocity Rance had never seen. To keep from crashing right in his lap, Jody nudged his horse to slacken the rope just enough to send Rance skidding on the dirt of the yard on his butt.

Once at a stop, Rance turned to Les. She, too, apparently had never made that trip before. A buxom blonde girl in braids shielded them from being trampled by the panicked cows. Rance looked up at Jody with a smile. "We did it."

A grunt as loud as a scream came from behind. Clyde Farnsworth raised a rifle with his left hand, steadied by his blackened right. His face bloodied, he limped out onto the porch and wobbly aimed the rifle at Rance. Instinct forced

Rance to dive atop Les. One shot rang out. Then another, then one more.

A peek above showed Jody holding the .44 at arm's length, the busty gal holding a rifle at her shoulder, both of the barrels wisping smoke. Rance edged his eyes to see the hulking body of Clyde Farnsworth facedown in the dust.

30

THE SMOLDERING FLAMES from the collapsed fort still sent enough black smoke into the sky to shroud the morning's light. Rance sat on a dead cow, wiping the sweat from his brow. He watched as Jody stood over one with long, wide horns. With a shake of his head, Jody patted the carcass and walked away from the smoke.

"That the one you called Brewster, I think?" asked Rance. Jody nodded and bobbed his head to the side. "I guess if you'd told me I'd lose him and that's all, I'd take it." He looked back at the bull. "Probably would have wanted to go that way rather than show up on someone's plate, if he had a say. Just the same, I'm going to miss him." Jody pointed at the empty holster on Rance's side. "Lose that crazy gun?"

Rance peeked at the holster. "Another sacrifice. I overloaded the charge. Figured they'd take it from me. Didn't want it to end up killing me. Knew I'd never hear the end of that. So I chose to have it save my life just one more time."

They both looked at the herd amassed out on the plain. Les walked toward them. Jody came to meet her, and they both stood in front of Rance.

"You look like you made it through without much damage," Jody said.

Les only glanced at herself but didn't appear relieved. "Yeah. Would have been better if I hadn't been left behind."

Jody wagged his head side to side. "I told you I had to. And I told you that I'd come back for you."

She pointed at Rance. "It was him that came for me, not you."

"And that's twice I ruined a coat in the process," Rance added.

They both faced him for a second. "Stay out of this," they said in unison, then faced each other.

"I did what I had to do," Jody said. "Believe me, Les, I didn't let a second go by that I didn't think about you here. I was going to come down here last night and get you out." He pointed at Rance. "It was him that said it was a bad idea."

Rance nodded. "That is true."

They faced him again. "Stay out of this."

Les looked up at Jody. "Well, you seemed too eager to follow that Indian woman."

"I had to. She got me out, didn't she? I charged the herd in here, didn't I? I'm standing in front of you now, ain't I?"

Rance had seen all this before. "Why don't you two—"

"Stay out of this!"

Rance held up his hands in surrender.

Jody settled his breath and stared at Les. "Look, I know this whole trip has been one problem after another. But we still have the herd. We only lost about a dozen. We're going to drive them to Colorado. Once we get our money, you'll change your tone when you see all the money we take back to San Antonio."

Les dipped her head to the ground. "I ain't going back to San Antonio, Jody." She looked up at him and met his eyes. "I made myself a promise. Prayed for it, if you want to know the truth. I'm going back to Abilene to live. For good." She shook her head. "Texas hasn't been what I thought it to be. Kansas has been my home for six years. I don't even really remember the place called New York." She swallowed hard, no doubt in some fear over his reaction. "I asked the man above to save me and get me back to Abilene. That's when I seen you coming with them cows. The way I reckon, I made a promise. One that can't be broke."

Jody huffed a breath. Slowly, he nodded his head. "Well, I told you once that I would take you there myself. After we get this drive to Denver, I'll have a mess of money to take you there." He paused, looking first at Rance, who waved him on, then back at her. "If you'll let me."

Les stood, folding her arms, running her eyes up and down him, but seemingly careful not to meet his eyes. "I'll let you."

Jody breathed a sigh. "Well, then, let's get to it."

"There you go, giving me orders again."

"It ain't no order. I was just trying to get us back on the trail."

Rance knew he'd be here all day watching this. "Now wait." They turned to him again, but he spoke first. "No, I won't stay out of this. Ever since that day when you learned she was a girl, you've held this tone with her."

"Yeah," Les added.

"The same for you," he said to her. "You were only too helpful when he thought you were a boy, but when you couldn't hide in those duds anymore, you expected him to treat you differently."

"Yeah," Jody said to Les.

Rance shook his head, knowing he'd sparked another argument. He rose and brushed off his pants. "I fold on you two. If neither of you can see that you two have feelings for each other, then I'm going to leave you to yourselves." He walked toward the outer plain. It took him until he was under the gate opening before he turned about. Finally it was the first time he saw what he knew all along. Jody and Les in a full embrace, pressing lips together just as the two young sweethearts they were meant to be.

Not wanting to watch what wasn't intended, he found his eyes catching sight of the tall blonde in the saddle. Now, there sat a challenge before him. As he pondered, Les and Jody walked by him arm in arm. "That was a long time in coming," he said as they passed. "So, I assume you're going to Colorado with him?" he asked Les.

She first looked to Jody, then at Rance, and nodded. "Kansas ain't that far from Denver." She arched a brow at Rance. "What about you? I know there's a broken heart in San Antonio."

Rance smacked his lips and shook his head. "You know, I think that girl is better off without me." He cast an eye at the blonde girl in braids. "As a matter of fact," he said then, facing the both of them, "Kansas is where I was trying to get to in the first place."